BUTTERFLY OF DINARD

EUGENIO MONTALE

Translated from the Italian by
MARLA MOFFA *and* **OONAGH STRANSKY**

Introduction by
JONATHAN GALASSI

NEW YORK REVIEW BOOKS

New York

THIS IS A NEW YORK REVIEW BOOK
PUBLISHED BY THE NEW YORK REVIEW OF BOOKS
207 East 32nd Street, New York, NY 10016
www.nyrb.com

This book was supported by a grant from the Italian Ministry of Foreign Affairs and International Cooperation.

First published as a New York Review Books Classic in 2024.
Originally published in Italian as *Farfalla di Dinard*.

Library of Congress Cataloging-in-Publication Data
Names: Montale, Eugenio, 1896–1981, author. | Stransky, Oonagh, translator. | Moffa, Marla, translator.
Title: Butterfly of Dinard / Eugenio Montale; translated from the Italian by Marla Moffa and Oonagh Stransky.
Other titles: Farfalla di Dinard. English
Description: New York: New York Review Books, 2024. | Series: New York Review Books classics
Identifiers: LCCN 2023050112 (print) | LCCN 2023050113 (ebook) | ISBN 9781681378169 (paperback) | ISBN 9781681378176 (ebook)
Subjects: LCSH: Montale, Eugenio, 1896–1981—Fiction. | LCGFT: Autobiographical fiction. | Short stories.
Classification: LCC PQ4829.O565 F313 2024 (print) | LCC PQ4829.O565 (ebook) | DDC 853/.914—dc23/eng/20231026
LC record available at https://lccn.loc.gov/2023050112
LC ebook record available at https://lccn.loc.gov/2023050113

ISBN 978-1-68137-816-9
Available as an electronic book; ISBN 978-1-68137-817-6

Printed in the United States of America on acid-free paper.
10 9 8 7 6 5 4 3 2 1

NEW YORK REVIEW BOOKS
CLASSICS

BUTTERFLY OF DINARD

EUGENIO MONTALE (1896–1981) was born in Genoa. In his teens, he studied accounting at vocational school and pursued his passion for poetry at the library. After serving in the infantry in the Great War and training to be an opera singer, he published his debut collection, *Cuttlefish Bones*, in 1925—the first of many books of poetry that would establish him as the leading Italian writer of his generation. A sworn anti-Fascist, he spent most of the Mussolini era barely making ends meet in Florence, where he got to know, among others, Carlo Emilio Gadda, Tommaso Landolfi, and Irma Brandeis (the subject of some of his most ardent love poems). In 1948, Montale moved from Florence to Milan, becoming a regular contributor to the newspaper *Corriere della Sera*, where many of the prose pieces in *Butterfly of Dinard* were first published. After taking a hiatus from poetry for much of the 1960s, he returned to it in the 1970s with a series of books remarkable for their unstudied epigrammatic elegance. A selection of this work, titled *Late Montale*, is published by NYRB Poets. He was awarded the Nobel Prize in Literature in 1975.

MARLA MOFFA was born in Massachusetts and has been living in Italy for more than twenty years. A theater director, writer, and translator of Italian literature, she has published two children's books: *Il leone con gli occhiali* (2019) and *Non ti senti speciale?* (2021). Her first collection of short plays, *Tre pièces da Borges*, is forthcoming. Her father, Mario Moffa, a professor of Italian language and literature at Mount Holyoke College, was the author of *Eugenio Montale, Lettura della Farfalla di Dinard* (1986).

OONAGH STRANSKY has translated novels by Domenico Starnone, Carlo Lucarelli, Giuseppe Pontiggia, and Erminia Dell'Oro, as well as works of nonfiction by Roberto Saviano and Pope Francis. She has published short translations and essays in a number of journals, including the *New England Review*, *Exchanges*, and *The Massachusetts Review*. Stransky studied Italian at Middlebury College, UC Berkeley, Università di Firenze, and Columbia University, and currently resides in Italy.

JONATHAN GALASSI is the chairman and executive editor at Farrar, Straus and Giroux, as well as a poet and translator of Italian poetry, including the work of Giacomo Leopardi and Eugenio Montale. He lives in Manhattan.

CONTENTS

INTRODUCTION

1956 WAS a banner year for Eugenio Montale. He turned sixty, and what is generally considered his greatest book of poems, *La bufera e altro* (*The Storm, Etc.*), was published. Alongside it, relatively quietly, appeared the first edition of *Farfalla di Dinard* (*Butterfly of Dinard*), a collection of occasional stories and sketches written over the previous decade for Italy's leading newspaper, *Corriere della Sera*—an almost sotto voce counterweight to the apocalyptic Dantean blast of his greatest, most lacerating poetry.[1]

Montale was born in Genoa in 1896, and moved to Florence in 1926, soon after the publication of his first book of poems, *Ossi di seppia* (*Cuttlefish Bones*), which won great praise for its taut embodiment of the anxieties of a new generation confronting Fascism. He spent the war years in Florence, earning a meager living as a librarian, critic, and translator and writing his second, equally radical book, *Le occasioni* (*The Occasions*), which confirmed him as the dominant poetic voice of his era. In 1946, he began writing for the *Corriere* and was hired as an editor there in 1948. Montale described in an introduction to an earlier English translation of *Butterfly of Dinard* how it was that he came to write these prose pieces over the course of several decades:[2]

> After ten years of unemployment due to political reasons—I didn't belong to the "Party"—I joined in 1948 the editorial staff of an important Milanese daily. [...] There was no question of my being sent out as a foreign correspondent, since others were already doing that job. But, still, I had to write something.

What? I haven't got the imagination of a born novelist; nor can I invent anything. But being a great admirer of the English essayists and having the sense of humor that is seldom wanting in the Ligurians ... I thought that I could perhaps talk about myself and my experiences without boring readers with the actual autobiography of an ordinary man—a man who has always tried to move through the history of his times in a clandestine way.

This is how these short stories—*culs de lampe*[3]—of *The Butterfly of Dinard*—came to be written. Only a few are set in Liguria, but a great many take place in Florence, where I lived for twenty years in close contact with the English colony, which in those days was quite large. During those years I tried to do something quite impossible—to live in Florence like an Italian, exposed to all sorts of vexations from the political regime, and at the same time to live like a foreigner,[4] aloof from local troubles. After something like twenty years of hard but unsuccessful struggle I gave up. In the meanwhile I had moved to Milan—the center of business, not art. I had brought along with me a long trail of memories which demanded written expression. If I was not a born storyteller, so much the better; if the space at my disposal was limited, better still. This forced me to write in great haste. To cater for the taste of the general public, which is little accustomed to the allusive and succinct technique of the *petit poème en prose*, created no problem. [...] To write about those silly and trivial things which are at the same time important: to project the image of a prisoner who is at the same time a free man: in this, if I may say so, lies whatever merit these instantaneous flashes which are *The Butterfly of Dinard* may have.

Montale is at pains here to explain the relaxed timbre of *Butterfly of Dinard* and its distance from the often-hermetic intensities of his poetry and the *prosa d'arte*, or prose poetry, which he seemed to feel was expected of a writer of his stature (and at which he excelled, as several examples in *La bufera* attest).[5] He wrote, almost apologetically, to his friend and literary conscience the critic Gianfranco Contini in November 1946: "you mustn't ignore my first and most serious difficulty: the nature of this paper: the most ill-suited to a prose in which I can preserve the tone of my conversation...I write the articles in two hours, with no trouble, but when I'm out of ideas (and it happens often) I feel truly lost."

Nevertheless, he soon found a genial conversational tone for his sketches, or *elzeviri*, as they're called in Italian—atmospheric pieces intended for the *terza pagina*, the third or opinion page of a daily, and, as he admitted later, "it wasn't a sacrifice." He quickly adapted to the format, often filing two or more pieces a week in the 1950s. This style of writing helped him express himself "with fluency and ease" as he moved with remarkable suppleness and variability, equipped with humor, irony, self-irony, and a ready supply of nostalgia, across fictional vignettes, memoir, literary and cultural opinion, travel writing, and music criticism.[6] What emerges is a self-deprecating portrait of a sophisticated, at times even snobbish, sensibility—the art critic Roberto Longhi is reported to have quipped that "with Montale, we're always in the shadow of a luxury hotel"—a defender of what he views as an endangered bourgeois humanism whom some called an "apocalyptic conservative," ill at ease with postwar society's readiness to forget the past, both the good and the bad. Montale's *terza pagina* persona may not have replicated the sharp, telegraphic wit of the poet's conversation, but it made him a major, if controversial, presence in postwar Italian culture.

Butterfly of Dinard, then, is a collection of quasi-autobiographical pieces, "*racconti/non-racconti, poesia/non-poesia*": stories that aren't exactly stories but are not quite poetry, either. The structuralist critic Cesare Segre, in what is perhaps the most astute reading of *Butterfly of Dinard*, argues that the book should be seen as falling "between Montale's poetry and the poet himself...at an imaginative level that is no longer autobiographical and is not yet or not entirely or no longer poetry." Segre notes that where Montale's poetry is terse and intense, characterized by great concentration and difficulty of vocabulary and syntactical density, the language of *Butterfly of Dinard* is journalistic—clear and even repetitive, its syntax loose and free. As he puts it, "we are at the antipodes of the poems."

Many of the pieces in *Butterfly of Dinard* return—almost involuntarily, it has been suggested—to the locales, characters, and themes that populate Montale's verse. Fiction was not part of his arsenal as a prose writer; as he said about his poetry: "I always start from the truth." He also declared that if someone "really wanted some news about my life, he should read *Butterfly of Dinard*, and he'd have a great deal, all of it true . . . and not false, as if my life had been written by someone else."

The book's first, and most charming, section recalls the writer's youth in his native Genoa and in Monterosso, the village in the Cinque Terre on the Ligurian coast where the Montale family had a summer house, the locale and source for *Ossi di seppia*, a book "attracted and absorbed," he wrote, "by the fermenting sea." The author's alter ego in these pieces, named Federigo in one story, Zebrino in another, but always recognizably the same character, returns to the settings of his childhood—the family house, with two palms in the garden, and a wizened, bearded woman working in the kitchen, the pretentious "zabaglione-colored villa" built by rich returnees from South America. "A few days of vacation in the company of my dearly departed" will pass quickly, our narrator promises himself, but he is soon overwhelmed anticipating "the flavor . . . that gets handed down, generation after generation, that no cook can ever destroy. The kind of continuity . . . that endures in the oil of the soffritto." The same autobiographical substrate appears, in more concentrated form, in the poems, many of them written twenty or thirty years earlier— though some are contemporary with the vignettes and others belong to his latest work. The stories aren't keys to the poems; they emerge from the same psychic magma; this is Montale's stuff. One of the most telling sketches here, "The Best Is Yet to Come" (1950), describes an elegant restaurant meal in which an unnamed diner who might as well be the grown-up Federigo, on being offered "eel Livornese," is visited by memories of "the muddy ditch near my home . . . where the eels were, the best in the world." His dinner partner, who knows his foibles inside out, accuses him of wanting to stay "mired in that dish, fishing around for your eels." The humble domestic fish appears in his earliest poems but finds its apotheosis in "L'anguilla" ("The Eel") of 1948, regarded by many as Montale's greatest, most singular love lyric. Idealized in verse as "an undifferentiated life force" at once "immanent and transcendent," as one critic puts it, the familial eel of "The Best Is Yet to Come" is paired with the warbler from our hero's childhood garden on his "mythical, infantile menu," just as "Il gallo cedrone" ("The Capercaillie") of 1943 sits beside "L'anguilla" in *La bufera*. Likewise, the names of the boats competing in "The Regatta," *Lampo* (lightning flash) and *Grongo* (Ligurian for eel), evoke two of the poet's most significant and enduring images. "I have lights that go on and off," he writes in one late poem. "It's all my baggage."

Butterfly of Dinard's second section portrays denizens of Florence's expatriate colony before the war—years that Montale called "the most beautiful of my life," which came to an end with the advent of the Fascist hegemony. "The Florence that interested me was in the course of dissolving," he lamented in an interview; "I had to feed myself on memories fed by the memories of others" —outsiders who displayed "a dandiacal humanism in their search for a viable alternative to the present," in the words of one critic. Remittance men, gold diggers, translators, social climbers, would-be mystics: they are characters the writer feels a sometimes bemused affinity for, averring that "each and every one of us has had at least one friendship that we don't know how to explain, not even to ourselves." In one of the most charming of these scenes, he reports that he has applied for membership in the Slow Club, dedicated to "a decisively anachronistic way of being." "'In a few years you will receive news regarding your application,' the secretary said, accompanying me to the door. 'If you manage to stay out of the papers, it is very probable that you will not be blackballed. I have arranged a carriage for you.'"

Part three, set in the same period, focuses on his life with a shadowy female interlocutor, very likely the same one who castigates him in "The Best Is Yet to Come" and closely resembles, as Montale himself acknowledged, his companion and eventual wife. Drusilla

Tanzi, known as Mosca, was his long-suffering chief tormentor and conscience, sometimes referred to by his friends as "Hellish Fly." Segre calls attention to the difference between "the supernatural and dazzling feminine apparitions" who animate Montale's major poetry and the everyday world of *Butterfly of Dinard*, where women seem for the most part "aggressive, masculine, or querulous companions, tolerated with stoicism: as if their poetic idealization amounted to visionary retaliation for an annoyance with earthly femininity, linked to the misery of living together." The narrator writes at the end of "Would You Trade Places With...?": "Late at night they calculate who has racked up the most points, which of them is unhappier, who would more willingly trade places with someone else." Their relationship is embodied by talismans: odd animals—bats, and okapis ("half donkey, half zebra, half gazelle, or half angel")—but also by household objects and a parade of domestic pets: "dogs, cats, birds, blackbirds, turtledoves, crickets, worms," symbols of the persistence of memory that also find their way into Montale's poems of the period. "Our life is a menagerie, or, better yet, a seraglio," his partner observes dryly in the sardonic portrait of a marriage that is "Relics."

The book's last section offers a mosaic self-portrait of the writer himself, a bumbling yet proud, memory-obsessed Chaplinesque antihero, who sees himself as the only surviving, if unwilling, witness to a disappearing world. In one of the funniest of these, "On the Beach," the narrator, having received a letter from a certain "A.B." with whom he appears to have once had a flirtation that she remembers more vividly than he does, tries in vain to place her—was she Anactoria, Annagilda, Annalena? "I was aware," he confesses, "that I kept locked away in the treasure chest of my memory a multitude of possible ghosts whom I avoided evoking precisely out of the fear of reawakening specters who were not always welcome but nevertheless kept surfacing in my conscience, somehow enriching it."

Montale sometimes referred to *Butterfly of Dinard*, which he viewed as an undervalued part of his work, as a novel, or a novel manqué. He told one interviewer in 1960 that he would have liked to write a novel, but that he hadn't even begun it; to another, he spoke of "some approximations of pages of what could be a novel of mine (never an anti-novel)." But he also described the book as, "albeit in fragmentary mode, an autobiographical novel of mine; everything in that book is autobiographical, I have almost written a novel, then; it's a 'new' novel, not a traditional novel." At times he described his poetry in similar terms. He called the "Mottetti" ("Motets"), a sequence from the 1930s that is central to *Le occasioni* (1939), "an entirely unmysterious autobiographical novel" (and, elsewhere, a "novelette"), though he bemoaned its "lack of all pretext to quasi-narrative development"; the "occasions" of the "Mottetti" are moments or "flashes" (see above) of intense awareness, "snapshots" of supernatural clarity in which effervescent feminine presences bring sudden life to a deadened world. They had multiple instigators in Montale's life, but they eventually coalesced in the figure of Clizia,[7] an amorous and moral ideal who over time becomes emblematic of resistance to an inimical reality and the focal heroine of his poetry, his Beatrice, as it were. Her primary inspiration was a young Jewish-American academic named Irma Brandeis, who had come to Florence in 1933 to write a novel, and with whom Montale became passionately and secretly involved. She returned to the United States for good in 1938, after the promulgation of Mussolini's racial laws, and her relationship with Montale eventually ended. But the figure of Clizia lies at the heart of his poetry. In *La bufera* she metamorphoses into a salvific, though absent, "visiting angel," a source of purpose, hope, and admonition as the poet endures the crucible of the war.

By 1949, Montale was planning a new book of poems, largely about the war years, which he was considering calling *Romanzo*, possibly influenced by *La vita nuova*, Dante's "novel" of sublimated inspiration. Montale's book, which was eventually published as *La bufera e altro* in 1956, has been called "the novel of Clizia." But earlier that year Montale had met the young poet Maria Luisa Spaziani, who became a romantic presence in his life and work, and whose avatar, called Volpe (the she-wolf), represents a new kind of eroticized, earthly fulfillment. The Clizia-Volpe opposition, embodying the ambivalence between present immanence and remote transcendence, reflects an unresolved dynamic tension in *La bufera*. *Butterfly of Dinard*, which was largely composed and compiled in the 1940s and early 1950s and is concerned above all with the real, and the complex and paradoxical contrast between then and now, is a book that falls under the aegis of Volpe, as well as of Mosca.

Montale pays homage to the inspiration of a certain English fictional style in the stories of *Butterfly of Dinard*, writing that Ivy Compton-Burnett "has perfected that art of saying and not saying, which from Chekhov to Mansfield down to certain *New Yorker*–style stories constitutes one of the secrets of modern narrative." Short fiction by Brandeis appeared in *The New Yorker* in the 1930s and 1940s, and Niccolò Scaffai suggests that some early versions of Montale's *elzeviri* may have been written as coded bulletins meant to keep Brandeis informed about his Florentine life when she was in America. (The two also briefly discussed collaborating on a novel.) One of the most complex of the *Butterfly of Dinard* stories, "At the Border" (1946), is a rewriting of a narrative Brandeis published in *The New Yorker* in 1935, based on an experience of Montale's he described in one of his letters. The Clizia who is the protagonist of the 1949 story "Clizia in Foggia," however, is a young student who is much more like Maria Luisa Spaziani than the protagonist of *Le occasioni* and *La bufera*.[8] Indeed, Montale wrote to Spaziani that "90 percent of the story is yours," and asked her to write another, "Clizia ai Bagni" ("Clizia at the Baths").

Butterfly of Dinard comes at a crucial point in Montale's work, after the highly rhetorical *poesia-poesia* of the first three, Dantean books that conclude with *La bufera*, to be followed by the more ruminative, ironic, laconic work that issued from what the poet called his *retrobottega*, or "back of the shop," ultimately collected in *Satura* (1971), and the diaristic notebook poems of his final decade. The more prosaic, disabused tone of the later poetry reflects a vision of history as no longer a cosmic cataclysm but something that is actually over, "observed from below," as Scaffai says, and it was greatly influenced by the observer and raconteur who wrote the *racconti/non-racconti* that make up this enchanting, fascinating, episodic book. *Butterfly of Dinard* is no more a novel than anything else of Montale's but has much to tell us about its temperamentally reticent yet somehow garrulous author, and it has been translated here with care and finesse by Marla Moffa and Oonagh Stransky. *Satura* contains great poetry, including "Xenia," the haunting elegy for Mosca, and another brilliant "novelette" about an old man's infatuation with a much younger woman, "Dopo una fuga" ("After a Flight"), but, as the poet writes, "the accent's different, the color's changed." And as Montale enacts his rites of aging and loss, the inspiring heroines of his earlier work tend to merge. "Alas, / my mind's confused," he writes in a late poem, "many figures get added / into one whom I can barely / discern in my sunset." Only in the reminiscent jottings of the final years do the saving phantasms of his "adored ghosts" briefly reappear as themselves.

The closing *cul de lampe* of *Butterfly of Dinard* is also its title piece. This brief, deft sketch of an evanescent butterfly's apparition in an empty square in Brittany is addressed to an unnamed woman whom we can be forgiven for imagining as Clizia (or is she also Volpe, since Montale's butterfly is both Dantean *angelica farfalla* and iridescent, symbolist creature). Some have called the piece a motet in prose; it is the closest thing in the book to the vaunted *prosa d'arte* the poet more or less left behind when he became a journalist. But "Butterfly of Dinard" is not a companion piece to "The Prisoner's Dream" that closes *La bufera*, in which the poet persists in telling his long-sought-for, absent beloved, "The wait is long, / my dream of you isn't over." Here, as Segre points out, the emotions and symbols that raised the ghostly butterfly of Dinard have already been dissected critically, even self-ironically, in the *non-poesia* of the book that precedes it, "leaving us on the inhospitable terra firma from which the butterfly (or its symbol)" has taken flight.

—JONATHAN GALASSI

NOTES

These pages are indebted to the critical acumen of Marco Forti, author of *Eugenio Montale, La poesia, la prosa di fantasia e d'invenzione* (Mursia, 1983) and the editor and introducer of several compendia of Montale's prose writings in Mondadori's Meridiani editions; Cesare Segre, whose "Invito alla *Farfalla di Dinard*" (1966; collected in *I segni e la critica*, Einaudi, 1970) offers incisive keys to the exploration of this fascinating work; and, above all, Niccolò Scaffai, whose exhaustive critical edition of *Farfalla di Dinard* was published by Mondadori in 2021.

1   Expanded editions were published in 1961 and 1969.

2   The translation, published by London Magazine Editions in 1970, was by Ghan Shyam Singh, a scholar of Italian literature at Queens University, Belfast, who created the first English versions of much of the poet's later work. Mondadori published a final extended edition of *Farfalla di Dinard* in 1973, which included five new stories; this current translation is the first to include these five stories in English.

3   Typographical ornaments or pendants, often with symbolic connotations, printed at the end of a text, so-called because they resembled corbels, architectural supports for lamps. By extension, brief, interpolated literary-journalistic pieces.

4   Montale wrote about W. H. Auden in 1951, "I leave him full of envy. I will never experience the joy of being a foreigner living in Italy. God knows I've tried, but when you're born here, you haven't a chance!"

5   See, for example, "Where the Tennis Court Was..." and "Visit to Fadin" in this writer's translation of Montale's *Collected Poems, 1920–1954* (Farrar, Straus and Giroux, 2012).

6   Other collections of Montale's prose writings drawn from his newspaper work and published in his lifetime include *Auto da fé: Cronache in due tempi* (Auto da Fé: Chronicles of two eras), 1966, cultural criticism; a collection of travel writings, *Fuori di casa* (Away from home), 1969; and *Prime alla Scala* (Openings at La Scala), his collected writings about music, 1981. (Montale had studied to be a singer as a young man and served as the opera critic of the *Corriere*'s sister publication, the *Corriere d'Informazione*, from 1954 to 1967.)

7   "Two Jackals on a Leash," (1950) translated by this writer in *The Second Life of Art* (Ecco Press, 1982), is a genial evocation of the predicament of

"almost every lyric poet who lives besieged by the absence/presence of a distant woman," here referred to as Clizia, and how news of her provides the impetus—the occasion—for his poetry.

8   An earlier piece, however, "Solitudine" (1946, later collected in *Auto da fé*), is cast as "one of those Lettres à l'Amazone which Clizia"—who here bears a far closer resemblance to her poetic namesake—"says she is expecting from me."

BUTTERFLY OF DINARD

PART I

A STRANGER'S STORY

"MAYBE you'll recall seeing the *Amico delle famiglie* at my house. Every Saturday morning, through the bars of our front gate, the postman would pass me our copy of that innocuous gazette (whether parochial or missionary, I'm not sure) to which an aunt from Pietrasanta had given us a lifetime subscription. I would open it, nervously steal a glance at the puzzle section, and then declare in triumph, 'Buganza!'

"My father's groan of deep satisfaction could be heard from within.

"Although he and I had a fraught relationship, we shared a desperate need for the Reverend Archpriest Buganza's name to appear, without fail, each and every week among the 'solvers' of the *Amico's* logographs, rebuses, and other word puzzles (one of whom would be chosen at random to receive an edifying book as a prize). It represented a bond, a thread that tied me to my father. There was a correspondence between the harmless obsession of the old priest, who clearly felt obliged to respond to that weekly competition, and our own ever-hopeful and always-rewarded expectations of him. Back then, crossword puzzles as we know them today did not exist, but what transpired between us was a perfect illustration of crisscrossing destinies. Let me tell you the rest of the story.

"I couldn't say whether it was my father or I who first became interested in this rather odd matter. The priest was a complete stranger to us: he didn't live in our city, we never took the time to find out anything more about him, and we merely assumed that he was old. The fact is that for a number of years (how many?) his name was always there, so much so that its presence became vital for us, one of our most jealously guarded habits. What would he have thought had he discovered that he was responsible for pushing us toward the edge of the abyss? He probably would have considered it the work of the devil. And yet, back then, our tribulations were mild in comparison to what was going on around us. The city was changing, becoming more modern in the worst of ways. Cafés were being transformed into bars, which were in turn taken over by strange youths who perched on stools day and night in frock coats and bowlers consuming potato chips and Americanos, as well as other strong cocktails. Theaters were also feverishly cropping up, with Viennese operettas taking the place of *La gran via*, *Boccaccio*,[1] and similar comforting performances of our forefathers. Chorus girls had yet to arrive on the scene, but variety shows, with starlets and chanteuses, and the first attempts at cinematography led to numerous opportunities for the corruption of young people. Even I—who did not frequent those places—had stuck a picture on my mirror of the enchanting star who would go on to lead a venerated sovereign of Europe to be nicknamed Cleopold.[2] When my father discovered the clipping, a violent argument broke out between us. I threatened to pack my bags and strike out on my own. But I didn't have a penny to my name, and how could I possibly leave on a Friday, before the visit from the archpriest? The next morning, Buganza, who had won himself the life story of Saint Benedict Joseph Labre,[3] appeared, sealing—*in hoc signo*!—our reconciliation.

"And thus, our life went on, unchanging. Just as he had united us for months, Buganza continued to unite us for years. My father split his time between home and office (where my brothers, who truly were independent, lent a hand); I split mine between home and the porticoes of the new streets, still unemployed. I was, of course, looking for a job that was worthy of me and my skills, though what these skills actually were, neither my father nor I could ever ascertain. In traditional families, there was usually one son—often the youngest, the favorite—who was not expected to engage in any real occupation. The last-born son of a widower, sickly as a child, but filled with all sorts of vague ideas and non-profitable vocations, I turned fifteen, and then twenty, and then twenty-five, without ever choosing a profession. Then came the war, and not even that managed to tear me from my home. Then came the postwar period, the recession, and the great revolution that was supposed to save us from the horrors of Bolshevism. Business was bad: one couldn't obtain import permits without purposefully forgetting stuffed envelopes on the desks of commendatores in Rome. But Buganza continued his visits, undaunted. There was something unshakable in our lives, something that *held*.

"One Saturday morning, my father and I had an argument. A few thugs had beaten me up on the street because I hadn't raised my arm to salute a Blackshirt, and my old man approved of it and said that they had done well, that my foolishness deserved nothing less. The *Amico delle famiglie* arrived. I casually opened it, only to come upon something quite incredible, something that would change the course of our lives: *Buganza's name was missing*!

"'Farewell, Buganza!' I exclaimed, after a short pause, and then I went to my room and prepared to leave. My time had come: the thread had broken, the chain had snapped. With the disappearance of 'basso continuo Buganza' from our lives, everything could change, and it had to. It was time to begin a new life and it didn't matter that I didn't know how or where. My father took the blow with dignity, without comment. But I noticed that while he was watering the dahlias in the garden, he looker feebler and glummer than usual, although he knew nothing of my decision. I worked all day, part of the night, and into the following day, destroying old papers (even the clipping of Cléo de Mérode, rediscovered after years) and packing up others. I carefully prepared two suitcases. More resolute than ever—what did I have to fear? By next Saturday I would be gone and, in any case, a foreseeable reappearance of the phantom-priest was not to be feared. Buganza had interrupted the flow, broken the pact: he went back to being an extra in my life and now I could exist without him. Having planned everything, I felt safe from all hidden dangers and enjoyed prolonging my departure and savoring it sweetly. I retraced my steps down every one of my childhood streets; I revisited the route I had taken for years to walk to school. I had no friends, but I managed to get in a few farewell visits; without talking about my plans for leaving, I still surprised everyone with my odd comments. I told my father that I needed to go away for a few days. I can't be sure if he suspected anything. We exchanged only a couple of words that whole week. The days I had allowed myself flew by, almost without my noticing. I didn't realize that another Saturday had arrived until the mailman whistled at the gate and I saw the greenish cover of the *Amico*. I opened it up nonchalantly: What did it matter if the ghost appeared or not? The name was indeed back in its place, but a note that accompanied the puzzle section dealt me an unexpected blow. 'We regret,' it said, 'that on account of a lapsus by our usually diligent typesetter, the name of the Very Reverend Archpriest D. F. Buganza was omitted from the last edition. We thus extend to him our apologies, etc., etc.'

"The *Amico delle famiglie* fell out of my hand.

"After a brief moment of silence, I went over to my father, who was immersed in reading *Il Caffaro*,[4] and I announced, 'He's back.'

"'Who? Buganza?'

"'Yes, he was never gone. It was a printing error. It did seem rather odd…'

"'To me, too,' Father said, with a sigh of relief.

"Half an hour later I began unpacking my suitcases. It was pointless! The chain that I had deceived myself into thinking I could break had become stronger than ever. And now that my father is no longer with us and the *Amico* and likewise the archpriest are gone and only my house still stands, a large bomb could… but apparently not today, it would seem. Did you hear that? The all clear. We can go back up."

The whistle of a hoarse siren, a slightly waning F-flat, reached us from outside. I watched the stranger stand up, take his friend by the arm, and set off to finish his story in the open air.

THE YELLOW ROSES

"PRETEND to be my assistant," Gerda said to Filippo, looking at him through her loupe. "Imagine that instead of meeting by chance, two hours ago, in this pensione, you replied to an ad I placed in the paper, and now you are being subjected to a test. Not an exam, but rather a kind of experiment that I want to conduct, now that I've heard you speak. It's just after four; by eight o'clock I need to have sent by airmail a quintessentially feminine short story that will appear simultaneously in twenty-five American magazines. Nine hundred words, a thousand at most. Unfortunately, I'm not what you would call feminine," she said haughtily, flipping back her flaxen hair. "In cases like this, a man comes in handy. You seem like the right type. What's that? You don't know much about literature? Never picked up a pen? Even better; that's exactly what's needed here. Dig down and find the material for a good Italian story. Isn't there anything here in this room or in the view out the window that triggers some intense memory, no matter how old or fresh, whether disturbing or pleasant? Don't dwell on it. If it's there, let it out."

"Yes, there is," Filippo said, pointing to a lovely bunch of roses in a vase. "But it's a minor detail. Those red rosebuds remind me of other roses, yellow ones, which I couldn't bring home out of fear of arousing suspicion or jealousy."

"Yellow roses," mused Gerda, narrowing her eyes. "We're on to something. You say it's a minor detail, but if it had been, you wouldn't have remembered it. Who gave them to you?"

"A poor, lame girl in Piazza Duomo in the city of M. Let me tell you the story."

9

"But don't try and put it in any kind of order. Just tell it as it comes."

"My wife and I are, or were, standing in the main piazza. There's a lot of fog. We're waiting to see our former housekeeper—both humble victim and tyrant—who was with us until the world as we knew it collapsed. We had come expressly to see her, though we didn't tell her so, and, as soon as we arrived at the station, we called to arrange a meeting. Would she show up? She had to do the dishes first and then find an excuse to venture out. She's not some modern-day housemaid like the other ladies in their felt hats; she never goes out. What were we thinking, asking her to meet us in this weather, at two thirty in the afternoon, in a large, foggy piazza? Teodora (let's suppose that's my wife's name) will soon tire of standing and waiting. But no; she suggests we go meet Palmina at the stop where the tram arrives from San Clemente, the neighborhood where she now lives, two miles from the center. But does it make sense to wander off? We discuss the matter, a small quarrel ensues (though I'm not sure the quarrel actually took place)."

"We're in Italy, the more quarrels the better," Gerda said. "Keep going."

"We come to a compromise. I'll walk around the piazza behind the church and Teodora promises not to move. Fog and shadows, merchants and middlemen, pass in the distance. I walk around the church, under the porticoes. Brief parenthesis: I feel unsettled by the mere thought of seeing Palmina again. What if she doesn't come? In love, the one who flees, wins... And even if we're not talking about love here, she may well be shrewd enough to apply the poet's adage to her own situation. Perhaps she knows how much we missed her during my illness. But it couldn't go on, all of us together, she gave everybody hell: Teodora, deliverymen, the doorman. She really was stormy weather, though in no way vulgar. When Teodora was out, she used to sing at the top of her lungs, 'senza un soldo per dormir, senza un soldo per mangiar, non mi resta che...'5 Wait! How does it go? Damn memory! Such enchanting voices belong only to those who suffer extreme adversities or deformities. Then she came down with bronchitis. When she thought she was cured, the doctor disagreed, so she turned to extortion: no convalescence at our expense. Either she'd leave the hospital and come back to us, or she'd go home. The English were about to enter the city; there were endless bombardments. To our surprise, she made her way back to us, exhausted from carrying her belongings. A squabble promptly broke out and I failed as peacemaker, so I let her leave. That's when the dark period known as Liberation began for us. Hunger, disease, calamities of all kinds. Perhaps it had been a stroke of luck for Palmina to have made it to the other side of the Gothic Line.⁶ A year later, we received her news. She had managed to escape only two hours after we had argued, finding a ride in a truck that was later blown up as it was crossing the Apennines. When she reached home, she had nothing but the clothes on her back. With her news, a semiclandestine correspondence started up again—between me and her, between her and Teodora—that was both cruel and kind. Would she or wouldn't she come back to us? In any case, the thread had not been broken. This, by the way, is the end of the backstory.

"I stumble aimlessly around the Duomo. When I turn back, I can just make out Teodora's fur coat, next to an officer (she is, of course, inquiring about the tram from San Clemente). Then I see a small figure come rushing out of the fog, and the two shadows merge in one long embrace. It's her, Palmina. She hands me a long cardboard tube stuffed at one end with a bouquet of yellow roses. The two women walk off and I follow them, carrying the mysterious tube in my hand. We need to find a café. Palmina never comes into the city, so she doesn't know any, but finally we find one, a huge empty place with billiard rooms. The two women talk, bicker, embrace, and make up. In the meantime, I discover that the tube holding the bouquet is actually a bottle of wine for me; the roses are for Teodora. A sparkling red wine from Sorbara. I mumble my thanks. Teodora decides she has a few errands to run; Palmina offers to accompany her. I can't possibly walk through this fog with a bottle and a bouquet and so I decide to wait for them at the café. I wait for an hour, alone in a corner littered with sawdust, in the shadows of billiard players. Palmina appears to have fully recovered: her cheeks have a healthy glow (rouge,

Teodora says) and she still sways from her limp in that graceful way of hers. I wonder what the two are saying to each other. It's probably just as well they left me alone here. Women are especially bad at searching for lost time. On my own, I relish the thought of diving into a life that I once imagined finished. Will it begin again? Nothing begins again. Palmina was very astute, especially at speculating on my natural predisposition to doubt myself. She was the true head of the household, but she always used to say 'us poor servants,' as if she were being mistreated. Her extraordinary vitality made her quite attractive, despite her deformed figure, like a lizard whose tail grows back after it's been chopped off. But her presence also had a way of making people who didn't normally feel ill at ease feel far worse than she ever did. Only imbeciles, parvenus, and governesses who rolled their *r*'s expressed their surprise that we kept her on, though in fact the whole building thought it scandalous. I look at my watch; only twenty minutes before the express train leaves. We're going to miss it. I'll have to stay in M. until midnight with a bottle and bouquet of roses in my hands. Ah, not to worry, here they are, bickering and embracing. If we hurry, we'll make it. Palmina ushers us onto an overcrowded tram and comes with us to the station. I look at my watch. It'll be a miracle if we make the train. (What on earth were those two up to? I feel both the desire for and the threat of Palmina's possible return. I'll ask later. No time now.) We reach the station, I rush to get a platform ticket for Palmina, and we wait together while the train pulls in. There's some bustling, embracing, I embrace her too, for the first time, then we wave goodbye from the window as the train starts to leave. We're still standing when a sudden jolt of the train causes the bottle of Sorbara to slip out of my hand, fall to the ground, and lose its cap. An acrid sugary sourness fills the aisle. Everyone looks at me, annoyed, trying to step over the wine as it flows toward the luggage. The train speeds onward, it's dark and cold. Teodora finds a seat, and remarks that other bottles from the madwoman had also broken. An hour and a half goes by, the train approaches our city.

"'Don't even think about bringing those roses home,' Teodora says. 'The new girl will run off if she suspects that we met up with the little witch, so keep quiet. Give the bouquet to Professor Ceramelli, he's standing over there, in the back; tell him it's for his wife, she'll appreciate the gift. But don't make any gaffes, don't say we can't take it home.'

"The professor, a respectable person whom I hadn't seen in ten years, is surprised by the unusual present. He doesn't quite know what to make of it. He hesitates and I invent some excuse, but it doesn't seem to convince him. He finally accepts the flowers, also because he hasn't got any luggage. The train pulls into the station, the fog is gone, the professor waves goodbye, and walks off with the bouquet. For a few moments, I observe the bluish reflection of a neon sign on the pale petals of the yellow roses. One is bent, its head bowed. Then, in the dissolving mist . . . Is that enough? Perhaps with some order . . ."

"No, a bit more disorder," Gerda said, glancing at her watch. "Shame I didn't have my Dictaphone. In a couple of hours, I'll have my first Italian story: 'The Yellow Roses'. A perfect title. Thank you."

DONNA JUANITA

THE INTERMITTENT buzz of radio static came through the open window. Gerda closed it impatiently and turned toward Filippo with a piercing look, like a tiger eyeing its prey.

"Don't abandon me now, not after our first successful experiment. I need a second Italian story for my series. After all, this is how I earn my living. Look around. Doesn't anything here—painting, book, vase, flower, photograph—set the tone for you? Let go, open up; I want to trigger something spontaneous in you. Spontaneity is not my forte, as you well know."

"No," Filippo said. "Nothing moves me in here, besides you. But outside, oh, outside! You can't imagine whom you've just shut out."

"Who?" asked Gerda, looking out onto the street with curiosity. "A kidnapper?"

"No, a woman: *Donna Juanita*. The music that you just brusquely interrupted was her, or rather, the symphony of the comic opera by Suppé with the same name. But it felt like she had reappeared in person."

"A young love?" asked Gerda.

"A more persistent sentiment than that. Childish hatred, then virile compassion, and eventually oblivion ... until I heard that music.

"Donna Juanita used to come down to the beach for a swim around midday, wrapped in a large robe and protected by a broad-brimmed straw hat tied under her chin. Dark and shapely, she wouldn't tolerate amorous glances, and when she went to get undressed in the bathing hut, she came out wearing more than she had been before. Bathing skirt, petticoat down to her ankles, gloves, espadrilles, dark glasses, a dark turban in lieu of the hat—an entire arsenal that, coming into contact with the water, puffed up around her, making her look more like a giant jellyfish than a bather. She didn't swim. She just sat on the surface of the water and floated about, with much dignity. The beach sloped steeply and everyone knew that a few feet out you could no longer touch the bottom. She had a well-established itinerary: with a flick of her tail, she'd reach the first rock, the *carregún*,[7] as it was called, because of its throne-like shape, and there Juanita would sit, her bathing shoes in the water, proudly looking up at her terrace, which jutted out over the sea. Then Juanita would slip back into the bosom of Thetis (the only bosom visible in those circumstances) and, stretched taut in the wind, the folds of her tunic would carry her to the 'little rock', which represented a second rest stop; and on to the 'middle rock', a sort of low platform, almost an atoll, full of prickly sea urchins and sharp clams. There too, half in and half out of the water, Juanita would stop to rest a short while. Then, the final flight to the 'big rock': ten meters of actual swimming, followed by a scramble up the pyramid-shaped boulder to its pointy peak, from which she could enjoy a full view of her grand, cream-colored villa, built on a towering cliff, thanks to heaps of money and dynamite.

"The return trip followed the same itinerary, in reverse order. Back on land, the sails of Juanita's airship drooping and dripping, she'd throw on a second robe before the garments could adhere to her body and reveal anything of her shape. She'd then make her way back up the stony path to her house where an obliging *criada*[8] would close the oxblood-red gate behind her. How old could Juanita have been? Forty, maybe younger.

"I used to spy on her from a pine grove that overlooked her garden as she sat ensconced in a deck chair—her two daughters, Pilar and Estrellita, by her side—sipping maté and reading *Caras y Caretas* and *Scena illustrata*, the only publications that reached the household.[9] Don Pedro, her husband, didn't read even those. With his long, flowing mustache and freshly shaven chin, he'd stroll up and down the terrace in a panama hat, raw-silk shirt, and gaudy tie. His principal occupation was looking after the construction of the family mausoleum in the town cemetery. He wanted a Carrara-marble temple with lots of spires, as befitted his bloodline. To this end, they invited a sculptor from Pietrasanta to come stay with them, the same man they had entrusted to design the grand statue of Neptune and other sea deities on the shoulders of which rested their immense oyster-shaped terrace. But every so often, the statues, battered by coastal storms and southwesters, would lose a hand or foot, so his stay lasted for years. It all concluded in a long, drawn-out lawsuit, because Don Pedro, who suddenly developed a passion for politics, spent his money running on a conservative-party ticket—narrowly losing the election to a radical candidate who had spent far less—and thus was no longer in a position to meet the demands of the starving artist. Don Pedro de Lagorio (please use another name) did not survive the blow. He was taken to a mental asylum, where he promptly died, roaring mad (an outcome no one could ever have predicted, especially not the supporters who had christened him 'the lion of two lands' to impress those who, like him, had made their fortunes three thousand leagues away).

"And so the zabaglione-colored villa was closed up. Donna Juanita took the girls—her *cocorite*,[10] as she used to call them, who were never seen at the beach—and returned to Boca, the Italian suburb of Buenos Aires where the lion had sharpened his claws and taken his first steps toward wealth.

"A return to her native land? No, Italy was her homeland and even the lion was one of our own. He had gone to Boca as a young man and, after making enough scratch (hard cash, that is), he had sent for his Giovannina, from their hometown, with the intention of marrying her, a cousin he knew only from photographs. The transformation of Giovannina into Donna Juanita took place there, on the shop-lined *avenidas* where Genoese dialects from Cicagna or Borzonasca were more often heard than *criollo*. From this chrysalis came our plump butterfly: she never became fluent in her new language and forgot most of her native tongue and her Italian, which she had never known particularly well in the first place. As a girl, she had always been a prisoner, both at home and in the convent, and knew nothing of real life. She learned about music from the puppet theater she saw as a child, *Il diluvio universale* with Barudda (be sure to spell the name correctly, he's a kind of Ligurian commedia dell'arte character). In the show, God himself made an appearance, in the form of an eye on a cardboard triangle. A ray of light (created by a flickering candle) glowed from the center of the pupil, but, instead of the song of the angels, a barrel piano with a crank handle spewed out the only tune it could: the aria of the three brigands from *La gran via*.[11]

"As you can tell, following her death, I delved into Donna Juanita's past, managing to discover the very operetta that marked her destiny. She came back to the villa after their exodus, not with three brigands in tow, but two: she had temporarily plugged the hole in her sinking ship by marrying off her daughters, who came back to live with her. *El casamiento ingenioso!*[12] Yet the solution was short-lived. The two sons-in-law, Ramirez and Bertrán—tall, voracious, and sporting long sideburns—wreaked havoc on everything that remained and held the three women captive, beating and insulting them. Scenes of great ferocity unfolded in the dining room, under the autographed and framed photos of the great presidents, from Porfirio Diaz of Mexico onward. And when there was nothing more to loot or plunder, they all picked up and left 'for the Americas' (as their compatriots used to say) where it was rumored that they led a sad life and met with an even sadder finale. Donna Juanita was the first to die: she was in a hurry, afraid that someone would usurp her place on the celestial *carregún*. She may have even reached the throne on the notes of the "Cavaliere di grazia" arietta if *La gran via* had left any trace in her. I don't think the daughters ever aspired to much, either in life or in death. They had neither home nor homeland, neither language nor offspring. They never lived a proper life and probably never even suspected that another life was possible. I can't say who's entombed in the mausoleum, which was constructed at such expense and effort. Maybe other lunatics, fringe members of the family, or perhaps the artist himself came to repossess his creation.

"Is that enough? I expect you'd like to know the actual place, the shore from which the lion sailed for the New World. I imagine you'd like to insert the figure of the child hiding behind the reeds who threw pebbles at Donna Juanita and her *cocorite*, blaming them for building a palace worthy of Semiramis in a cove up until then inhabited only by his father. You'd probably like to know where, in what lands inhabited by recluses, victims, and alcoholics, such tales were still conceivable at the dawn of a century, a time when the mask of prosperity and progress had yet to be lifted. You'd probably like to know…"

"No, not for the story, at least," Gerda interrupted, scribbling the title "Upstarts" on a piece of paper. "Do come back to see me soon. And who knows? Maybe I'll even be able to offer you a cup of maté. But don't deceive yourself—any resemblance to Donna Juanita would end there."

THE REGATTA

The whole of Verdaccio—a small, natural harbor protected by rocky cliffs and hemmed by a semicircle of old houses that were either attached or separated by dark alleys and intricate backstreets—could be seen from Zebrino's third-floor room of the villa in Montecorvo where his family spent their summers. Located, as it was, on the far side of the bay, three miles or more as the crow flies, only a telescope could detect the dust being kicked up in that raggedy and picturesque cluster of dwellings, that den of pirates and hawks that not even the Saracens had dared to approach. There were no trains, no passable roads, no lodgings. If some outsiders happened to come ashore and venture down the narrow *caruggi*, the townspeople wouldn't hesitate to empty their brimming chamber pots on them without the classic warning of *vitta ch'er beuttu*! (watch out, I'm about to dump it!), generally reserved for passersby of distinction.

This was the legend that had reached the attentive ears of Zebrino, for whom, however, Verdaccio was nothing more than a hole in a distant cliff with one large leafy tree, a walnut that challenged all proportions and grew practically harborside, and a white splotch with turrets built on a rock off to the east. This was the home of the Ravecca family, the feudal lords, or the undisputed nobility at least, of the village. These were people who sent their children to the trade school in the provincial capital, people who wore proper shoes even on weekdays, people who read the paper and who frequented the city in winter. In other words, they were very different from the other folks in Verdaccio: women dressed in satin and yet barefoot, shifty and hirsute men, sailors of small craft, smugglers, and vintners without vines.

But did the Raveccas actually exist? Zebrino had never met them. Montecorvo and Verdaccio didn't enjoy the best of neighborly relations, and their two dialects had few words in common. The Montecorvini expressed themselves differently when throwing their by-products out the window, and their customs were also dissimilar. However, there was one thing that Zebrino was quite certain of: his father, some thirty years earlier, had been on the verge of getting engaged to the youngest Ravecca daughter, a woman now widowed, encumbered by children, and residing in the ghost town of Fivizzano. Most likely she was an unhappy, penniless domestic martyr, in no way superior to Zebrino's mother, but the news itself, having filtered down to the boy through a puzzling game of allusions, insinuations, and petty quarrels between his parents, made a lasting impression on him. If things had been different, Zebrino might have been born there, in that white tower, and Verdaccio wouldn't have held any secrets for him. If his father had married a different woman, he, Zebrino, would have been a different Zebrino. Maybe he wouldn't have even had that nickname, Zebrino. Would that have been a loss for him, or might it have been better if that were the case?

The sycophants in the family, the panhandlers who made their way to his house each Saturday in a kind of procession, the book peddlers from Pontremoli who stopped even in Verdaccio, and Battibirba, the friar, who came all the way from Sarzana just for handouts, all swore that Zebrino's father was one hundred cubits richer and far more generous than all the Raveccas put together, who were destitute and perpetually in debt. The elder Zebrino did not particularly appreciate any allusions made to the possible fall of the Raveccas. He didn't want the status that he could have enjoyed in his youth to appear in anything less than a favorable light. Most of all, he didn't want to be divested of a weapon, the *if* weapon, with which he systematically blackmailed his faithful partner in life. Although he got along with his wife just fine, if the *trenette* with pesto weren't dressed to perfection and seasoned with Sardinian pecorino or if the stuffed *cima alla genovese* seemed loaded with stale bread instead of pine nuts and *laccetti* (otherwise known as sweetbreads), Zebrino Senior wouldn't miss the chance of playing his wild card and, pointing at the white house on the far side of the bay, would insinuate that there, yes, *over there*, such things would never happen.

With the passing of time, the myth of the Raveccas began to fade in the soul of the young boy, taken as he was with other discoveries and concerns . . . but not before an incident erupted, the hidden meaning of which only he was able to glean.

On the twentieth of September each year, a rowing regatta took place in Montecorvo. *Lampo*, the skiff belonging to the Zebrinos, won every time, with no exceptions. It was faster from the start, due to its tapered shape and high bow, which drew very little. With the rowers' first stroke, *Lampo* always shot ahead, gaining one and a half yards over the others, and, at that point, it was all over, the boat seemed impossible to overtake. But that year—Zebrino had grown and was already twelve—a new threat loomed on the horizon. *Grongo*, the Raveccas' gillnetter, rowed not by its legendary owners but by three muscular fishermen from Verdaccio, made its debut at the regatta, posing a serious risk. Once the initial entertainment was over— the greasy pole, the sack race, and the anticlerical speech by the resident anarchist, Papirio Triglia—six bows aligned themselves on the horizon, waiting for the starting gun. The entire course was about a mile, with the finish line a hundred yards from the shore, near the first rocks. A crowd had gathered on the beach. Zebrino, his brothers, and their parents followed the event from their terrace, leaning over the balustrade. Who would win? *Lampo* or *Grongo*? *Lampo* was crewed by four local veterans—three rowers and one helmsman—and as such presented no direct risk to the family honor, but even so Zebrino was jittery and his parents seemed uneasy. One could see the bows side by side in the distance: *Lampo*'s high up, red and white, while *Grongo*'s was low down, a somber green, like a bird of ill-omen. They were the first and third from the left. The starting shot was fired, immediately followed by the sound of all the oars slapping the water simultaneously. For a brief period, the boats appeared evenly matched.

Binoculars were passed around but no one could get the lenses to focus. The boats appeared immobile, the oars padded. Small crafts, sculls, and swimmers crowded the finish-line rock, where Papirio Triglia, the local authorities, and the jury all sat bare-chested.

The bells tolled five p.m. The sun glowed on the vast arc of sea between the promontories of Mesco and Monasteroli. A puff of smoke from a cargo train rose from an opening between the rocks. The sound of whispered imprecations and the steady rhythm of oars intensified the silence that fell over the harbor.

"*Lampo*," Zebrino's mother said confidently, lowering the binoculars. "Ahead by almost two yards." It seemed she sighed with relief.

"Yes," Zebrino's older brother agreed, making a fist with his hand and peering through it like a telescope. "But this time it's down to the wire."

"Let's hope those hooligans give it their all," muttered the other brother, shielding the light with his hand.

"Argh!" groaned Restin, the local farmer's son, his lynx-yellow eyes fixed on *Lampo*. "Too bow-heavy today, she's no spring chicken anymore."

The boats were neck and neck, the rowers and helmsmen hunched over and swearing. They were at the halfway point.

"Those *Verdacciani* are pulling like mastiffs," Father said, straining to keep the binoculars steady. "I'm afraid we're going to come up short," he said, casting a sideways glance toward the white spot on the distant shore.

"We're done for," confirmed Restin, squinting and biting his nails. "*Grongo* is staying the course better; its crew is lighter."

"It's not over yet," Mother said, without even looking.

"I'm telling you it is," Father insisted, annoyed. "No, it may not be over yet," he corrected himself, "but it's a matter of inches."

They could hear the clamor from the shore. *Lampo* and *Grongo*, high bow and hidden bow, were seesawing in the spray, far ahead of the others. The shouting helmsmen drowned out the crash of the oars. Only fifty yards to go, maybe thirty. It seemed to last forever. Zebrino's heart was about to explode. Then came a piercing shriek:

"*Lampo*!" Restin frolicked like a squirrel as the red bow, with a final jolt from the helm, swerved under the finish line. The oarsmen dove into the sea, as winners traditionally do. Half-submerged by the swells, *Grongo* also crossed the finish line, and the crew from Verdaccio, defeated but not convinced, proceeded to scream horrific insults at the jury and the boats full of spectators.

"No one beats *Lampo*," Mother said proudly.

"By a hair," Father teased, wiping the sweat from his brow. "That's the last time I'm trusting it to those drunks. Now we even have to buy them drinks. Are you happy, Zebrino?"

Hand on his heart and as pale as a ghost, the child did not reply. He just stood there, facing east, staring at the white spot that loomed over the port of Verdaccio.

THE *BUSACCA*

IT'S NOT always that children, who are both the most natural and trusting friends as well as the foes of animals, have the opportunity of seeing rich and varied fauna, such as the city zoos had before the bombs came raining down, setting free rattlesnakes and tropical beasts. Some youngsters, most of whom live in so-called civilized (though perhaps not for long) countries, have a limited imaginary bestiary and for them the animal kingdom's Pillars of Hercules are represented by the dog, the cat, and the horse, and not always the greatest of specimens of them at that. This was the case for the boys of my generation, who were unfamiliar with the sport of soccer or with complex mechanical toys and relied on their imaginations, or even on the stories old people used to tell. With no menagerie to speak of, they built their own. A boy I once knew, whom we all called Zebrino because of the striped shirt he often wore (a nickname that was also a prescient indication of his inclinations and tastes), resided in a village that was wretchedly poor in terms of unusual zoological species, and so he turned to the old folk and their lore for inspiration, profiting plenty. Once school let out, he spent his summers on a strip of land that faced the sea, cut off from the rest of the world by walls of rock. The village had no through roads and the train didn't even stop there but made its way instead along narrow and remote tunnels, the only sign of its passing a tremor in the ground and clouds of smoke from the openings in the rocky coastline. A safe yet stark harbor, it provided something of a transient home to badgers, squirrels, and birds. This was not a land of wolves or wild boars, which require open expanses and deep woods. Zebrino had not yet become a hunter and rarely went out on a shoot with the men of the village. Various kinds of migratory birds were only names to him, and not of great interest. But a few resident species—the goatsucker and the *busacca*—had been his feathered favorites since he was young. To say that he had actually seen one of them might be something of an exaggeration: at least once he had come across a dead goatsucker, with its large, bristly, and beakless suction-cup mouth, like that of a leech bird, which in itself was quite something, considering that these "goats" were exceptionally rare. And the busacca, you ask? Well, the mere existence of that species had been called into question by certain serious men, the kind who had spent time in big cities. And none of the hunters that Zebrino had met could proudly say they had ever killed one. It was, or was said to be, a bird of prey, larger than a hawk yet smaller than an eagle, equipped with sturdy wings, the short span of which did not allow it to take flight from the ground. When surprised by a hunter, it would dive off a high rock and soar through the air like a glider or kite, before landing somewhere higher up or lower down, depending which way the wind blew and the seriousness of the situation, but always on a perch from which it could then dive off again. An uncatchable devil, it was as shrewd, robust, and bulletproof as a tardigrade. Poachers would often pull dead hawks, kestrels, and hoopoes out of their satchels, as crumpled and droopy as used handkerchiefs, but never a busacca. No, that was an unachievable dream.

It was this very dream that turned Zebrino into a hunter for a day. He had no rifles at his disposal and a gun license was unthinkable for someone his age. Although Zebrino felt pity for dead birds and did not intend to follow in the way of Saint Hubert, he reveled in the idea of breaking new ground: to kill the busacca on his first day out and then never hunt again. He would get help from Restin, the son of one of his family's tenant farmers, who was as young and defenseless as Zebrino but knew more about munitions and explosives. The two boys worked for several days, taking a lead pipe and rigging it, with the help of many nails and much twine, to a piece of wood shaped like the stock of a rifle. In the bottom of the pipe, where it connected with the wooden breech, they made a hole for a fuse. Then they loaded the weapon with black powder fetched from the mines and stuffed a handful of lead bits severed by scissors into the charge. To seal the explosive and bullets inside the pipe, they stuck a wad of paper pulp in it and tamped it down with a stick. It was a one-shot deal. No room for mistakes. And so, one morning before dawn, they set out, equipped with matches and a length of fuse pilfered from some local miners.

The plan was to close in on the busacca, light the match, then the fuse, and at the first signs of alarm from the prey, aim the gun at the flying bird for ten or twenty seconds, until the shot went off... and then watch the bird fall. Zebrino assigned himself the role of marksman while Restin had the job of lighting the match and fuse at just the right time, and without a word. The division of roles was perfect and the honor would be equally shared.

They walked for more than two hours, leaving behind vegetable plots and twisted olive trees that were home to peaceful warblers, entered a pine grove, then reached the high boulders from which they could see the central valley, normally cut off from view by the great wall of stone. The sea shone in the distance. The sound of hammering reached them from the quarry.

The miraculous encounter came sooner than expected. A large and enveloping shadow skimmed the earth and something landed in a gorge on a cliff, dispersing a flock of small, shrieking birds.

"The busacca," Zebrino said knowingly. (Usually people said "*a* hawk," or "*a* blackbird," but it was always "*the* busacca," singular by definition; pure folly to think that more than one might exist.)

"Are you sure?" Restin asked, trembling, unable to hide his excitement.

"Completely. I'm going to aim. Get ready. Light the first match."

They tiptoed toward the undergrowth. Restin lit a match, then a second, and finally a third, scrunching up his nose at the smell of sizzling sulfur. He followed Zebrino like a shadow. They were almost at the cliff's edge. There was a rustling, a hiss, the shrubs shook as if something heavy was passing through. Restin brought the match up to the fuse before it went out.

"Yes...yes," Zebrino said, extending the weapon to his partner before re-shouldering the fumigant appendage. It was a moment, and yet eternal. Smoke curled up through the air. Then a modest little bird—a sparrow or greenfinch—flew up from the ground and landed on a bare branch of a cluster pine. A few seconds passed; the thunder was about to explode. Zebrino didn't have the courage to look around. Almost involuntarily, he pointed the harquebus at the small bird, and the shot went off. A great explosion caused the weapon to fly out of his hands and break into two, practically throwing him to the ground, and giving rise to a large cloud of pestilent smoke. The rumble echoed deep into the valley.

"Are you hurt?" Restin asked, deathly pale.

"No, but that was pretty awful," Zebrino whimpered, seeing the two sections of the weapon nearby.

The greenfinch sat on its branch, chirping at them with curiosity.

They heard footsteps. A miner in an old alpine trooper hat and a friar in clogs—the kind who traveled to town to ask for handouts—came hopping down from one rock to the next. They asked the two boys if they were all right and, after Restin told the story of the busacca (Zebrino didn't want him to say anything and kept signaling to him angrily to hush up), the miner said nothing but gestured toward other lands beyond the waves that broke along the coast of the peninsula.

"Ah, the busacca..." he said, suggesting that it could only be found in faraway places, on distant shores.

The miner opened some canned beef and offered it to the boys and the mendicant friar; the four of them then descended silently down the hill toward the first ring of olive trees.

LAGUZZI & CO.

SIGNORA Laguzzi, who lived in the apartment above ours on Corso Asmara, did not enjoy the best relationship with my mother. Whenever an item of clothing she had hung out to dry fell onto our terrace, she never came to reclaim it, which would have been the respectable thing to do, nor would she entrust anyone else in her household to do so. She preferred to lean over her balcony with a long pole and flexible finial—a fishing rod, in fact, fully equipped with a line and large hook for catching bonito. Thus armed, she would initiate an undertaking that only after much struggle resulted in the retrieval of the fallen garment. I was a child and not terribly fond of life by the sea, even though I spent three months at the shore each year, and consequently this form of fishing, deriving from Signora Laguzzi's stubbornness, left an indelible mark in my boyish imagination. Ever since, I haven't been able to look at a fish hook without having visions of stray handkerchiefs, slips, or bras being caught by that barb. More virtuous than Shakespeare's Autolycus, who was known for snatching other people's garments off hedges, the very proper Signora Laguzzi used her hook to rescue her own clothes, to which no one else laid claim. No one but the child (which is to say, me), who did his very best to move the prey out of range.

Our terrace was large and L-shaped. My father used to stroll up and down it after dinner, until it got dark. I spent a little time out there too, but in the morning, around eight o'clock, watching for the arrival of the horse-drawn omnibus from the Vittorino da Feltre Institute that would carry me and the other privileged few to school. Corso Asmara was a steep, winding road with little traffic, somewhat on the outskirts of the city, and not in a very elegant neighborhood. Nonetheless, from my terrace, I could catch a glimpse of the front gate of a noble home belonging to a family that boasted a distinguished name, their very own horse and carriage, and servants in livery. A world that was inaccessible to me, far beyond even the rosiest expectations. The only person I knew on Corso Asmara was a tobacconist, whom I often visited in order to buy Cavour cigars for my father (his favorite) and a stick of licorice for me. And the only two people I might meet along the way were wobbly Uncle Ugh, so named because of his repeated grunts (Ugh! Ugh! Ugh!) as he labored to push his ice cream cart up the hill, and Pippo Bixio, a childhood foe who would sometimes beat me up, robbing me of both cigars and licorice.

A few years later we moved to another neighborhood, into a new apartment with lower ceilings but full of modern comforts, including an elevator, a radiator—which was almost always turned off—and a bungalow-style dining room, somewhat reminiscent of a whale's belly. Middle school ended, and in no time I was eighteen, then twenty, and I began going out at night. I used to stroll under the porticoes with no specific destination in mind. I didn't know anyone and hadn't gone up Corso Asmara since we'd moved. One day, a young sculptor, whom I met entirely by chance, decided to take me under his wing. He said I had "an interesting character" and promised to introduce me to his milieu. He kept his word and turned up at our next meeting in a bowler hat and patent leather shoes. Half an hour later, the carriage and driver he had hired dropped us off in front of the very same fortress I had spied on for years from my terrace. I thought I must be dreaming.

I was introduced to the lady of the house, one of her relatives, and a German governess—all portly women whose hands the sculptor kissed. Then came the fair-haired children: two boys and a girl, who seemed to be on very familiar terms with the sculptor. The apartment was lavish, decorated with striped and dotted paintings, or what people then called modern art. We visited the garden, which overlooked the port, offering an unparalleled view of it. We then had tea from a samovar, a shiny and burbling ramshackle contraption. Everyone spoke proper Italian with great distinction, though with an appalling local accent. A discussion ensued about an article in *Il Caffaro* on Fogazzaro's *Leila* and a man with a mop of white hair sang "Zazà, piccola zingara" accompanied by the governess.[13]

I spent a couple of hours there, which, on account of my shyness, seemed like eternity, before deciding to take my leave. They hoped, I was told in a polite whisper, to see me again. Giacinto, the youngest son, walked me out, as the sculptor had enviably been asked to stay for dinner. More or less my peer, Giacinto was gracious enough to accompany me toward Corso Asmara. We ended up directly beneath the terrace of my youth. Here, as the young man shook my hand in something of a patronizing manner, I looked up and saw, or rather, *recognized,* Signora Laguzzi's pole hanging from her laundry line. I felt a tug at my heart. Apparently, the immortal biddy had ruined her relationship with our successors too! A thought came to me in a flash: Giacinto and his family (and the sculptor) were *unaware of my past,* and I was determined to keep it that way.

And so, as bold as brass, I asked, "What in the devil's name...? Do they fish?"

"It would seem so," Giacinto said, distractedly. "I've seen the pole before, walking by. Who knows why... they're common folk, riff-raff..."

He thrust and I parried. At that point, only the little thief Pippo Bixio could give me away, were we to run into him, but that dreaded encounter did not take place, not then, not ever. A whole new life for me had truly begun.

THE HOUSE WITH TWO PALMS

THE TRAIN was about to arrive. In the brief flash between one tunnel and the next—no more than the blink of an eye for the express train but an eternity if it happened to be a local train—the villa appeared and disappeared: a faded, yellowish pagoda, seen from the side, with two palms out front, symmetrical but not identical. Twins when they were planted in the year of grace 1900, one had had a growth spurt and shot ahead of the other but no method was ever identified to slow down the first or to accelerate the second. That day it was a local train and, consequently, the villa, although somewhat hidden by more recent constructions, was visible at length. On the western side was a small flight of stairs partly concealed by a hedge of pittosporum, at the top of which someone (a mother, aunt, cousin, or niece) used to wave a dish towel to greet the arriving guest and, if the person on the train replied with a flutter of a handkerchief, the family would hurry to put the gnocchi on to boil. Six or seven minutes later, one of any number of relatives would walk through the door, exhausted and famished. Five long hours of train travel and smoke!

That day no one waved a white dishrag from the top of the stairs. A feeling of emptiness came over Federigo, and he ducked his head back inside just before the train made its way through the last tunnel. He then took down his valise from the mesh rack and waited, gripping the door handle. The locomotive hissed as it slowed, darkness was followed by light, and then, with a sudden jolt, the convoy came to a halt. Federigo got off the train and lowered his luggage with some difficulty. The station was small, situated in a gap between two

tunnels, and faced a sheer bluff lined with vineyards. Those journey-
ing onward were immediately thrust back into darkness.

"Porter?" a barefoot and sunburned man offered, approaching the
only passenger in shirt and tie.

"Yes, thank you," Federigo said, handing over his suitcase while
wondering who this man was. His face was familiar and it came to
him instantly. "Ah, Gresta! How are things?" he added warmly, rushing to shake the hand of the man who was now bearing his load.

Gresta was a childhood friend, a hunting and fishing buddy whom
Federigo hadn't seen in thirty years and had completely forgotten
about for at least twenty. A local, the son of farmers, he had been
allowed to mix with the children of the gentry back when Federigo
was, or thought he was, the son of a gentleman. They made their way
down the stairs that led directly to the sea, with only a low stone wall
and row of wispy tamarisks standing between them and the waves.
On the left, another tunnel led to the village, out of sight. To the
right, a few scattered, abandoned houses were set into the cliffs and
surrounded by withered gardens. They had to turn down that road
and then take a right again along a dry ditch to reach the villa from
which no one—truly no one—had fluttered a white cloth. Walking,
they talked, with Federigo rediscovering in himself a dialect that he
had thought entirely forgotten. And since Gresta, whose nickname
derived from a crest of his hair, of which there was now no longer a
trace, was completely same in all other aspects, just as the road
and houses around him were completely the same, that immersion
into a world that was no longer his own—an almost unreal return—
seemed something of a miracle. For an instant, Federigo thought he
had lost his mind, realizing what it would feel like if he could replay
his life from the beginning, in a *ne varietur* edition, over and over,
as many times as he wanted, like a record that had been cut once and
forever.

On second thought, there were some variations (the absence of
the salutatory dishrag, for example), and so Federigo's bewilderment
was short-lived. Gresta, meanwhile, seemed oblivious, rambling on
about anchovy fishing, the harvest, the passage of the wood pigeons—

not to mention the passage of the Germans and their atrocities—mixing old and new, contradicting Federigo's first impression that the temporal order of things could be reversed.

The sight of a house the color of saltpeter, with an attempt at a bungalow-style room on the second floor, instead reinforced his initial sensation, with every stone and every patched-up spot, even the surrounding stench of rotten fish and tar, tugging him dangerously down the well of memories. Yet even here, Gresta rushed to save him from embarrassment, informing him that Signor Grazzini, the pot-bellied and barefoot owner who had made his money swallowing diamonds in South African mines, had died years ago and the property had passed into other hands. Just a few steps further on, was the rental villa the color of blood sausage. Federigo was afraid of seeing the paunchy Signor Cardello, a well-respected man, despite his having killed his first wife with a kick in the gut. His fear was for naught as, apparently, there wasn't a trace left of the Cardellos in the entire area.

What about Counselor Lamponi, who induced his younger brother to commit suicide so that he could collect his life insurance? (A bottle-green, turreted chalet.) Or Cavaliere Frissi, who repeatedly set fire to his store in Montevideo in order to cash in on it? (A monstrous agglomeration of towers and pillars, a tangle of snakes and vines that brought swarms of insects and mice inside, from which came a wretched din: a phonograph blaring "Ridi pagliaccio," "Niun mi tema," or "Chi mi frena in tal momento?" along with random exclamations of *Caramba*! from the quick-tempered drunk.)[14]

For a moment Federigo was afraid he might cross paths with his two old neighbors: one in short pants, belly drooping down to his thighs, a gold chain on his hairy chest, and the other sulking under a straw sombrero, surrounded by ladies in black crepe, a tangible halo around his head, thanks to the social position he had attained as well as the charity he dispensed. But not to fear, Gresta mentioned other names, other owners, and only the shapes of the peeling houses and the blades of an old windmill brought Federigo back to the days of his youth.

Finally, the last stretch: the dried-out gully and the small path across it, the red bridge, the rusty gate, and the uphill lane that led to the villa protected by the two old palms. The gravel crunched under Federigo's shoes. A titmouse, perched on a branch of the fig tree, filled the air with its vocal squiggle and, from the well where women did their washing, a white-haired, though not elderly, lady stepped forward to say hello.

"Oh, Maria," Federigo simply said. Again, it was as if thirty years had vanished and he went back to being the man he once was and yet still had possession of the wealth he had subsequently acquired. But what wealth did he have to speak of, really? No diamonds, no torched shops, no relatives sent off to join the realm of their forefathers, no import and export of local goods. But rather, an endless and involuntary process of uprooting, a long circumnavigation through ideas and modes of life there unknown, an immersion into time that could not be marked by Signor Frissi's sundial. Was this Federigo's wealth? This it was, and not much more, despite the weight of his baggage.

At the end of the ramp, Gresta was dismissed with a tip and a handshake, and Federigo turned to follow the old girl, who had spent her whole life with his parents. They talked in their familiar way yet avoided remarking on how much the other had aged. They spoke of the living and even more of the dead. When they reached the front of the villa, Federigo turned and took in that vast amphitheater, with its rumbling sea and the crooked poplar near the greenhouse, where he'd shot his first small bird with a Flobert. He looked up at the third-floor windows, the room where the portraits of his ancestors hung. He went into the ground-floor dining room and let his gaze fall across the bare walls. Gone was the panoply of spears and arrows, a gift from the officer of the lookout post who had spent several years in Eritrea. Still present was the etching of a young and austere Verdi. Federigo rushed through the house and when he encountered, at the base of a certain porcelain seat, the trademark THE PREFERABLE, SANITARY CLOSET, he felt his heart stop short as if he'd seen a family ghost. His first words in English. There in that cubicle truly nothing had changed. Elsewhere, however, there were differences:

beds added, empty cribs, new sacred images tucked into mirrors, signs that other existences had replaced his own. He visited the kitchen where Maria was blowing on the coals, hung a mosquito net over what would be his bed, pulled up a deck chair and stretched out in front of the house, one-fifteenth of which was his.

"A few days of vacation in the company of my dearly departed will pass quickly," he told himself. But then, with some apprehension, he considered the flavor of the food that he'd be served. It wasn't bad by any means, but it was *that* flavor, the one that gets handed down, generation after generation, that no cook can ever destroy. The kind of continuity destroyed elsewhere that endures in the oil of the *soffritto,* in the potency of the garlic, onions, and basil, in the fillings ground in the marble mortar. Even his dearly departed, condemned to consuming far lighter meals, must have come back from time to time to savor it.

"But you have a place by the sea," his friends would comment with surprise when they saw him at some fashionable beach where even the waves looked gift-wrapped. He did indeed have a place by the sea (well, one-fifteenth of one) and now he had come back to visit.

From within, the soft tinkling of crystal informed him that dinner was served; not the conch shell that his brother used to blow to gather the family together. That was gone. (Where was that horn? He must look for it.)

Federigo got up, aimed his finger at the titmouse that had dared follow him all the way to the poplar by the greenhouse, and mentally fired a shot.

"I'm being ridiculous," he mumbled. "It's going to be perfectly delightful."

THE BEARDED WOMAN

THE MIDDLE-aged man dressed in a proper grey suit who stood watching the schoolchildren as they exited the Barnabite Institute did not initially arouse any suspicion among the few adults waiting outside. Only the custodian mumbled, "Never seen him before, what's he doing here?" The children appeared in twos and threes, or even alone; very few of them were met by a "grown-up" who took them by the hand. Much to his disappointment, the middle-aged man did not see any servants among the grown-ups. A couple of young housemaids in felt hats, yes, but no servants.

"As I expected," brooded the middle-aged man—whom we shall call Signor M., for brevity's sake—as he meandered off toward the porticoes of Via XX Settembre, which were more or less the same as they were forty years earlier, and even the school building hadn't changed much. But Signor M. had changed a great deal and he knew it. By avoiding his reflection in shopwindows, he managed to persuade himself that forty years hadn't passed in vain. He reached out to the woman who came toward him, handed her his lunch basket and bundle of books, neatly wrapped in a piece of oilcloth and secured with a rubber band, and let himself be led in the direction of Via Ugo Foscolo, down a busy stretch overrun with carts and cars rebelling against the man waving the baton, the *bacchifero*, as the traffic warden was called in their city. At the foot of the deserted, zigzagging hill named after the poet of *Le grazie*,[15] Signor M. let go of the old woman's hand and ran ahead on his own. She followed, hunched over and holding his basket and books in her trembling hands. The distance between the two of them increased gradually; it was impossible to keep up with that *batuso*, that little rascal.

Signor M. was perfectly aware that he was no longer a batuso, nor did he ignore the fact that Maria had died some thirty years earlier in a private nursing home, which they had chosen for her when it was no longer possible to keep a deteriorating, not to mention putrefying, eighty-year-old at home. He knew all of this but since the street and houses between the Barnabite Institute and his home of forty years ago were practically identical, he didn't think it at all odd that he had evoked the body and spirit of the deceased chaperone who had accompanied him throughout his childhood. Why had he wanted to watch the children leaving that school, if not to see her again? The places where he could summon up Maria were but two: along that route and in the kitchen of his paternal home in Montecorvo, where Signor M. hadn't set foot in years. A similar exercise would be unthinkable in any of the other homes he had occupied, now destroyed, or inhabited by new tenants.

Signor M. stopped in front of the massive walls of the Acquasola and sat on a bollard. "Better wait for her," he said to himself. "She's fallen behind."

Old from the day she was born, illiterate, hunchbacked, and bearded since time immemorial, Maria had been the tenacious custodian of the M. family fortune long before the paterfamilias had married and extended the branches of the family tree in a not-unworthy manner. From the age of fifteen until she was eighty, Maria was both the rule maker and the referee of the household. Of course, she had once had her own home, although she could only return there during their summer vacation in Montecorvo, from which it was a ten-hour walk. In the early days, for two or three seasons, she undertook the journey, but when she realized that people no longer remembered who she was and even considered her an outsider, an intruder, Maria cut the cord once and for all to her ancestral hovel. She had two homes that were essentially hers, one in the city and one in the country, and she had children to accompany to school as if they were her own. Evenly separated in age, ranging from two to fifteen years old, they needed constant care and assistance, at recurring intervals. Her only consolation was the promise of eternal rest. The pleasure of life comes from repeating certain gestures and habits, from being able to say, "I'll do it again and it'll be just like last time but different, too." And discovering those differences is as true for an illiterate person as it is for an intellectual.

"Here she comes," said Signor M., seeing her approach and then skipping off toward Via Serra, tackling, with a touch of asthma, the uphill climb in the direction of the convent of the Capuchin friars. At the top was the dairy where he used to stop to drink a glass of milk and nibble on a few Lagaccio biscuits. This time around he also sat down in the garden but was unpleasantly surprised to find himself in a modern café, filled with the acrid smell of espresso rather than that of fresh milk. Briefly uncertain as to what to do when the waiter approached, he uttered an abrupt apology and rushed out, much to the surprise of other customers.

Maria caught up, out of breath, and walked beside him part of the way. He liked teasing her, with innocent jokes that grew more cutting over time. Napoleon's troops had passed through her area, the Val di Levanto, when she was a young thing. How had she managed to defend herself? Or was the virtuous chastity she'd boasted of really a fib?

Naturally, Maria was born half a century after those troops had marched through her valley but she shrugged off this detail and dug herself a trench with tenacious and pointless denials. She just kept saying that she couldn't remember, there had been no soldiers or officers; at some point there had been a fiancé, but she had never let him so much as touch her. He had left their village in search of work and was never heard from again. Who knows how long ago he'd died.

Signor M. preferred not to touch on a topic that would have been incompatible with the ten-year-old child he'd become but no other subject came to mind. Although part of him had regressed into early childhood, he couldn't deny the part of him that had come later. He pictured Maria at the nursing home, incapable of standing on her own two feet and yet still bickering with her neighboring bedmates and the sugar-stingy nuns. He saw the words of the letter that announced her death, which arrived many years after he had left home. Where was the old woman buried? He'd never even gone to visit her tomb. He hardly ever thought of Maria but flashes of her had come to him in the darkest moments of his life. A useless existence: that raggedy and illiterate woman's life had had neither meaning nor purpose. Signor M. was surely the only person in the world who preserved even a flickering memory of her. At times he had fought against that memory, trying to get rid of it, like you would an old rag. In houses that have been in the same hands for long periods of time, there's always some jar or trinket that no one dares move. But now Signor M., who no longer owned a home, had no such curio, nothing with that status, nothing that could be perceived as taboo. All he had left was that faint and wheezing shadow that he had tried for years to repress, the very same who now walked beside him, panting to keep up as he strode ahead like a light-footed roe deer.

A useless existence? Such an error to think so. When all the old servants will have disappeared from the world, when all the gears of the universe will have a name, function, and self-awareness, when the scale between rights and responsibilities will be in perfect balance, who will be privileged enough to say that he walked home with a ghost, who will be able to overcome the horror of solitude thanks to the protective presence of an angelic and bearded wonder?

Signor M. leaned over the railing and looked down at the vast expanse of gray roofs, the port, the lighthouse, and the sea beyond the breakwater battered by the southwestern wind. Nowadays you could get all the way up there from the heart of the city in an elevator. Every so often, the doors would open and a group of people would stream out and cross the small piazza without even looking back to take in the all-too-familiar view.

A voice said his name, startling him. "Well! What a surprise! And what're you doing here, all alone? It's been at least thirty years."

An old schoolmate, but not from elementary school, a man his age, an insignificant face. Signor M. tried to remember his name, rummaging through the dark of his memory. Burlamacchi? Cacciapuoti? Something with four syllables...

"Oh, nice to see you," Signor M. said. "Yes, just passing through... alone...stopped here for a moment..." He was stammering. Had this man not noticed anything?

Signor M. turned and saw a few old women leaning against the railing with some children in tow, but they ignored him. Maria wasn't among them. She hadn't caught up yet. Or maybe she had gone on ahead.

"I have to rush back down," Signor M. mumbled, hurrying toward the elevator. "Goodbye. See you soon...or later...or who knows when..."

He disappeared behind the closing doors of the elevator car; and down it sank. The other man headed for the main road, shaking his head.

THE BEST IS YET TO COME

HER QUICK and resolute decision, made as soon as they were seated, was received with a bow of approval from the young waiter who had appeared menu in hand.

"A double consommé, a grilled paillard, a baked apple, and a Manzanillo."

"Manzanillo? What's that?" asked the gentleman who was with her. "The *manzanillo* tree kills those who sleep beneath it. Its shade is lethal."

"It's a drink that's all the rage. Some people say it's a carob infusion. It makes you feel slightly and pleasantly queasy. But one's never enough, you need three or four a day."

She gestured to an advertisement: smiling blond men and women dressed in evening clothes lay in the shade of a big tree, holding small bottles of the fizzy drink as if they were hand grenades.

The gentleman continued to examine the menu with trepidation. An older waiter, more clean-shaven than the first, came to his assistance with the wine list.

"Chiaretto, Bardolino, Chianti? A Tokai from Friuli? Clastidio? A glass of Paradiso from Valtellina? Or Inferno?"

"I'd prefer Paradiso. Nothing else for now. I need to think about it. You may serve the lady."

The waiters moved off while the gentleman remained hunched over the menu.

"Trout *au bleu*," he mumbled. "Sole à la meunière. Eel Livornese. Well, how about that! No, it doesn't tempt me, it reminds me of the muddy ditch near my home. Who knows if it's still there. It used to—and maybe still does—wend its way between rocks and reeds, it was hard to get to, except in a few places. Sometimes, after a heavy rain, a few pools of water would form and washerwomen would gather there. And that's where the eels were, the best in the world: small, yellowish eels, difficult to see under the greasy soap rings that clouded the surface. To catch one, we had to dam up the pool with pieces of slate we'd drive deep into the mud, then we'd scoop the water out with our hands, and before it could seep back in, we'd climb barefoot into the ditch and root around among the pebbles and slime at the bottom. If an eel appeared, it was relatively easy to spear it with a fork. We'd jab it and fling the bleeding eel onto the bank, where it would wriggle around, but not for long. If we didn't have a fork, it was a more serious matter. The eel would slip through our fingers, hide under a soap bubble, and disappear. It could take half an hour just to catch one that was only eight inches long, slimy, disgusting, its guts hanging out, inedible."

"And still you ate it?" she asked, spreading yellow mustard on her paillard, raw in the center yet zebra-striped from the grill.

"We'd split it among the three or four of us after cooking it to a crisp on a fast-burning fire made of straw and paper. It tasted of smoke and mud, delicious. But that was just the first course that preceded our pièce de résistance: a garden warbler. To catch it, we had to lie in wait for two or three hours under the crooked poplar tree on the narrow path that ran between the greenhouse of succulent plants and the pittosporum hedge. My friends had slingshots (*vulgo*, bean shooters) but I had a Flobert that I managed to load with three or four microscopic pellets.

"We'd see the small, honey-colored bird hopping on the fig tree. It fed on the fruit, splitting the figs open by pecking them with its thin, delicate beak. It hardly ever flew from the fig to the poplar but it was impossible for us to hide under the fig. However, two or three times each season, the warbler (for us there was only *one*), with a rapid flap of its wings, would fly over the narrow path and land in the poplar. If it landed too high up or if there were too many branches in the way, that was it, but if it landed down low, in the open, a few feet away from us, we'd all fire at it simultaneously, with both rifle and slingshots.

"It would fall diagonally to the ground, still alive, a drop of blood trickling out its beak, its bright black eye shining until a veil came over it, and then it was dead. We'd pluck it quickly, while it was warm, its light feathers filling the air. The slightest breeze would blow them away. Naked and yellow, its rump stuffed with fat, it looked like an awkward mannequin, with some fuzz on the crest of its little head but, after a few seconds over the crackling fire in the vegetable garden, that vanished too. Hanging off a stick, the bird sizzled, dripped, and buttered itself, while the eel charred in the embers. And thus began our feast. Those were special occasions; we ate like that but twice a year…"

"And to drink?" she asked, while gulping down a sea of Manzanillo, unfazed.

"Water from the well, drawn up in a bucket, speckled with maidenhair fern and flakes of plaster, with ten or twelve lemons squeezed into it, bitter lemons, the size of walnuts."

The gentleman fell silent, his thoughts elsewhere. He raised the full glass of Paradiso to his lips, took a sip, and flinched. "No, no," he said. "It's not the same."

"You should drink Manzanillo," the young woman said, rustling through her tortoiseshell beauty case for her eyebrow pencil. "It doesn't kill you, it just wipes away the memories. You'd feel like an emancipated woman, afraid of nothing, but you want to stay mired in that ditch, fishing around for your eels."

The waiter came back with a dour look on his face.

"A chateaubriand?" he suggested. "A velouté of scampi? A dozen or two escargots bourguignon? A fillet of Rhine salmon? Or would you prefer to start with some snipe on toast?"

"I would have liked," the gentleman said glumly, "the leg of a warbler roasted over burning twigs of holly and a sliver of eel marinated in soap. Impossible, I know. Too bad. Check, please."

He extracted a blue banknote from his wallet, rested it on the plate, and turned to the young woman. "Shall we? The next time, I promise, I'll start with a Manzanillo, too."

"But don't stop at one," she said. "It's never enough. The best is yet to come."

IN THE BASS CLEF

"Beginning with this D, close your lips slightly and bring your voice in the mask,"[16] the old maestro explained, while tapping on the piano keys. "Later on, you'll also open E-flat, if necessary, but for now say *u*. Like this: *O-o-uuuu* . . . Perfect."

I had the impression of emitting a groan from beyond the grave, an inhuman yowl, but the old maestro seemed satisfied. Short, huddled over the keys, at once venerable and ridiculous, he would modulate the notes with his tiny mouth, shaped like a pigeon egg, which opened with difficulty between the eaves of his long white mustache and the quivering gables of a snow-white beard worthy of Moses. He warbled like a hundred-year-old nightingale, his little eyes twinkling behind thick lenses.

The windows (we were on the top floor) looked onto a vast square dotted with large umbrellas and market stalls. In the distance, an Argentinian general heroically brandished his saber astride an eternally rearing bronze steed. The avenue on the right that led to the sea was quiet, punctuated with nameplates for midwives and obscure orthodontic offices. He lived a bit out of the way, the old maestro, but it was worth the effort. After all, he had spent time with Maurel and Navarrini and brought the house down at both the Imperial in St. Petersburg and the Liceu in Barcelona, so he alone could save me from the ghastly incompetence of conservatory teachers. The voice lessons started very early, at eight thirty in the morning and usually lasted thirty minutes. By nine a.m., I would be in the public library, which was practically deserted at that hour. The book collection wasn't extensive and the librarian couldn't stand to be disturbed, but on a shelf that was accessible to the public, I found fodder for several months. (It was there that I read countless books by Lemaître and Scherer, the latter introducing us to Amiel.[17]) In the meantime, my lessons proceeded regularly. Little by little, I started to accept that I would have to bid adieu to my bass voice as I had imagined it. No more Boris or Gurnemanz or Filippo II. I'd have to forget the notes beneath the lines, the sepulchral sounds of the eunuch Osmin or of Sarastro. The old maestro was firm on the matter. Not even in the new register did he give me any false hopes that one day I would be able to wear Jago's plumed fez or sport Scarpia's monocle and snuff-box. He abhorred all that was modern and was certain that it would lead me to ruin. My genre could only be the traditional bel canto: Carlo V, Valentino, Giorgio Germont, Belcore, Dr. Malatesta. Those would suit me.[18]

"Giardini dell'Alcázar, de' mauri Regi delizie, oh quanto…"[19] A succession of C notes struck again and again like a gong, followed by a hornet's nest of arabesques and flourishes, rising higher and higher to the grand fermata—a high F—traveling beyond the statue of the general, coming to its resolution on a middle C, with an irresistible effect. This is how Alfonso XII, the king of Castile, makes his entrance and how the old maestro had won his battle forty years earlier, when it was said that Dom Pedro of Brazil applauded so hard that his hands stung. How sad I was though, not to recognize my old voice any longer, nor to be able to judge my new one. I now possessed another instrument, one that was of no interest to me. At the end of my half hour, other pupils would arrive and I soon made their acquaintance: a bespectacled accountant for Lloyd Sabaudo, a marshal of the cara-binieri (Signor Calastrone), and a woman with a tiny waist, short legs, and a crown of fake ringlets; she was the wife of an industrialist who didn't understand her (she told me straightaway). They arrived to rehearse the terzetto from *I Lombardi alla prima crociata*.[20] One day, sitting outside near a mullet and calamari kiosk, I happened to hear their "Qual voluttà trascorrere" pelting down on annoyed pass-ersby. Signora Poiret invited me to her house more than once. She lived in a crenellated and turreted villa accessible via a drawbridge.

She was from Caravaggio, despite her husband's French name, and she used to address me with the formal *Voi* twenty years before that infelicitous practice became obligatory. She debuted in *Cavalleria* at Pontremoli and then disappeared from the scene. She lacked everything except voice. From her I learned that the old maestro, always so unforthcoming with me, actually considered me the only worthwhile pupil fate had bestowed upon him in three lustrums of teaching. The only one, with the exception of herself, of course. I thought I must be hallucinating. Were they poking fun at me? I cautiously interrogated the old maestro, who dispelled all doubts. I had to accept it: neither Signora Poiret (you can't be serious!), nor the tram engineer (who howled his Amonasro, causing the fishmongers to look up in surprise), nor the daughter of the director of a mental institution (an aloof Mignon and corpulent, feline Principessa Eboli), nor the accountant (a tremulous and coy Nemorino), and least of all the woeful Signor Calastrone (most definitely not!), none of them were worthy, in his opinion, of lacing up my boots.[21] Voice, according to the old maestro, was nothing. What counted was what he called in dialect *axillo*, also known as *arzente*—that ardent flame—or put simply, a little pepper under one's tail. If everything went well, when they heard me sing the role of Valentino, the adolescent hero with hemp-colored hair, and perform the "Santa Medaglia" aria in the scene with the crosses, the scene of his death, they would hail me as the new Kaschmann.[22] I left that meeting with the aforementioned tail between my legs. Why was I—an incurable bookworm—fatefully granted *axillo*? And to what end, if they only entrusted to me the dullest parts of the lyric repertoire?

With or without pepper, the tail turned out to belong to the devil. One day, upon returning from the briefest parenthesis of a vacation, I was informed that the old maestro had suddenly died. I saw him laid out on his single bed, dressed in black and framed by his great silver mane. He seemed to have shrunk. Diplomas, medals from the czar, wreaths of artificial flowers, and framed newspaper clippings decorated his room. His favorite pupils approached the corpse in turns, their "masked" voices squealing *mi mi mi*, like mice. Following the funeral, I left for the countryside and, shortly thereafter I was swallowed up by the Pilotta barracks in Parma.[23] The enchantment, not to mention the chant, had ended. I do believe the old maestro brought his vocal alter ego with him to the other side, that sonorous ghost he had industriously tried (without my knowledge and at my expense) to discover and develop in me, perhaps in order to recover his own distant youth. Years later, when I found myself in front of a piano and decided to put myself to the test, I discovered that both the deep and cavernous E of the Grande Inquisitore and the contra-bass D of the hefty Osmin had returned to their proper places.

But by then, what good were they to me?

SUCCESS

THE OTHER evening, at the opera, the *chef de claque* must have fallen asleep. The production—good, but not very popular—was soporific, making the doses of "well done" and "bravo" difficult to calibrate. This is the only way to explain how an aria sung by the bass, with two matching strophes, was interrupted by untimely applause at the end of the first strophe, a point at which no sonorous clause or vocal effect could justify a sudden round of clapping. What had happened? The chef de claque, upon awakening, gave his signal off tempo, it's as simple as that. There was some hushing and the aria resumed, but by then the trick was up and when it came time for the real vocal effect, with the bass descending "into the cellar," the feeble applause that broke out from what was by then a topographically suspicious point no longer convinced anyone.

One must be kind when it comes to claqueurs. I don't believe they earn much, and even if the audience should display an inexplicable indifference for the paladins of the lyric arts, they fulfill a role that is altogether necessary. An opera or a melodrama without applause neither warms the heart nor can even be considered a proper performance. To forgo seeing Radamès and Ramfis take their bows after their bellowing of "Immenso Fthà," which grants the audience a glimpse of their bathrobes and turbans up close, is to miss out on half the pleasure of *Aida*.[24] To deny a grunt of consent to the gargling emitted by Sparafucile when he recedes after Rigoletto proposes his ignoble deal, is, to say the least, to be insensate, stonyhearted.[25] While that slightly grating sound may not be difficult to execute, it's far more than just a sound, it's the meaning of life for those deep-sea divers. Whoever has slept in a rented room or second-rate hotel has heard thousands of similar "notes from underground," and I'm not referring to Dostoyevsky.

The applause the other evening took me back in time. Once, claqueurs were recruited from the ranks of barbers. They were not applauders by profession, but out of passion, and no harm done if they could turn that passion into some spare change. When I decided to study bel canto, I was initiated into the milieu by my barber and chef de claque, Pecchioli, a true connoisseur who rarely gave his signal, a snap of his fingers. With the more famous pieces, arias with obvious effects, he'd leave things in the hands of his disciples and the paying audience, intervening only in difficult cases: a pianissimo or rare diminuendo in a tricky vocal exploration. In such moments, he'd whisper *bravo* so naturally no one would ever suspect he was paid to do so.

Even before I entrusted him with my fate as a singer, I did not figure among his favored customers. I was one of those rare clients who asks only for a haircut, refusing all manner of shampoos, lotions, and expensive massages, and, consequently, we weren't especially close. Nevertheless, on one particular occasion he needed an extra pair of hands and thus I joined his team of claqueurs for the evening. It was a new and complex situation. A rich compatriot who had just returned from Argentina was giving a concert of his own work: José Rebillo, pointillist painter and composer of various musical pieces, was not, in the strict sense of the word, a musician. It was rumored that he couldn't even read notes but nonetheless he composed music for his pianola by cutting and punching holes in cardboard rolls with scissors and awls. What came out of that contraption was then transcribed, harmonized, and often orchestrated by others.

In those days, modern music was represented almost exclusively by Wagner, whose work most people had come to tolerate. But music such as that of Signor Rebillo, all dissonance and screeching, had never been heard before. Was he a genius or a madman? Judging from the titles of his compositions (I recall a *Ninfea morente* presented as a "musical still life"), I ought to have concluded that he was, at the very least, a precursor.[26] But back then, and even less so today, I couldn't decide.

And so, on the evening of the concert, I entered the Politeama with a complimentary ticket and the goal of fulfilling my duty. But just as the dying nymph was taking her last breath and I was about to clap my hands, a chorus of hissing and protests rose from the seats and balconies, and the weak cry of "Long live Rebillo!" was drowned out by an almost unanimous booing that soon climaxed in "Death to Berillo!" vengefully distorting the musician's name. Was this a case of counter-claque? Or did Signor Rebillo have his share of enemies in the city? I never found out. Caught up in the tumult and far from Pecchioli, I rushed to take sides with the majority and vilely joined in with those who were heckling the artist with cries of "Basta!" The evening ended with jeering and laughter and I disappeared before my boss could find me.

Months later, in the company of others, I went to the house of the musician I had booed. He lived in a neo-Gothic tower accessible only by a malfunctioning drawbridge. Rebillo spent his days punching holes in cardboard and splattering spots on vast canvases. He spoke a dialect from the Riviera intermingled with a few Creole words and only read *La Prensa* and *Scena illustrata*.[27] No one could really say where his obsession with the avant-garde came from. Big, fat, bald, mustachioed, and ignorant, he was probably the most creative man to ever walk the earth. Maybe in Paris, twenty years later, he would've been taken seriously, but in that commonsensical and commercial city it was unthinkable. Rebillo's consorts, however, were not only scroungers and claqueurs, people who needed a meal or money; his best friend and confidant was a postal clerk, Signor Armando Riccò, a small and glabrous man who wore a monocle with a ribbon and wrote Parnassian sonnets by the dozens. Each and every one of his verses contained at least two diaereses, allowing him to declare that he had surpassed his God, the great Ceccardo Roccatagliata Ceccardi. According to him, a true poet could never write a line of prose without tarnishing his reputation. He had a predilection for choice expressions, employing the word *humans* instead of *men*, and yet feigned contempt for D'Annunzio. He lived a long life, always disdainful and never published. He used to say he wrote for posterity. Around midnight, the barbers and others said their farewells and Rebillo and Riccò were left on their own. Hissing and sneezing, the pianola was cranked up and Riccò would recite his verses in a reverie, emphasizing the diereses with eyes half closed.

On calm evenings the waves of the sea would break gently against the escarpment that protected Signor Rebillo's neo-Gothic tower and they probably continue to break there to this day, though the tower no longer stands. I have no idea what happened to the mountains of cardboard rolls that filled the artist's studio after his death. How to dispose of the verses of Armando Riccò, who died in anonymity, was a lesser problem.

From encounters such as these I learned a truth that few people know: art bestows its consolations *primarily upon unsuccessful artists*. This is why art occupies so much space in our lives and why Rebillo the musician and Riccò the poet, unintentionally evoked for me by the maladroit claqueur the other night, deserve a word of remembrance, which every grateful soul owes his teachers.

"IL LACERATO SPIRITO"

I RECENTLY saw, and listened to part of, a collection of old records, works for voice and piano dating back to the period between 1903 and 1908. The elderly gentleman who initiated me into the secrets of his musical archive took ownership of these vocal relics late in life. When he was young (some forty years ago), the death knell for bel canto had already rung. During the golden age of that era, records did not yet exist; when the new invention allowed for the surviving heroic voices to be canned (the first wax cylinders truly looked like tinned tomatoes), flaws in the apparatus meant that only a wisp of their sound was preserved. As a result, the voices came out strident, discontinuous, and altered in timbre. Especially unrecognizable were the deeper voices. Today only an expert can critically reconstruct the invocation from the *Ebrea*, "Se oppressi ognor," as sung by the massive Navarrini, who stood over six feet tall, age and glory weighing him down in the dawn of the new century.[28]

The stars of that period looked askance at the newfangled device, and with good reason. Faced with the prospect of being presented to posterity in such an artificial manner, they preferred to be forgotten rather than remembered in such a way. But soon a few gave in and others were recorded on the sly. In 1903, at the opening night of *L'Africaine* at the Metropolitan Opera in New York, someone hiding in the wings managed to capture what he heard of Vasco da Gama's disembarkation and its inspiring arioso "Beau paradis" as executed by tenor Jean de Reszke, including background noises and a thundering ovation.[29] The record went on to be cut and reproduced in numerous copies.

I listened to what is considered to be the only remaining edition, an object of inestimable value. Anyone familiar with that piece by Meyerbeer and its innumerable complexities can make sense of it, while others will only hear a general hum interrupted by various vociferations, concluding with a hard and tuneless B-flat, followed by a crashing wave of exclamations and applause that come across as insults. Nothing further remains of Jean de Reszke. The elderly collector knew of no other recordings.

A few years later came a recording of the aria "Io son l'umile ancella" from *Adriana Lecouvreur*, as performed by the great diva Angelica Pandolfini, who created the role, and of the bold serenade "De' vieni alla finestra" from *Don Giovanni*, sung by Victor Maurel. Scraping away the many layers of rust, one can still discern Angelica's extraordinary interpretation, but the arbitrariness and vulgarity of the voice of the penultimate survivor of Italian bel canto in France is somewhat stupefying. A squeaky "Home Sweet Home" executed by then sixty-year-old Adelina Patti is altogether indecipherable,[30] while one can still detect a few sparks of greatness in the (mosquito-like) voice of Tamagno in his version of the death of Otello.[31]

My listening experience went on for a rather long time; beyond the significance of those petrified voices, my curiosity was directed toward the elderly gentleman's hidden secret. Before taking my leave, I managed to pry it from him with relative ease.

An opera buff, as indecisive as Leoncavallo's clown between the stage and real life,[32] both shy and insatiable, proud and cowardly, he had spent the better part of his life trying to deliver a perfect execution of Jacopo Fiesco's famous aria from *Simon Boccanegra*.[33] Every day, from the age of eighteen until he was fifty, standing before the mirror with a lathered face, his brush and razor to one side, he would take a few steps back and raise his fist toward the doors of the marble palazzo opposite the Duomo di San Lorenzo in Genoa and thunder forth "A te l'estremo addio, palagio altero!" going on to soften his voice for the following line, "Il lacerato spirito del mesto genitore" before sinking into the final deep rattle (F-sharp below the lines) that seals the "Prega Maria per me" imploration.

While not a difficult aria, it does require an extremely mature voice. When the elderly gentleman was young, he knew his voice was not mellow enough; an immature bass is like an unripe fruit, inedible. The years passed quickly. Countless houses, hotels, barracks, clinics, hospitals, and rented rooms rumbled with the invective, allowing his voice to mature and open up, losing its choke point (or *tuba*, as it is known), only to realize that its timbre and consistency were also at risk. The elderly gentleman (who wasn't even that old at the time) knew he had to grasp this opportunity, seize the few days of perfection left to him, astound everyone with the famous line, and then withdraw forever in dignified silence. A doctor friend, who had abandoned a brilliant medical career, often came over to rehearse with him the "Suoni la tromba" duet from *I puritani*. More often than not, though, the guest fingered the piano and with furrowed brow attempted alone the bitter and snickering confession of Jack Rance the sheriff in "Minnie dalla mia casa son partito" and its explosive finale "Or per un bacio tuo getto un tesoro!" which had the unfortunate effect of arousing the inevitable complaints from the neighbors and the concierge. The ex-doctor had also been holding off his debut, waiting for years for his voice to mature, until one day a slight rasp made him lose his patience—and his marbles—and the aspiring sheriff jumped out the window and landed on the spikes of the iron gate in the garden below, dying instantly.

The future record collector took heed and gave up. At the age of fifty, the moment he had been waiting for had probably long since passed without anyone (least of all himself) noticing. From time to time, while shaving, he still finds himself taking a few steps back and beginning his "Il lacerato spirito" in a quavering voice. But then, in that very moment, the ghost of his doctor friend appears and his voice peters out. Besides, whom would he sing for today? The arts are in swift decline.

THE OSTRICH FEATHER

PEOPLE are a bit like books: you read one casually, without foreseeing that it will leave an indelible mark, then you pounce on another with fervor because it appears promising, only to discover a few months later that the effort was worse than useless. At that initial moment, the first impression, the question of what the end result will be—the ultimate profit or loss—is always unknowable. I often wonder not which books, but which living or deceased beings, might involuntarily flash before my eyes if I were to find myself in front of a firing squad (God forbid) or about to drown. Favorite people or beloved animals? Men or women who were dear to me, or people who were just passing through, individuals I merely brushed up against, acquaintances who would never suspect they'd taken up so much room in my unconscious?

If the instants that precede sleep, which ought to be filled with prayers and meditation, might resemble in some way the last moments of one's earthly life, I would have to say that for the *Homo sapiens* of our times—disassociated, devastated, and demeaned by a society where the more concern one shows for the rights of the community, the more inhumane it becomes—the surprises are sure to be many.

The other evening, before falling asleep, while focusing on the ultimate meaning of life and saying to myself "remember you must die," two strange figures whom I had entirely forgotten came to see me. Startled out of my reverie, I felt like a traveler who sees himself through others' eyes, and, upon discovering that his reactions to facts and events of the past have changed, gains a new awareness, embracing the old axiom that no man steps into the same river twice.

I was about to turn off the light when I heard a knock at the door, followed by a deep, cavernous, "May we come in?" (in at least a low B), announcing the arrival of a big, old soldier armed cap-a-pie, like the ghost in *Hamlet*,[34] with a long ostrich feather descending in an arc from his helmet all the way down to his spurs, and a servile and obsequious white-haired man who communicated more through gestures and lemur-like grimaces than with words belonging to any comprehensible dialect.

"Marcello," I said to myself, recalling the loyal servant of Raoul de Nangis in *Gli ugonotti*.[35] The memory of the character, inevitably associated with the singer who had famously interpreted the role, led me to recognize instantly the man who produced the most sepulchral, lowest notes the Italian theater has ever known, and who died years ago in Montevideo: the basso profundo Gaudio Mansueto. When I first met him, he was a broad-shouldered *camallo,* a longshoreman in the port of Genoa, but he went on to have a successful career as an opera singer, equipped with a natural intelligence that allowed him, when in character, to completely dominate the stage.

"Marcello," the soldier admitted, twisting the ends of his pointy mustache à la Marco Praga.[36] Approaching the piano, which was always open in my room, he ran his hand over the keys and hinted at the "Pif, paf" to evoke the siege of La Rochelle. The windowpanes rattled heavily.

"Ah," I said flatly. Then, turning to the other, "And forgive me, but you are ... ?"

"This evening I come to serve you in the role of Dulcamara or Alcindoro,[37] also known as Astorre Pinti, comic bass or buffoon, if you prefer."

"Astorre Pinti? Why, of course I know you, Signor Astorre. We spoke at great length in the shelter on Via Lamarmora, in those hellish days leading up to the Liberation of Florence." (Hirsute, famished, always in pajamas, his chest heavily adorned with pendants and medals, voice perpetually "in the mask"[38]—a *mi mi mi* spread across three octaves from groundhog squeal to death rattle—he and his large family had gone without food for a number of days.) His presence made the situation even more complex. Was he alive, or dead like the other fellow? I hadn't heard anything of him since.

"You surely won't recall, Commendatore Mansueto," I said to overcome my embarrassment, "but we were introduced some thirty years ago by Pecchioli, the barber in Galleria Mazzini. You took me to see the piano tuner, who was also the *chef de claque*, and listened to my rendition of 'Il lacerato spirito,' suggesting I continue to study bel canto."

"Ahh, ahh," Mansueto thundered and, "Ahh, ahh," sneered Dulcamara, a perfect third above.

They sat together at the piano, taking no notice of me. They played arpeggios and took the score of *La forza del destino* down from the shelf, turning directly to the section they wanted.

"If I recall correctly, Cavalier Astorre," I added, "you predicted the total destruction of Florence, city of blasphemers, which happened only in part. As for you, Commendatore, I had the pleasure of seeing you again in the role of Zaccaria[39] at the Chiarella in Turin, then I lost all trace of you."

"Ahh, ahh, ahhh," echoed Mansueto, and, "Ahh, ahh, ahhh," Astorre insisted, setting the tone for the two conspirators in *Un ballo in maschera*.

"I won't flatter myself to think," I continued, "that you, true luminaries of the lyric arts, might remember me, modest wordsmith that I am. However, if you dear sirs would be so kind as to explain to me the reasons for..."

"Giudizi temerari..."[40] Marcello exploded, hurling his hat to the ground and beginning his part in the duet of the two friars. A piece of the now broken feather fluttered behind the piano. The last syllable gurgled so deeply in his throat that it sounded like an organ, muffling even the screeching of the late-night tram. Someone upstairs pounded loudly on the floor, in the name of silence. The neighbors had most certainly been disturbed in their sleep.

"I'm so pleased," I went on, bringing my hands up to my ears, "so very pleased, dear Commendatore, to hear that your deep register has conserved, in spite of your age and altered conditions…of life, all its vigor. Nevertheless, considering the late hour and my neighbors' habits…though it may seem inopportune…yet surely, you'll understand, being so worldly…"

"Del mondo i disinganni…"[41] Mansueto burst out, swiveling around on the piano stool and playing his own accompaniment on the piano, while the other joined him with a mocking and stinging countermelody, in the hope that his piercing voice would make its way through such a storm.

It was a full-blown hurricane. A tempest of highs and lows, sounds from a bottomless pit counterpointed by trilling embellishments and belly laughs from an uncouth, paunchy friar: Padre Guardiano's lesson in humility and Melitone's objections and bawdy jokes. I tried to intervene, but my voice was drowned out. The storm went on until it finally extinguished itself in an ultra deep and visceral F upon which Astorre attempted his coy flourish—two octaves higher—but failed.

When I unplugged my ears, I heard a loud knocking at the front door. The entire building was in a state of commotion. Loud voices and cursing could even be heard in the street.

"Basta," the Commendatore said, closing the lid of the piano with a thud. "Basta," Astorre repeated, picking up his top hat, which he had placed to one side. The two men stood and bowed.

"Servitor," they issued in unison, like Gounod's Mefisto,[42] descending to an F-sharp that seemed to come directly from the underworld, and then crossed over the threshold, apparently deeply satisfied with their nocturnal lesson.

I remained in a state of agitation for quite some time as the complaints from outside began to fade. The departure of the armorer and the pipsqueak had apparently passed unnoticed; that they left on a broomstick seemed altogether improbable. I slept very little after, mumbling "Del mondo i disinganni" over and over and trying to understand the hidden meaning of that nighttime visit. Had I witnessed an encounter between a dead man and a living being, or the evening excursion of two ghosts? And if the two knew nothing of me, why had they come to my house? And lastly, if I was to consider them a mere product of my subconscious, a hallucination, why hadn't I generated someone of greater importance?

I then realized that a link between the two figures did indeed exist within me. When I first met Marcello, I hoped one day to emulate his glory and follow in his footsteps. Some thirty years later, while sharing days of deprivation with Astorre, I thanked God I was not him, despite the fact that I went on to incur my own more humiliating troubles. The two men represented the beginning and end of an arc: my own personal and private parabola. Meanwhile, they continued to ignore the man for whom, objectively speaking, they existed most fully. We do not always succeed in living on in the person of our choosing.

The following morning, I telephoned my neighbor upstairs to apologize. He drily replied that he hadn't heard any noise during the night. Later, upon careful interrogation, the cleaning lady who comes to tidy my room admitted to having found a feather between the wall and the piano.

"A small feather," she specified. "Chicken or pigeon, not ostrich. The wind must have blown it in."

PART II

THE ENEMIES OF MR. FUCHS

FOR A LONG time, I was impressed by the enemies of Mr. Fuchs. I didn't know them personally but he often spoke to me of them: high-ranking, powerful, shadowy figures, or just humble men and women. How could they possibly hate the monument of respectability, the leviathan of learning, the nonchalant scholar of snobbery that is Mr. Fuchs? Tall, thin, poorly dressed, with a long, yellowing mustache that drooped down around his gluttonous mouth, of elusive age and origin, the multilingual Mr. Fuchs is well-known in certain rarefied and intellectual circles, both in Italy and abroad. Penniless like all true poets (which he considers himself, although he does not write verse), his principal occupation is that of professional guest, one who is hosted yet never hosts. He seeks out rich families (aristocrats when possible) willing to provide him with a room and two meals a day in a castle on the Loire, a tower in the Vosges, a villa in San Sebastian or, worst-case scenario, a cozy apartment in Florence, Venice, or Milan. He seeks and finds, or rather, used to find, for after two world wars the rich have surrendered their castles to the state and the tradition of patronage has fallen into disuse. And so, even the greatly sought-after Fuchs is forced to succumb from time to time to a second-rate hotel where he is expected to cook his own meals on a small kerosene burner. A meal for him is always a *quatuor*, a quartet (Fuchs is known to express himself in French). For example, a pork chop, some boiled beets, a piece of cheese, and a pear—a meal that for you or me might seem quite ordinary is for him music worthy of Mozart. Not a day goes by that he doesn't tell his friends about his most recent quartet. Yes, because Fuchs, in addition to having a fair number of enemies also has many friends who, although unable to invite him back to their villas, ask him out to restaurants in the city and buy him lunches that are grander than his, although not in keeping with the rule of four. He is an expert in the art of making those who extend him an invitation feel as though they're bestowing an honor upon themselves, and a great one at that. Everyone falls into the trap, including myself. For a few months I was his friend and invited him more than once to my house or to a restaurant, seduced by his lively conversation and spirit. Then, one day, our friendship ended in an almost tragic way, and I discovered the truth behind the mystery that had exerted such fascination over me.

It was a cold winter in Florence, not long after Liberation Day. Coal was nowhere to be found, or maybe the other residents in my building could not afford it, I can't recall. The fact remains that I used an electric heater equipped with four coils, or elements, that only worked in pairs.

I was having lunch with Fuchs in my apartment when he began to complain of the excessive heat. I got up from the table and turned off the two elements that he considered extraneous. Not long after, Fuchs, gnawing at the leg of lamb (a miracle from the black market), raised his mustache to let me know that he was freezing. I leaped up from the table and reinstated the hearth of the four coils, apologizing profusely. Not a moment had passed before Mr. Fuchs issued the opinion that three—not two, and definitely not four—elements would create the ideal temperature for conversation.

"I'm sorry I cannot accommodate you," I said. "But my heater runs in either second or fourth gear and I do not own another."

Our conversation went on, with me jumping up from time to time to turn the switch on or off, but by then Mr. Fuchs had grown sulky, apparently mistrusting my skills as stoker. Eventually he got to his feet, bent over the heater, and fiddled about for a few minutes, turning switches on and off, until the heater fizzled out with a long hiss.

"It would appear that I've broken your heater," he said while smoothing his mustache and stepping back from the still-warm coils.

"Let's hope not," I said. "In any case, it doesn't matter. We can finish our conversation in a café that is more adequately heated."

My comment seemed to anger him terribly.

"There can be but two possibilities," he said. "Either I broke the heater or I did not, and if I did not, you ought to be able to confirm it by getting it going again. Don't you know how?"

I made a few attempts without any success.

"You see?" he went on. "That means the heater is broken and that I'm responsible for it."

"Not to worry," I said. "A valve must be blocked. It has happened to me too, on occasion."

"*Me too*? What does that mean?" Mr. Fuchs quipped. "So, you're saying that I broke it."

"I'm not saying anything, Mr. Fuchs," I replied. "The heater isn't working, let's just say it's my fault, which indeed it is, since I am guilty of not having a better heater. The damage is negligible and tomorrow it shall be repaired."

"By asserting to your guilt, you're only complicating matters further by actually affirming that I am the guilty party. I trust you'll agree that the word *guilt* is a bit excessive here."

"I acknowledge that and I apologize, but I was referring to myself, not you."

"Until the matter is settled, the word also concerns me. I came here as a guest and I leave as a culprit. You'll concur that such degeneration in etiquette is both unthinkable and irreversible. When I broke the wall mirror belonging to Princess Thurn und Taxis, she dismissed the butler and the mirror was replaced immediately. And in that particular case, I really was at fault, while today the question at hand is still *sub judice*. Adieu."

Mr. Fuchs gave a small bow and made his way to the door. I tried to stop him, but in vain. No reconciliation was possible. Unwittingly and unwillingly, I had been enrolled in the ever-growing ranks of his enemies. I comforted myself with the thought that perhaps I was more useful to him that way.

MR. STAPPS

THIS STORY has an antecedent. On a late winter afternoon in 19—, Mr. Lazarus Young, MA, PhD, a short and shy man who always wore a magpie feather in his cap, saw a sparrow, more dead than alive, shivering on a snowbank in a street in the Bronx, New York. In an effort to save the sickly bird, he missed the transatlantic crossing that was supposed to have brought him to Europe. Placed in the hands of renowned specialists, the winged creature was saved from certain death and luxuriously accommodated in a cage fitted with a heating pad that had been expressly designed so the sparrow would enjoy a constant temperature of 71.6°F. The entire ordeal, including the missed voyage on the *Jacques Cartier*, cost Mr. Young two or three thousand dollars, while Snow Flake—Snow, for short—now flaunting hoary plumage, went on to astound guests at the villa in Florence on Via dell'Erta Canina, where Mr. Young lived for a month every five years or so, leaving the house furnished in his absence, complete with a gardener and cook awaiting his return. The year we first met, Mr. Young, surprised by the so-called iniquitous sanctions that had been enacted in Italy, left the city in haste after an even shorter stay than usual and returned to his native St. Louis, Missouri, to escape the unwelcoming atmosphere. An unusual guest stayed on in the villa to look after Snow: Mr. Josef Stapps, a tall, corpulent man with light blue eyes, aged somewhere between forty and sixty, always freshly shaved, his chubby cheeks textured with small bluish veins, and often flashily dressed in shirts with large raglan sleeves and a number of accessories, including cameo rings, inlaid walking sticks, kangaroo driving gloves, lavish scarves, ascots, Dunhill pipes and cigarette holders, and the like.

Mr. Stapps settled into the light blue room, a long chamber (with en suite facilities) illuminated by four large porthole windows that looked out onto an olive orchard and garden that extended all the way to the street, and he girded himself for the atrocious period that lay ahead. Our friendship—born of chance, unforced, and inexplicable—is cause for reflection: if other people's love affairs (and especially those of our friends) appear at times incomprehensible, to the point of seeming exaggerated and contrived, as though a praiseworthy capability was being wasted, the same can be said with minor variations about friendships. Here, too, our judgments tend to be both tyrannical and proverbial: "A man is known by the company he keeps," and so on. But the premise is unjust, as each and every one of us has had at least one friendship that we don't know how to explain, not even to ourselves.

Mr. Stapps was one of these. According to him, I was the only one in my circle worth associating with, even though he was by no means a misanthrope and never missed an opportunity to allude to noble acquaintances, old bonds, and intimate collusions with people from different, worldly spheres, now on the run or being held hostage. I honestly think I was the only person he saw during those six months in Florence, and the same was true for me. He was my sole companion throughout that long and trying time spent waiting for the end of the world that never came, or rather, which did come, only it was six or seven years later. How was it possible that one man alone, and a mediocre man at that, could take the place of an entire universe? And yet, my good man Stapps, the only sentinel still standing in a city that used to be one of the beating hearts of European civilization, lived up to the task I had mentally assigned him.

To be frank, Mr. Stapps was a man of vague origins and lifestyle. He claimed he was Bohemian, that he had been married three times, was a Czech diplomat (often quarreling with his friends Masaryk and Beneš),[43] and yet he didn't know the language of his country well.

For that matter, he didn't speak any language in a fully comprehensible manner. Most of the time he relied on a mix of bad English and bad French or an even more fragmented Esperanto. "I have *delivrato* the falcon," he declared the day he freed a small falcon that he had recently purchased. He had no contact with Mr. Young's household help. A perfect cook, Stapps prepared lunch for himself, improvising savory dishes. In the evening he dined with me in local *buche*,[44] tossing back jugs of Chianti and preparing complicated dressings for his salads with the inevitable splash—*oh rien qu'un soupçon*—of Worcestershire sauce, while griping about the poor quality of the mustards and caviar. On returning home late at night, before getting to work, he'd stop to listen for Gilly, the ghost of a suicide who could be heard driving a carriage over the gravel around midnight.

What kind of work? It was untenable that he could be a writer, for the aforementioned shortcoming: no language was in any way congenial or familiar to him. I believe he drew on a miscellany of poets from around the world, from the T'ang to Rilke, all in their original languages, which he presumed to understand. It was a deeply personal volume, a sort of commonplace book, the kind Robinson Crusoe would have compiled as the sole survivor of a shipwrecked culture. Whatever it was, Stapps (part cowboy, part dandy) was a high priest of its culture, and this may have been the bond that united us. While radio-transmitted lies belched out a slop of harsh insults along the streets of the old part of town, and swastikas and German books were prominently on display, and the belt of our sudden national folly tightened around our collective girth, Mr. Stapps, with his gold teeth and the fatuous smile of an artificial forty-year-old, kept right on "delivrating" falcons, cutting and pasting Sumerian poems, feeding Snow Flake hypophosphates, and preparing his famously spicy stews, always calm, cool, wrapped up in a cloud of allusions, reserve, worldliness, and lousy literature. Yes, Josef Stapps was where he was meant to be and, for as long as he was there, I felt I could still have great expectations.

One late autumn afternoon, Antonio Delfini and I went up to the villa to taste a version of the goulash Mr. Stapps had prepared in

19— for President Stamboliyski in Neuilly. The dreamy climb to the house through orchards and gardens combined with the meal he prepared (and which we served) filled our bellies with fire. A beakful of the yellow paprika stew was even given to poor half-blind Snow, eternally cheeping in his boiler room. Juicy conversation in our usual argot followed, together with music from the phonograph, liqueurs throughout, and a nightcap of chamomile tea. At midnight, we paused our merrymaking to listen for the ghost of Gilly; even I heard the wheels crunching on gravel. Later, Antonio and I staggered back down to town, smoke coming out of our ears, entirely convinced that a window on the world still remained open, certain that around the globe that same evening a number of other Stapps had also unquestionably paid homage to the vestiges of culture that were straining to survive under the leaders of our day.

That was the last time I saw Mr. Stapps; the time during which I needed him most was waning, supplanted by grand songs of victory. A few evenings later, I climbed Via dell'Erta and saw that the porthole windows had been shuttered. I learned from the caretaker that Mr. Stapps had departed suddenly and had asked to be remembered to me. I have had no further news. As for Snow, the poor thing didn't survive the lapse in the strict diet that had been expressly prescribed for him by an ornithologist from Johns Hopkins and, the day after his taste of goulash, they found the bird dead, whiter than ever, balled up on the perch of his cage of fire; he was exactly eleven years and three months old. Mr. Stapps, prior to his departure, buried Snow with his own hands at the foot of a tree in Gilly's garden.

DOMINICO

RECEIVING a letter from Dominico in Brazil constituted big news for me. It was written in that half-American, half-Sicilian language of his which always made talking with him so arduous. I could only imagine how his newly acquired Brazilian patois would get mixed in, creating as yet unknown combinations! "Write me," he says, "*una vostra lettera sera [sic] muito desejada por min.*"[45] And to think that just yesterday I came across a photo of Dominico, *primus inter pares*, naturally, in a group of party officials and other big shots from his Florentine stay of ten years ago. Back then, with an exhibition opening or some kind of cultural ceremony taking place nearly every day, followed by a generous buffet of pastries and drinks, Dominico—always ready to take part for gastronomical reasons—was one of the most photographed and popular of men. Nobody actually knew his name, but there wasn't a party or "rally" (a word very much in vogue) where Dominico Braga wasn't in the front row, grinning at the harsh magnesium flash, a hefty wedge of puff pastry in his hand.

Here he is, in a photomontage, sitting next to the prefect and the federal secretary, wearing his usual yellow sweater, a pair of torn pants, and yawning sandals, his long mustache draped over his fleshy mouth and protruding chin. His beady eyes shine with satisfaction. To one side of his image is a list in block letters praising Florence's merits as a city of learning, with an eighteen-hole golf course, picturesque sightseeing in Tuscany, the traditional *Scoppio del Carro*,[46] the grape harvest festival in Impruneta, and other delights.

It was a grand life for Dominico, as long as it lasted. It wasn't a bad deal to feel half Italian, with no worries or obligations, protected by an American passport and the easily shouldered cultural baggage that combined Dante, Lorenzo de' Medici, Garibaldi, and Mazzini with Lincoln, Jefferson, Whitman, and Ulysses Grant to form his own "picturesque sightseeing," a backward glance into a universe now blinded by the lights of the new imagist poetry, of which Dominico Braga (the American son of an apothecary from the Sicilian town of Linguaglossa who in turn relocated to Bridgeport) claimed to be— after Ezra Pound—its most illustrious representative. As already mentioned, he knew very little Italian, and his English was not exactly refined. He was most familiar with the language of Linguaglossa, but even that had been forgotten or contaminated. And yet, at the age of twenty, "the call of Italy" had made itself heard and Dominico embarked as an apprentice scullery boy on the *Dardanus*, a cargo ship bound for Holland. En route he had a true lucky break when the ship's baker, an inveterate pessimist and avid reader of Schopenhauer and Hartmann,[47] killed himself by jumping overboard; Dominico took on the job, which paid him well enough that he purchased a Pegaso motorbike in Amsterdam and traveled across Europe. Then, when the Pegaso collided with a cow in the San Bernardo valley, Dominico wriggled out of the wreck by offering the owner of the wounded beast what was left of his two-wheeled contraption, and he continued his journey on foot.

In Florence his yellow sweater was soon ubiquitous. Within a matter of days, Dominico became known as the most voracious annihilator of cream puffs anyone had ever seen at a public function. He lived off cream puffs, and the occasional bowl of soup ladled out by friars, who pretended not to notice Dominico's repeated presence in the soup line. He enjoyed the fictitious life of a city full of students and foreigners. His vaguely democratic principles did not impede him from finding entertainment in the carnivalesque regime the Italians had instated and that appeared to him to be perfectly in tune with the pageantry of the Palio, the reenactments of *calcio storico fiorentino*,[48] and other traditional events. After all, "when in Rome" It's worth mentioning that Dominico was never one for subtlety, even more so since his maestro, Ezra, had assured him that the only thing missing from Italy were peanut plantations, but that otherwise, the country represented a model of permanent and efficient authoritarian democracy.

What could Dominco Braga possibly complain about? He ignored his new friends' laments and liked absolutely everything, especially attending mass spectacles and, in particular, the open-air performances in the Boboli Gardens. He never missed a show nor, for that matter, ever purchased a ticket, emerging from the bushes amid the sprites conjured up by theater director Reinhardt[49] and slipping into the front row in his yellow sweater, a big smile on his face. An unfortunate incident occurred the day he hosted two new friends in his gloomy attic on Via Panicale, people he'd met, unfortunately, through me. The three of them slept in one small bed: Braga; Morluschi, the proletarian writer; and Angelof, the Bulgarian painter. The typographers on the floor below reported hearing angry voices during the night ("Gangster! Traitor! Spy!"), leading them to believe that a violent ideological quarrel had broken out among the three drifters. Apparently, while taking turns napping, the two guests discovered that Dominico belonged to the abhorred "reactionary" forces and so they tried to kick him out of bed. But they finally made peace, and maybe during that appeasement, the ridiculousness of it all gained the upper hand over any political conviction...Whatever the case was, Dominico left Florence shortly afterward. Later I learned that he continued his obstinate ways on the other side of the Atlantic, publishing his prose and verse every four years in the ephemeral magazines that spring up like mushrooms during preelection periods.

What could I possibly tell him in my *muito desejada* letter? Linguistic difficulties are nothing compared to those arising from divergent spiritual backgrounds. How could I possibly make him understand what is happening in Italy today? A pure and innocent soul, Dominico Braga is one of those men who makes the notion of humanity without a homeland, borders, or laws (the kind described in classics of utopian literature) look both incomprehensible and undesirable. People like him manage to dodge the established order of things and slip through the fine net of history, thanks to the conformity of the majority, those legions of beings that stand in support of a label, a face, or a destiny that is shared and not individualistic.

Then again, is the liberty of a single human being—a liberty that is not one for all, but one *against* all—even of interest to us? I fear that Dominico, in saving only himself, also lost himself. He who fails to grasp the religious meaning of collective life also fails to grasp the better part of individual life. To be fully human, a person must engage with other people; a being must accept other beings. But what a struggle it would be to try and explain this to Dominico in a language that I'd have to invent just for him, at a period in our history when any form of selfishness, any form of self-declared anarchy seems preferable to the specious, social, and material deliberations of the remote superpowers who are currently calling the shots for us and our infelicitous peninsula...

ALASTOR'S VISIT

ON A COLD and deserted street on the outskirts of town, the arrival of a Lincoln belonging to Patrick O'C. drew some attention. The man who got out—tall and husky, no longer young but still robust, with thinning, reddish-gray hair—checked his address book and asked a grocer to give him directions. Number 117B Via delle Stringhe was a rundown building with an inner courtyard filled with the noises of children shouting and dogs yelping. Was this really where Ponzio Macchi, the most indefatigable, and perhaps the subtlest, of his foreign translators, lived? The street name and building number were correct. Patrick O'C. chided himself for his reaction; how unexpected that things were not as he had imagined, but life is hard for those who do not follow the well-trodden path. Patrick O'C.—known to the rest of the world by the pseudonym Alastor—tried to make peace with this maxim as he knocked back a shot of grappa. Then, after paying the grocer generously and asking him, more through gestures than words, to keep an eye on his automobile, Patrick O'C. headed toward the stairs, at the top of which a brass plate was inscribed with the much-anticipated name of Ponzio Macchi. The woman who came to open the door after he knocked more than a few times (the bell must have broken) was surly and held a sniveling child in her arms. Most likely the translator's wife, she was wan, carelessly dressed, and of an undefinable age. Was Signor—or rather, Professor—Macchi in? Yes, no, yes: it was hard to understand, since Patrick didn't speak a word of Italian, and the alleged lady of the house could not communicate in any language known to him. Finally, the Irish American man handed her one of his business cards with his name printed on it, followed by a coda of capital letters (MA, PhD, and others), indicating a noteworthy cultural and social résumé, and "Alastor" added in pencil, in parentheses.

Ushered into a gelid sitting room where at least four of his volumes stood out among the books on a small shelf, Alastor waited for some time. When he had walked in, the clickety-clack of a typewriter in an adjacent room had suddenly stopped. Was the professor working? Alastor shivered with cold.

A few minutes passed. From the room next door came an animated discussion, then the sound of a window being closed, and, finally, silence. Shortly afterward, the presumed Signora Macchi reappeared, and Alastor was admitted without further delay into the study of his commendable translator. The room was dark, the shutters firmly closed, and, when the light was turned on, Alastor saw a man lying in bed with an old wool scarf wrapped around his head. From under a pile of tattered blankets, a colorless face emerged. The marble-topped nightstand was piled high with manuscripts, perhaps indicating a new translation in the works.

The ill man's wife stayed for the meeting. Alastor bowed slightly, and jumped right in. He asked if he was in the presence of Professor Macchi (yes, the professor replied, in English), and if he had the misfortune of finding him sick (yes). He went on to express a regret of sorts for the untimely visit (yes), along with his gratitude for the work of translation and divulgation to which he, Ponzio Macchi (yes, yes), had dedicated such a precious amount of time that surely could have been better spent (yes, oh yes). The monologue lasted no more than a couple of minutes. The patient must be in a great deal of pain, did he want company? Did he prefer to be left alone? Did he need medicine, assistance, advice, suggestions? Was he in the hands of a good doctor? Was another visit opportune? Or was it better to forgo? Each of these questions was met with a yes; at which point Alastor announced that he thought it best to take his leave and, with another small bow, made his way out.

At the top of the stairs, he bid farewell to the woman who did not seem particularly flattered to be called Mrs. Macchi, and, a few minutes later, the American was drinking his second shot of grappa with the grocer before he quietly started the engine of his enormous Lincoln.

Through the slat of a semi-closed shutter of number 117B Via delle Stringhe, his departure was observed by Ponzio Macchi, now fully dressed, together with his wife and three overexcited children.

"He just dropped in here out of the blue," Ponzio said wiping his brow. "Doesn't even know a word of Italian, that dunce! Now what? Is he coming back? Did he say?"

"If he does, you'll just climb straight back into bed," his wife sneered.

"If he does, you'll have to tell him that I'm not here, that I've left, that I'll be gone for a couple of months. It'll be easy. I'll teach you the two or three words you need to know."

"If you knew two or three words, you wouldn't have made such a fool of yourself."

"Who, me? I talked the whole time, didn't I? I did fine."

"You'd do better by getting back to work! If he comes back, I'll deal with him. You should've just pretended to be deaf."

Meanwhile, Patrick O'C. was at the wheel and fast approaching his hotel. He was leaving the following day and was no longer thinking of his translator. Had he realized the absurd truth—that a character worthy of one his stories was lurking inside that man—he, a glutton for such prey, would have surely gone back for more, whatever the cost.

HONEY

SIR DONALD L. used to enjoy taking trips, especially ones to Italy. He had led a long and comfortable life that was, at least for the first half, entirely Edwardian: the life of a man rising in a nation that was itself on the rise, in continuous progress, never doubting himself or the social class that had recently welcomed him into its bosom. Son of a brewer from Newcastle, most likely a Jew, but not quite Jewish enough or rich enough to be able to glean the advantages of his birth, Sir Donald was a sickly child, far from precocious, welcomed to Eton with diffidence, and flogged to a pulp there by the older boys. He went on to graduate with honors from Oxford after a four-year struggle with both tutors and pupils who wanted nothing to do with him. He then entered the civil service and, after the first of the world wars, left with a title and a deep desire to live alongside his counterparts, the gentry. Thence began his epic journeys to a number of magnificent El Dorados as a self-styled man of the North who has heard the call of the South: Greece, Spain, Morocco, the Balearic Islands, the Azores, and, above all, Italy, which he got to know from top to toe. Southern Italy was where he wrote his books (of which there are no traces) and where he has, or rather, had, a few tenacious friendships. Ah, the good old days . . . gone, due to political and social revolutions that he despised; an interminable crisis; the madness of an Italian dictator who was initially so mild-mannered and charming, but in the end so cruel; and a second interminable war that led the English government to forbid its citizens from going abroad with more than thirty-five pounds. All this forced Sir Donald to spend year after year (the last of his life, the most precious!) in a gloomy three-room apartment, rich in books and memories, but poor in sunshine and human warmth. His neighborhood, St. John's Wood, was filled with trees, visible from each and every window. Homeowners and renters also had their own small gardens, and while they might have been only a few yards wide, each was enclosed by a front gate, where unusual advertisements (HOME WANTED FOR LOVELY PARROT—someone clearly wanted to get rid of a bird) were posted. Despite the neighborhood's proximity to the heart of the city, itself the beating heart of the best organized and most civilized example of cohabitation that exists the world over, Sir Donald still felt like a prisoner. He needed someone with whom he could both admire and criticize the gears of the universe of which he considered himself one of the decorative cogs. Whom could he talk to about such things? Certainly not the young bucks who sought his company: pseudo painters, pseudo writers, pseudo stooges, always ready to give him advice, drive his Austin (on rationed gas), or eat slices of his toast, in short, always ready to exploit the melancholy of an old bachelor who didn't know how to be alone. No, it was impossible to talk with such parasites, though at times they were useful. His ideal companion could only be an Italian on a visit to London, young enough to allow Sir Donald to say, "Back when you were still in swaddling...," and cultured enough to sustain a quasi-Platonic dialogue.

For forty-eight hours, I was this companion. On the first day, he took me around the city. While apologizing for not being the perfect cicerone (in Italy, it would have been easy; after all, what did I, a mere greenhorn, know about the real Italy?), he tried not to omit anything he considered either horrid or sublime: the docks, the slums, the changing of the guard at Buckingham Palace, pubs and chemists with seventeenth-century beamed ceilings, antique shops, a visit to his club, and endless parks and gardens, where recently imported gray squirrels had devoured the previously abundant red squirrels and now their own numbers were dwindling. Were they being eaten too? By humans? I told him that red squirrels were actually quite delicious, having tasted one myself in Italy. From here the conversation diverged, and we began to discuss the culinary arts. Sir Donald took offense that I was impressed by the billboards depicting bowls of carrots and yellowish sauces with headlines that boasted THE PERFECT SOUP or A MARVELOUS SAUCE in gargantuan letters. He thus decided to invite me to dinner. He wanted to prove to me that, despite the difficulties facing his peers, he, as a man of the isles, was skilled in the art of getting by, having learned it under other skies. He would prove it on the spot, without any further ado. No, actually, he needed some time to reflect. It was too much to ask him to perform right then and there. The endeavor warranted some preparation and fore-thought. We weren't going to solve it by just walking into a restaurant, much less if it were an Italian trattoria. There, they'd surely bam-boozle a visiting Italian like me, but not him, he knew better. He'd invite me to his house. Not right away, not that very evening, for crying out loud! He had to alert his cook, Honey, who lived in Man-chester but came to prepare his meals every once in a while. Isn't that too far? No, no, just a four-hour train ride. A telegram would reach her in a flash, and the following morning his sweet Honey would be there. A small banquet could be ready by nine. I was asked to come early; he would expect me at seven. Could I bring an Italian friend? Of course, even two. I was then dropped off at my hotel and had to content myself with a light standard meal, whereas the next day...

The next day, around six thirty p.m., I stood on the corner of Oxford Street and Park Lane whistling for a taxi, hoping to move a driver to pity. At that time of day, in London, it's not easy to find a taxi. A hotel porter, having pocketed a few shillings, whistled better than I ever could and saved me from disgrace. By seven o'clock, my friend Alberto Moravia and I were climbing the narrow stairs that led up to Sir Donald's, to make the acquaintance of Honey. The angel from the city of coal was as dark as coal herself. She was one of those women who, when asked how old they are, replied, "of legal age." She was round, fat, oily-skinned, curly-haired, and friendly. Sir Donald and his disciples gathered around her, laughing merrily. In-troductions and complimentary praise for the forthcoming dinner followed suit. Honey did not remain in the kitchen, as one might expect. Maybe the food was already prepared and simply brooding in the oven. Not your typical Englishwoman, she too must have been of mixed blood, and she was fiery, straightforward, and hardy, always ready for banter, quick to catch witty double entendres and salacious innuendos. Her Cockney accent made it hard to follow everything she said, but nothing stopped Alberto and me from doubling over with laughter, partially because we were good guests, but also because some stiff drinks had put us in a good mood. The meal was mentioned, but only incidentally: an appetizer of gulls' eggs (not subject to rationing), followed by a roast chicken, and finally a nice jam tart. It was ready, but then someone turned a key and opened a television cabinet, whereby the initial scenes of a murder mystery diverted Honey's attention, and that of everyone else.

I took advantage of this distraction to retreat to the living room with Alberto. We were worried.

"Gulls' eggs! I suppose that means seagull!" I said. "There's no way out now. I've heard they're as dark as Honey and taste brackish."

"Let's hope the chicken isn't actually a roasted gull," remarked Alberto. "*Coraggio*!"

From the other room came shouts and laughter. "Murder! Murder!" cried an overexcited Honey. We went down to the courtyard, where, for more than half an hour, no one came to look for us. Evidently the drama was reaching its climax, because we heard Honey shrieking and gasping in turns, until her cries grew guttural and then stopped altogether, at which point we heard the sound of people trying to rouse or rescue someone. The drama either had come to an end or it had been interrupted. We rushed upstairs.

The lights had been turned back on; Honey had fainted on the sofa. Everyone stood around her, fanning her and patting her cheeks. The show had been brilliant, but the resurrection of the cadaver in the trunk had given her one thrill too many, and she had collapsed. We would have to eat in a hurry and then accompany Honey to her son's house, just around the corner, about half an hour away, no more. In the meantime, the dinner had burned in the electric oven. Oh well, we'll make up for it another time. Three young Ganymedes brought from the kitchen the hard-boiled eggs on a platter; they were black around the edges and bright green inside from overcooking. Sir Donald warned us against them. Best to move on to the chicken (which was the real thing), but alas that, too, arrived charred on its nice bed of pickled vegetables and radishes. The tart wasn't too bad and we toasted with half a carafe of Australian wine, the "fill your own bottle" variety. It was getting late, time to go our separate ways. Honey had returned to her merry self and was beginning to pack up her things. She was showered with dainty air kisses and compliments for the extraordinary dinner. One young man went out to call a taxi. We left in two groups and to opposite directions: Sir Donald, Honey, and two of the young men took the Austin, while the other two guests accompanied Alberto and me in the taxi as far as the Tube station, where we smiled and said our goodbyes. As I descended belowground on the escalator, I glanced at my watch. It was twenty past eleven. Too late to find a restaurant still open, and, regrettably, we had forgotten to thank our host.

CLIZIA IN FOGGIA

THE TRAIN tracks glowed incandescent under the torrid sky of Foggia. Hovering in the gleam, amaranth-red railroad cars, a dry fountain, and a pile of bound timber (an absurd hint at a future winter), all seemed on the verge of melting. A glimpse of the train's caboose departing prompted the thought that a short, hundred-yard sprint would be enough to reach the last car but, in the time it took Clizia to realize what little strength she had left after two days in sweltering Foggia, the hundred yards became one hundred fifty, two hundred. Too many. It was three in the afternoon. Clizia rested nervously on the edge of a chair in the waiting room and examined her timetable. No more trains until seven in the evening, and even then, only a local, which would take twenty hours to transport her all the way north. She looked up instinctively in both resignation and despair, like a devotional figure in a countryside church who glances to the heavens for protection from extreme danger, as if trying to seize some symbol of inner faith. But the ceiling of the waiting room did not open up to reveal any consolatory apparition. What she did see, however, in all its lubricious and mournful pomp, was a long ribbon of yellow flypaper dotted with black spots that were not merely buzzing, but practically screaming and thrashing in collective agony. Stuck to the center of the syrupy strip was a large, black, immobile spider. How had it made its way to the middle? Clizia stopped to consider a number of hypotheses. She concluded that a draft had probably caused the tragedy; hanging from a thread made of its own saliva, the spider, swinging through the spaces of its aerial architecture, had been caught by surprise in a twister that had swept it toward the sticking point of its fatal landing.

Having solved the mystery, Clizia stepped out, into the piazza. Her cardboard valise was light but nonetheless made her overheated hand feel as though she had brushed up against stinging nettles. City cafés are not cheery places in the middle of summer, teeming as they are with bluebottle flies that collect around customers and drinks. Unfortunately, Clizia had already checked out of her hotel room. For a moment she felt at a loss. Then, salvation came to her in the form of a green poster pasted on a wall. In a conference room of the town hall (which she immediately imagined as cool and full of comfy armchairs), renowned professors Dobrowsky and Peterson, from the University of Baton Rouge and the Avatar Institute of Charleston (South Carolina) respectively, were holding an important debate on metempsychosis. Willing audience members could participate in practical demonstrations of the highest caliber. The entrance fee was only a few lire.

Shortly after, Clizia was walking through a front gate decorated with pine branches and stunted lemon trees, following arrows that guided her to the conference room. The welcoming shade of the hall was refreshing. A gathering of about fifteen people sat at a prudent distance from the table where the speakers were positioned, eager to begin. The two men were very different from one another: one was bald, lanky, bespectacled, and dressed in black, while the other was chubby and ginger-haired, and wore a raw silk shirt and a pair of Bermuda shorts.

An attendant, or, better yet, a disciple of the two teachers, made his way through the audience selling pamphlets. Clizia purchased one. On the cover was a drawing of a robed Pythagoras pointing toward a shield on the wall of the temple of Apollo in Branchidae. In a speech bubble above his deeply masculine and sculpted face, like those of the youths who encircled him, were the words: "This is the shield I, Euphorbos, slayed by Menelaus, used!" The pages inside the leaflet explained the episode in detail and also summarized the life and work of the great philosopher. Clizia read two or three pages. Her neophyte zeal began to wane as the cool temperatures of the hall surrendered to the heat coming in through an open window, with swarms of menacing flies looming large.

She moved a few rows back, into the darkest corner of the room, avoiding the inquisitive stare of Professor Peterson. Little by little, she lost contact with the outer world, sinking into her own black swamp with a not altogether unpleasant feeling.

At first it seemed as though the world no longer exerted any gravitational force. She felt light and springy on her eight very long legs, the extremities of which were covered in a gentle fuzz that softly cushioned each step, if such a word could even be used, since her forward movements could hardly be defined as steps, but rather fractions thereof carried out first by this leg, then the next, in a natural flow that happened all by itself, without her having to make any effort to give them impulse or direction. Now she saw the world horizontally, not vertically, which, she seemed to recall, was the case for human beings, who, planted on two stilts, proceeded at right angles with respect to the earth. Her new perspective was enhanced by the prone position of her body, extended at the base like a soldier engaging in open-order exercises, as well as by the strange positioning of her eyes, of which she had eight, like her legs, and they were arranged in a semicircle around her head, so that—and this is something that humans do not know—she could see much of the world around her all at once, augmenting her sense of both space and freedom. The vision in one pair of eyes was blurry, as if she were nearsighted, but Clizia discovered there was a reason for that too, one that granted her even more freedom. As soon as it got dark, that pair went into action, lighting up the darkness and facilitating her spinning.

Her web was beautiful. It was solid and well spun, the most beautiful one in that white marble courtyard, where a small fountain burbled night and day, happily spraying the soft moss below. Now and then a young man dressed in a white robe (where had she seen him before?) strolled through the courtyard. He held a book in his hand that he leafed through as he walked under the portico, ignoring everything else around him. Every so often, he'd come and examine the web. Once he even came to look at it at night. It seemed as though he appreciated the way the dew in the moonlight highlighted the thin weft of its outline. As he examined her work, the young man's large face took on an engaged and intense expression. It was as if the web were a continuation of his thoughts, as if it wended its way into the topics addressed by the book that he was reading as he paced from dawn till dusk.

At times, the young man with the pleasant, square-jawed face would receive visitors. They would sit with him near the fountain, or on one of the plinths of the colonnade, and not infrequently, right under the capital where Clizia lived. They spoke, leafed through books, and unfurled scrolls, their gestures creating small ripples of air that reached the web, causing it to sway, reawakening the flies entangled therein, already sluggish with agony (judging by the little resistance they offered upon being caught, there must have been something in the spider's saliva that diminished their vitality, making them facile prey, easy to embrace and suck dry). Often the young men would have a little something to eat, and, after they left, the spider would descend and carry off the spoils of crumbs, seeds, and sugary fruit peels. And so it happened that one hot afternoon, the spider, resting on the base of the column, noticed a line of plates brimming with a yellow, sweet-smelling pulp. Hanging onto her web, she greedily lowered herself down by the silken thread—alas, a tad too quickly!—unspooling it further and further. Looking up from the bottom with drunken pride, her strand appeared taut, shiny and strong. By the time the spider realized what was happening, it was too late, her horrible destiny was sealed. The soggy, golden nectar had stuck to the bristles on her back, and although she swung and shook and spat out saliva in an attempt to strengthen her thread and return upward, her head was already trapped. Soon after, a leg sank into the slimy swamp too. A nauseatingly sweet smell rose up thickly around her, making her body go rigid. With a cry of final despair and infinite revulsion, the spider was about to throw back her head and speed up her own death when a hand on her arm brought her out of her slumber.

The two men were leaning over her.

"Signora," said the man in Bermuda shorts, "you truly are an exceptional subject. Please come up to the podium and tell us what you dreamed. Could you start by telling us your name and a little something about yourself? Do you live in this city? Do you work, study, travel?"

"No, I sing," Clizia replied, just to say something (it was true, she did often sing, to herself).

"Signore e Signori," thundered Professor Dobrowsky, in terrible Italian, addressing the audience. "Here before us, we may very well have a reincarnation of Malibran or the divine Sappho. No, it couldn't possibly be; it would be too bold of a temporal leap. Could you please tell us, Signorina, who you dreamed you were? This dream will reveal who you were in your previous existence. Let yourself go, speak freely."

Clizia stared out in front of her, noticing that the crowd of fifteen had doubled in size.

"Well," she said, seized with a degree of embarrassment, feeling as though her privacy had been violated. "Well, I believe I dreamed I was a spider. Yes, a spider in the courtyard of Pythagoras. Or, at least, I think it was him. I recognized his face."

The audience burst into laughter and Professor Dobrowsky flushed up to his ears.

"Signora," he said, "how dare you make a mockery of science! You aren't worthy of my hypnosis. Do you realize the level of perfection required to progress in one single stride from the stage of spider to human being? Please, be serious. Tell us *who* you dreamed you were."

"A spider in the courtyard of Pythagoras," Clizia repeated. The audience sneered, laughter echoing all the way to the rafters. Professor Peterson took her firmly by the arm and led her straight to the door, telling her curtly that she should not take part in experiments if she didn't intend to take them seriously.

Soon after, she found herself out in the street. Trilling with life, she angrily clutched her valise and glanced at her watch. Only fifteen minutes before the train was to leave; her afternoon in Foggia had come to an end.

LADY WUTHERING

THE NEWS that Giampaolo had married Signora Dirce F., twice a widow, and his senior by many years, had not given rise to any unpleasant remarks around town. Life had been hard for Giampaolo, and to know that he was settled down once and for all (despite certain inevitable sacrifices) was a relief to his innumerable friends, none of whom dared insinuate that he was sponging off his consort. The wedding was followed by celebrations and banquets of remarkable sumptuousness, after which the two newlyweds retreated into the shadows. The couple was still a topic of conversation, but in slightly more elusive terms. It was said that Giampaolo "worked"—on what, and how, it was impossible to say—and that his significant other had created a heaven on earth for him. But soon it became clear that the couple led a somewhat isolated life. People referred to visits and invitations that dated quite a way back and, while praising the culinary skills and generous hospitality of the lady of the house, they also revealed the desire not to subject themselves to a repeat performance anytime soon, or, better yet, they hoped to postpone it *sine die*. Nothing explicit or untoward escaped their cautious lips, and, as they commented, "Signora Dirce and Giampaolo . . . what a precious couple," their faces revealed both a hint of anguish and firm resolve not to let the cat out of the bag.

Federigo had not picked up on these reservations or elements of understatement prior to the morning he found himself strolling absentmindedly along Via del Forno. He hesitated in front of number 15, recalling that this was the building where his old friend Giampaolo now lived, the very same friend who had vanished from his circle after his propitious marriage. Federigo was poor and shy and had no intention of trying to keep up with Giampaolo and his new status, nor was he willing to pick up the crumbs after the lavish banquet. In no way a sycophant or supplicant, Federigo felt only pure friendship in his heart. A mix of discretion and pride had kept him away from his more fortunate friend until, by pure chance, here he was at his house, and, almost without realizing it, Federigo had rung the bell, hoping for a half-hour tête-à-tête, the likes of which they had often enjoyed in the good old days, and one of the reasons that the city of A. had grown so dear to him...

Greeted by a growling watchdog and a stubbly faced butler, Federigo was ushered into a parlor (which they called a "living area," he soon learned) full of paintings, statues, tapestries, pewter vases, and silver eagles. In the brief amount of time it took him to relay his personal information and for it to be communicated back to headquarters, his ears were assaulted by rapid-fire exclamations.

Federigo Bezzica? What an unhoped-for honor! For two years— no, three!—ever since she began her beguine with Giampaolo, when her dearly departed, which is to say, her second dearly departed, was still alive (she pointed a finger to a large oil painting of a bald man), she, Signora Dirce, had heard so much about Federigo, and was so full of intense admiration for his life and character. Ah, Federigo Bezzica! If she'd met him before Giampaolo, well, there's no saying... Why, he was the dearest, most dignified, most reserved of all of Giampaolo's friends. Naturally, he ought to be scolded for having waited so long to pay them a visit. Was he shy? Or was he simply a lover of the quiet life? She understood (and how!) his desire for *beata solitudo*, and it was this very affinity that would be the basis for a good, solid friendship. Giampaolo? Yes, Giampaolo was working but he'd surely pop in soon. In the meantime, they could exchange a few words and get to know each other better. Would he care for a glass of port, a dry martini, a Negroni? Fabrizio, oh, where had that idler disappeared to? Fabrizio, run along and bring our guest a glass of port.

Federigo had not yet had a chance to look at the lady of the house. The room was dim and shadowy and she had sat down far too close for him to crane his neck to observe her. But a large wall mirror—a *trumeau*, she called it—reflected a strange, hovering bird of prey, the nostrils of her beak-like nose quivering, her hair a mélange of blue and mahogany. Her bister-colored eyes blazed like the briquette she kept in her tortoiseshell *trousse* to light her guests' cigarettes.

After a bit, Giampaolo, casually dressed in his shirtsleeves, came in and kissed his spouse's hand. He didn't dare say more than a few words. Next came sallow, scrawny, and diffident Antenore and Gontrano, sons with her first dearly departed (she pointed to another portrait of a mustached official) followed by Rosemarie, a daughter with the second. It was already one o'clock. The Signora decided that Federigo must stay and do penance with them. They went into the dining room where an elegantly embroidered cloth lay over a glass table positioned under a bronze statue, which veered in a nosedive toward the guests. After waiting for the gentleman of the house to slip on his jacket, the butler served them a bowl of consommé, a cheese soufflé, a mélange of fried prawns and zucchini, and a basket of dried fruit. For coffee they went back into the parlor; the drip filter was a lengthy process and the choice of liqueur to accompany it was equally complex.

When Antenore, Gontrano, and Rosemarie asked if they might be excused, Federigo made his own attempt to leave, but having foolishly expressed the desire for a nap (a sensible postprandial habit shared by Signora Dirce), he was thrust onto a nearby sofa and entreated to rest, no standing on ceremony in this house. He lay nervously in the dark for two hours. Not a sound could be heard; perhaps everyone was napping.

What could he do? Two hours seemed interminable. He was consoled by the sound of the pendulum striking four. Federigo got up, opened a shutter, tidied the sofa where he had lain, and tiptoed out, in search of the foyer. Unfortunately, vigilant Fabrizio sounded the alarm, the result being a rapid new round of proposals that reached Federigo from the deepest recesses of the living room.

It was almost teatime! Why leave so soon? Urgent business? Nonsense! What's that? Not feeling well? A tonic will do the trick. Or, maybe a restorative intramuscular *piqûre*? The very same she regularly administered to Giampaolo. Had his doctor prescribed it for him too? All the better. No moment like the present. And no pharmacy was needed, at least not for now. She'd take care of everything. She was a trained nurse, and a good one at that. For heaven's sake, this was no time to be formal, not among such good friends. She'd be with him in a flash.

She returned fully armed. Federigo was to stretch out on a heap of pillows and expose a bit of himself, just a few inches, so she could administer the jab. Exhausted by it all, he felt obliged to stay a moment longer. In the meantime, Fabrizio dragged in the tea wagon. Giampaolo peered in and, admitted to the ceremony, announced that the weather had turned ugly, that it was now raining. Federigo was without an umbrella.

Signora Dirce quickly made up her mind: He would stay for dinner. No trouble at all, it was a pleasure for everyone. Was he declining the invitation? Preposterous, unthinkable. Why, it would be tantamount to a declaration of war. (A threatening light gleamed in her eyes. Federigo managed to make only the faintest gesture of protest.)

But no, by all means! He wasn't refusing, he'd gladly stay on. It was now pouring. Antenore and Gontrano came home with the dog, a vermouth was provided, and after another hour or so of pleasant conversation, Fabrizio appeared in white cotton gloves to announce that dinner was served. Federigo was taken by the arm and led to his place for a *minestra del paradiso* with lumps bobbing about in it, rabbit in aspic, and a few peaches in syrup. Fabrizio stood by, watching over them, Parmesan grater in hand, ready to sprinkle their bowls. The conversation turned to the topic of love and became even juicier when the youngsters took their leave. At ten o'clock, thunder and lightning shook the house.

Impossible to leave in such bad weather. Fabrizio would have driven him home by car but, unfortunately, hadn't had time to repair the differential gear. Not to worry, the guest room was ready, it had been done up with exquisite taste, just gorgeous. She had decorated it herself. Would he care for chamomile tea, a mint infusion, a bromide?

See you in the morning for caffe latte. But first, around eight, Fabrizio had been instructed to bring a cup of black coffee up to his room. Did he need anything else? The bathroom was on the right, the light switch to the left. And thank you for the delightful visit, the first, no doubt, of many. Thanks, thanks again; goodnight, nighty night.

It had stopped raining. Leaning out the bedroom window, Federigo calculated that it was too far to jump. Besides, there was the problem of the garden gate; the danger of being bitten by Tombolo, the dog; and the potential for other minor setbacks. What if they mistook him for a thief?

Wavering uncertainly, he closed the window and noticed the pajamas laid out on the bed for him: Did they belong to the second dearly departed or to the first? He picked them up, then dropped them quickly when he heard a knock at the door. Giampaolo had brought him a pair of old slippers.

"See you tomorrow," he said. "A bit on the late side, because I have to work. And what about you? When are you going to tie the knot?"

KARMIC WOMEN

MICKY, who these days goes by Donna Michelangiola, used to be extremely thin, with a mane of ash-blond hair down to her shoulders, and a light, intrepid step that once radiated joyful hope and triumph. She had, back then, perhaps thanks to her high heels, a certain joie de vivre in her stride, like Ibsen's Nora. But now? The visitor stands watching her from behind a pillar in the cloister, which is straight out of a Nazarene painting. Like all her friends, she has black-painted nails, or nails so heavily lacquered that they look black, and an expression that shows absolutely no inclination toward laughter but instead appears strained by overwhelming ennui. Also like her friends, she shuffles about in a pair of old leather sandals, worn at the sides, and a few sizes too big. She's put on weight, her hair is shorter—now dusty gray—and she wears dark glasses even when there's no sun. She's dressed in a simple, long tunic and shell earrings.

"Have a seat," she says informally to the visitor, as if no more than five minutes have passed since their last meeting. "You did well to come. My old man leaves me alone for seven months out of the year, and it's a good thing, because he bores me to death. Just think, he doesn't even like spending time in the convent."

Her old man is presumably her husband. They say he's loaded, but who has ever seen him? The visitor looks around and takes in the ruins of the cloister, part of an ancient convent that the old Micky had restored, adjacent to the villa where she now lives. Or rather, where she used to live, since everything, for some time now, apparently takes place in the convent: the receptions, the luncheons (the refectory is a bit dark, but "it moves the soul," or so she says). She even sleeps there, she and her friends, in small bare rooms with chipped brick floors, each with an enormous black crucifix, along with a pitcher and basin in the corner. (Hidden in the wall, though, is a tiny door that leads to a large, green-tiled bathroom.) There's mold just about everywhere. The visitor is then ushered into a small room with a tall, marble stoup and Gothic arches. Every so often, the altar bell rings.

"Hear that?" Micky asks him. "I hired a gardener who used to be a bell ringer, he knows all about canonical hours. Compline, matins... it makes it all the more authentic. The only problem is that he rings the bell a bit too often." With a vague circular gesture, she introduces the visitor to her friends (Freya, Cassandra, and Violante, as austere in appearance as in name) and goes on to tell them about him. "What you all don't know is that years ago, I would've married this guy, remember, Piffi? But then one day he says to me: I'm too old for you. He was thirty-three and I was eighteen. What was I supposed to do? I didn't know what to say, so he left and I married Lucky. How funny! But, actually, he's something of an inconvenient witness, because back when we first met, I used to believe in psychoanalysis... I actually believed that earthly love could make me happy."

Freya, Cassandra, and Violante squeal in a chorus that covers exactly two octaves: "Really, Micky? How could that be?"

"I don't know for sure, that's just how things went. I already explained to you that I skipped from the fourth to the seventh in only a few years, a case of accelerated growth."

The visitor tries to get his bearings. "Micky... Michelangiola. Fourth? Seventh? What are you talking about?"

Her friends look at each other, speechless. Michelangiola takes it upon herself to explain. "Be patient with him, I truly believe he knows nothing about it. From the fourth to the seventh level of reincarnation, try to wrap your head around it. Don't you know anything about karma? Nothing? Total darkness. And yet you seem like an evolved type, not below six or so, I'd say. It's a long and tiring journey to perfection. For some people it just takes more time, kind of like when you're learning to drive and they say you need a few more lessons because you have a hard time handling the curves. While other people soar right through it, like I did. This is the last time I'll be reincarnated."

A poorly shaven servant enters and motions to her. Michelangiola excuses herself, gets up, and walks out with him.

Freya, Cassandra, and Violante again break out into a chorus: "Poor soul! With everything she has to endure, she deserves way more than the seventh!" (The altar bell rings. Silence.)

Michelangiola returns.

"How do you deal with your servants, Piffi?" she asks. "I had one, a subversive type, who said the most outlandish things. I'll save you the headache, since you still haven't had your tea. I mean, how can you ramble on about equality, exploitation, and rights, I asked him, when the problem is something else entirely? It's as easy as putting two and two together: If you have worries and hassles and money problems it's because of your karma. To expect anything more would be like trying to squeeze blood from a turnip. Wait your turn and see what the future has in store for you. People who are broke are all the same, they simply don't know how to wait, and instead they take out their problems on those who soar through it . . . or who have already soared."

Freya, the toughest of the bunch, interrupts her, "So? Did you give him the boot?"

"Obviously," Michelangiola said. "But if he thinks it's not going to leave a trace on him, he's wrong, poor dear! You see, Piffi, the soul is more impressionable than a layer of gelatin film. Keep it up, I said to him, keep on complaining. You have no idea what you're missing out on . . . no idea at all . . ."

The altar bell rings again. It's teatime in the refectory.

DANCERS AT THE DIAVOLO ROSSO

IN LATE August, the city hotter than a wood-burning stove, young Cavallucci, who aspired to literary greatness but was, for the time being, an insignificant accountant at the stenographic institute on Via dell'Anguillara, seemed to have been accepted—or at least benevolently tolerated—as an auditor of the elite circle that gathered around the tables of the café (name withheld out of discretion).[50]

That such a circle even existed was, let us be frank, a matter of opinion; perhaps in homage to a not-too distant past, but this was still just a theory sustained by scant evidence. Yes, it was true, men of various ages, mostly young, could be seen exchanging a few words at a cluster of tables in a corner of the café during cocktail hour, but if it was the case that among those habitués flowed something akin to intellectual discourse, an exchange of ideas, or even mere shared sympathies, it was harder to affirm. Yet Cavallucci, proud of having taken his first steps toward glory, was not one to linger on such subtleties. "The group" existed, it was now within reach, it included the city's Big Five (or even more than five), and he was allowed to sit on the sidelines and listen, which he did, all ears, to the few phrases that leaped from one chair to the next. There had been no formal introduction (that's not how it was done) but Cavallucci knew someone who was part of the circle, a minor figure, and consequently his appearance had been greeted with glances of ennui rather than suspicion, and everything had gone off smoothly. Once, twice, three times . . . things were shaping up nicely. Around eight in the evening, on the heels of the group's diaspora, scruffy and scurfy Cavallucci, with a zealous gleam in his weasely eyes, got to his feet, left no money on the table (members were not obliged to order anything), and rushed back to his rented room on Via delle Stinche that he shared with a lodger who was even greener than himself but no less hungry for literary experiences. Pigni, who had blown in from Borgo San Lorenzo without a penny to his name, was ostensibly a student, and for the past few months he had been employed as a tester of woodwinds in an accordion factory on Via de' Neri.

The conversation between the two, which took place while they carefully filleted kippers on mustard-yellow paper (straight out of a still life by Funai), naturally centered on the group and the lucky opportunity that had been granted to Cavallucci, who spoke of his initiation with the blasé attitude of a made man, but one who didn't want to assume (no, he couldn't possibly) the responsibility of taking on an initiate. Still, they needed to talk about something, and Cavallucci was happy to tell all, and did so with languid elegance, the way one would tease a cat, dangling bits of offal or tripe before the prehensile claws of his ravenous roommate! What of the two famous poets, Mondelli and Guzzi, the doddering old man and the younger fellow with the pointy chin? To be honest, they hadn't said a thing, they yawned continuously, exhausted perhaps by their excessive mental efforts. Lunardi, from Modena, had told him with a pat on the back that he could write a piece for *Cavalcata*, the literary journal that he published, independently of the group. Elegant Lampugnani returned his greeting while continuing to edit a manuscript. Funai, that master painter, had even sketched his profile on the marble tabletop. There were others, too, not all of them important, of course, some of them even chumps, but, all told, it was a lively get-together and, you know how it is, one thing always leads to another, and even Pigni, one day (whoa, easy now!), would be able to make an appearance. All in good time. Unfortunately, Pigni got out of work—panting and wheezing from his constant puffing—too late in the day, and after dinner there was an entirely different group, or just the inner circle. Sundays were unthinkable, with those crowds! But his time would come, he just had to be patient and do the work, hunker down (and here Cavallucci gestured offhandedly to his pile of notebooks). Pigni swallowed his bread and kippers and nodded, at once afraid and incredulous.

A few weeks went by with Cavallucci putting in sporadic appearances at the café, until one evening in late September, when the two friends decided to pursue a new kind of pastime. In fact it was more happenstance than a decision that led them to meet two robust scullery maids from Monghidoro at their local food store: two dumpy girls dressed in their Sunday best, two "mussed-up dames" as Cavallucci, the expert, called them, all puffery and lace, their long hair in ringlets, American style, and wearing short skirts that showed their knobby knees. The young men took them to dinner at Trattoria Làcheri (Pigni had received some back pay) and then for a stroll along the Arno in the sweltering heat and darkness.

After getting gelato and sharing two orange sodas at a kiosk, they crossed the iron bridge and were drawn to the neon sign of the Diavolo Rosso, a dance hall that was all the rage. A small garden with Venetian-style lanterns and a hallway coffee bar led to a triangular dance floor presided over by a large cage in which a jazz band dressed in Turkish garb poured out a steady stream of screeching, syncopated beats onto the dancers below. The entrance cost an arm and a leg but Cavallucci realized that he knew the doorman, so they all got in with an amicable slap on the back, like right and proper freeloaders. A second later and the two couples were dancing on the overheated dance floor with ten or twenty others, bothered by a sudden tempo change to a boogie-woogie, when Pigni, cavorting near his friend with the less chubby of the two, elbowed Cavallucci and pointed out someone in the crowd.

"Gosh, look who's there! What now?"

Cavallucci turned to see who it was, without letting go of his prey, and was surprised to see something (not entirely unsurprising) that could only be avoided if there had been a trapdoor (none existed). This was his chance, his golden opportunity. The two lions of the group, Piero Lampugnani and Gamba, the robust and four-eyed bull of a man, were advancing toward them with two willowy reeds in backless evening dresses, one in silver lamé and the other in red satin, both ladies wearing garlands of flowers in their hair. Murmurs of admiration rose up from the pandemonium around them: "It's the Rizzolini girls, the daughters of the Fascist."

Without thinking twice, Cavallucci pretended to trip and looked down at the ground, but Lampugnani, tall and rosy cheeked, smoothing down his silvery mane while holding on to his blond tightly, brushed up against him and, in spite of being nearsighted, recognized him with ill-concealed astonishment.

"Well, well! Look who's here! Good evening," he said, darting off like an eel. Gamba, meanwhile, slid by on the other side, pirouetting his brunette with her grape-cluster earrings, almost bumping into Pigni before looking back at Cavallucci with incredulity. Suddenly, the orchestra stopped playing. People looked up at the cage of fake Turks, clapping to get them to play, and staring breathlessly at the bright red devil painted above the entrance to the dance floor. When the music started up again, new couples took the floor, but Cavallucci and Pigni gave up trying and, hiding behind a hedge of spectators in evening dress, watched the two lions spinning and shuffling as the orchestra changed register yet again, unleashing the shrill telephone ring and sinister rhythm of "Miss Otis Regrets."[51] One of the Monghidoro girls sat on a bar stool powdering her nose, while the other had found a new fellow and threw herself into the fray with him. Gamba and Lampugnani cruised by again but didn't look beyond the ring of faces that encircled them. Composed, still tan from the seaside, the two men focused on the blond and brunette, whom they maneuvered like walking canes, with Gamba, the music buff, explaining the lyrics of "Miss Otis," and his sidekick staring off dreamily into space, like Baudelaire's Don Juan, "ne daignait rien voir."[52] Or at least that's how it seemed to Pigni, who felt he was beginning to get a handle on these matters, thanks to the French books piled up on his desk. In the meantime, Cavallucci leaned toward his roommate and delivered a parting shot, "I'm done here, but if you want to stay... They don't know who you are; you've got nothing to lose." And off he went, rushing toward the iron bridge. After about fifty paces, he turned around and, in the glow of a headlight, saw that Pigni and one of the unwanted girls were trudging along behind him, scowling.

LIMPID EYES

SORROW extended over Arcolaio, the grand villa composed of two old farmhouses that had been restored a hundred years earlier in the style of a whimsical folly and connected by a long, glass corridor covered in flowers and vines; sorrow overcame the inhabitants of the villa and its habitués. Gherardo Laroche, a rich industrialist with a fine ear for music, as well as an esteemed collector of antiques and a prudent patron of the arts, had died two days earlier. Despite the funeral notice requesting "no visitors, please," numerous admirers and friends of the family gathered that day around the widow, a tall, middle-aged, bony woman with chamomile-colored hair that now appeared black, due to all the mourning crepe she wore. Signora Gabriela received her guests in the garden with her young, blond daughter, Tatiana, and her spiritual guide, Father Carrega. A maid, also dressed in black, brought out a few cold drinks from indoors. It was hot, and the visitors sat around a chipped slate table under the shade of a loquat tree. In the distance the Arno shone brightly; a barge with a few cars on it crossed at the bend in the river at Rovezzano. The bells tolled. Sunday afternoon would be long and sad.

At first everyone was silent, sighing heavily from time to time with heartfelt participation. Then Father Carrega, in response to a gesture of deep bereavement from Signora Gabriela, decided to take the matter into his own hands.

"You must find the strength to live, Signora, you must carry on in the manner of the great man that he was, who gave all for the good of others. His friends, his disciples, his spiritual offspring (how many of them are there? Impossible to say!) will bear the fruit of the seed that he has spread. Not to mention your beloved daughter, just thirteen years of age, this pure flower that God ... this flower that the heavens ..."

Father Carrega paused, out of breath, and wiped his glasses. At this juncture, the others picked up the cue.

"Tatiana will always be like a younger sister to me," said Franca, the child's chaperone, who had always been made to feel at home in the villa following the death of her own parents, close friends of the Laroches.

Dark, curly locks ringing her face, not too thin—far from it!—and elegant (even if her studied neglect of the latest trends in fashion was rather ostentatious) the clear eyes of Tatiana's "big sister" easily sustained the opaque yet piercing gaze of the widow.

"I know how loyal you are, Franca," Gabriela Laroche said, opening a small pouch underneath the table, which was further shielded by her black veil. Her yellowish eyes narrowed. Scrutinizing the young woman while the others gazed at little Tatiana, who in the meantime had flung herself into the arms of her dear chaperone, Signora Gabriela delicately removed a piece of glassine paper that had been neatly folded in four, the kind of paper used by pharmacists to measure out doses of magnesia and Epsom salts. A handwritten label had been applied to it that read "F. July 7." It was the calligraphy of the late Laroche. She had found the piece of paper in her husband's wallet just after his fatal car accident.

Next to speak was Signor Billi, Esq., legal representative of the Laroche company, who went on to illustrate the business merits of the deceased vis-à-vis his manufacturing company. When she was certain that all heads were looking elsewhere, Gabriela flicked open the piece of paper, keeping her hand under the table, and peered at its contents: a dark, bluish-black ringlet of hair, neatly snipped off. While Signora Catapani, one of Laroche's former nurses, took the floor, Gabriela went on to make the comparison between the ringlet and Franca's head of hair, which was so black that it almost had a bluish hue to it. It could be hers, in a certain light, at a certain time of day, but how could she tell from such a miniscule, practically homeopathic dose, from that mere wisp?

"I will continue my research in the library," Laroche's private secretary, Fedora, affirmed, running her hand through her own lovely black, wavy mop of hair. "We owe it to him . . . to carry on his work."

"Three years of notable work, Fedora," Signora Gabriela said, shifting her gaze from the curl on the paper to the hair and vivacious eyes of the florid young woman. "Three years, isn't that right? Let's see, you started with us in . . . July 1936, so, actually four years ago."

"I interviewed with Signor Billi in September, Signora Gabriela," replied Fedora, tossing back a curl that was not unlike the specimen contained in the glassine envelope.

"And I started here in August, one year earlier," chimed in Miss Filli Parkinson, the art restorer who had brought back to life a few "ruins" of the Laroche collection. "Four full years. Who could ever have imagined? Oh, what a tragedy!"

She, too, had a limpid gaze and dark hair, hers tied back behind her ears. She, too, like Franca and Fedora, was rubicund, serene, unreadable, and not at all hindered by the floral-print shirt that only served to accentuate her prosperous bosom.

"We owe you much gratitude, Miss Parkinson," Gabriela acknowledged, raising her clouded gaze from below the table to the dark tendril that hung at the nape of the pretty restorer's neck. "My husband was actually planning to show you just how much on your birthday, which is in early July, on the seventh, if I'm not mistaken . . ."

"The seventh of July?" Miss Parkinson asked, her clear eyes opening wide. "No, it's March seventeenth, already passed, unfortunately. How time flies. It's true though, Signor Laroche always did remember my birthday."

With a dry snap, Gabriela closed her *trousse*, letting the glassine paper sink to the bottom. Then, interrupting Signor Babbucci, one of her husband's partners, just as he was speaking, she said, "Oh, how foolish of me! I don't know why July has always been a difficult month for me, perhaps because I spent July of 1938 in a clinic. If it hadn't been for my husband's assistance, and yours, Franca, the two of you always at my bedside, inseparable..."

"Along with Miss Parkinson," Signor Billi, Esq., added, repairing the gaffe.

Once again, the beady-eyed kestrel in mourning took in the crystal-clear eyes of Signor Laroche's two assistants, who stared back at her without flinching, passing the test. Franca, his third muse, spoke up.

"Indeed, the month of July was not a lucky one for him. I remember when we traveled to Zurich to deal with the Zimmermann bankruptcy..."

"Ah, yes," Gabriela said, examining her puffy, yellow eyes in her pocket mirror. "How right you are, that was July." She raised her head and leered at Franca the way a bird of prey stares at a chick. "The first week, wasn't it?"

"We left on the twentieth," Franca said flatly. "We worked like mules until the tenth with Fedora and Miss Parkinson on the refurbishment of the gallery. Naturally, he assisted. You, Signora Laroche, had gone to the spa at Porretta with your daughter, don't you remember?"

"Ah, yes, Porretta," said Gabriela. Then, slyly, hoping to derail at least one of them, she added, "I remember. Yes, I remember perfectly well when you arrived. It was raining. You were drenched, happy, disheveled, blond...wait! You were blond back then, weren't you?"

"Blond?" said Filli Parkinson, with innocent surprise. "No, I've always been dark haired, even darker then than now, with bluish-black streaks, you used to say..."

"Oh, yes, bluish black," Gabriela repeated slowly, casting her gaze across the heads before her: bald, graying, Tatiana's platinum blond locks, and the bluish-black curls of the three ladies, who now stood close together, forming a single mane of hair, a tiny bit of which (but whose, whose was it?!) had ended up on the glassine paper on the seventh of July.

Once again, there was the sound of a dry click as Gabriela put away her pocket mirror, closed the pouch, and rested it on the table in front of her. She then got to her feet, causing a goldfinch that had been perching in the loquat tree to take flight.

"I'd like to thank everyone, and I mean every single one of you, even those of you who don't have black hair or eyes as clear as a summer's day. I think we can all agree that my husband was a bit of a strange man. If he were alive, I'd like to ... thank him. But now that he is no longer with it us, it almost seems as though he never existed."

"Oh my!" exclaimed Counselor Billi and Signor Babbucci.

"Oh my!" exclaimed Signora Catapani, Signora Billi, and the three raven-haired ladies, in unison.

"You need some rest, Signora," Father Carrega whispered, taking her by the arm and leading her toward the house, while waving his left hand to indicate to the others to move along and not linger.

They all watched as Gabriela entered the house and eventually disappeared, but not before she stopped in front of a large mirror to peer into it closely, trying to see the bottom of her swamp-colored eyes.

The others, after a moment of hesitation, made their way toward the garden gate in single file and without speaking. Franca and Fedora brought up the rear, their arms sweetly linked.

Miss Parkinson called out to them as she led Tatiana to a back entrance to the house.

"I'll catch up with you," Filli said, waving to them. "Wait for me at the café at the bottom of the hill. A little ping-pong with Tatiana, and then I'm all yours. Toodle-oo!"

"OK, Filli."

There was a sudden whir of wings as the goldfinch came to rest once more on the swaying branch of the loquat tree.

IN A FLORENTINE *BUCA*

IN THE narrow corridor of the *buca*, a few penniless—or just plain stingy—diners sat together with two policemen in street clothes, eating shoulder to shoulder, backs against the wall. A flat-chested, stocky woman in glitzy evening clothes, with a feathered miniature top hat set at an angle on her reddish head of hair, quickly made her way past them, moving toward the spiral staircase that led to the cellar, with its world of music, lights, and good cooking. Trailing closely behind her were two obsequious men, the first sporting a monocle and dressed in gray, the second wearing a black uniform, with a cape tossed nonchalantly over his shoulder, in his hand a riding crop and bundle of newspapers.

"Signora Pinzauti," said one of the men, pale with admiration and bowing his bereted head over his dish of stewed *lampredotto*.

"Mrs. Bedford!" a fat diner corrected him, with some surprise.

"Donna Odilia Caponsacchi," clarified a bald, bespectacled young man who had recently arrived from Rome.

"Also known as Berta Chimichi, if you please," another patron said testily from beneath his panama hat, which was pulled down over his eyes, covering his bowl of tripe and trotters.

"What's that, now?" the first three exclaimed in protest. "Is this a joke?"

"Not at all. Her name was Albertina, but back when I met her, she went by Berta. A delightful woman," the spoilsport explained, setting the record straight.

The busboy, whom they referred to as the Minister, walked down the corridor and refilled the policemen's glasses with a splash of

Aleatico. Through the back door, beyond the partly closed roll-down gate, they could see the dark street. The war had just begun; nightlife in the city took place behind shut doors.

"Go on, tell us more," one of the policemen said, listening attentively to the squabbling four.

"She was very chic," confirmed the man with the panama hat. "And had an impressive..." he paused to make the gesture of holding something round, "temperament. I knew her well, we were schoolmates. At twenty-eight, she married Ferralasco, the industrialist, who couldn't keep her happy. He worked hard and gave her everything she needed but he simply didn't understand her. So the couple had an agreement, a 'covenant,' she called it, but Ferralasco didn't hold up his end. She wanted to be like the nymph Melusina, who only agreed to marriage on condition that one day a week, in this case, Saturdays, she could carry out her transformation into a serpent from the waist down. On that day, her husband was not permitted to see her nor to be seen."

"I understand where this is going..." the first of the commentators observed. "And the husband wanted to know how she spent her time."

"Not right away, no. He was away on business several days a week. But when he was home, he wanted to be the boss and keep a handle on her spending. There were significant disagreements. They say that Ferralasco caught her in the arms of an architect who was supposed to be building a pavilion in their garden, up in Pian dei Giullari."

"On a Saturday?" the bald man asked anxiously. "The nerve of him! A woman like that in such hands. I don't know her husband, but..."

"Actually, they say it was a Friday," the man in the panama hat said. "Either way, not much room to maneuver with a brute like that. She got lucky: Ferralasco died a few days later, intestate."

"So," the lampredotto eater asked, "you're saying that the wedding with Pinzauti took place later? After she was twenty-eight?"

"I can't say for certain; I spent a number of years in Africa."

"This Pinzauti fellow, was he the architect?" the second cop asked, with avid curiosity.

They were interrupted by the noise of the roll-down gate being raised, admitting a newsboy and an ice vendor. The Minister returned and doled out some dishes of beans, which he doused with just the right amount of oil from a jug, and went on to fill the officers' glasses with Morellino. From the cavern below a hoarse voice was heard singing "Funiculi, Funiculà."

"Forget about the architect!" the man in the beret remarked. "That was just a fling. Imagine a woman like that marrying an artist, a bum! Odilia—that's the name she went by when I knew her—married Dr. Pinzauti when she was still rather young. I don't understand why you said she was twenty-eight when she first...Well, anyway, he was a homeopath and had made quite a bit of money working with the English. For political reasons, he was internally exiled. Instead of following him to Lampedusa, she, in order to protect her reputation, traveled to Hungary to obtain a divorce. Her husband covered all the expenses—quite a costly undertaking—without a word. And yet he was a greedy fellow, a small-minded man who spent most of his day in his medical office."

"Ah, so that phony worked with the English?" the fat man said, fingering his lapel pin. "Perhaps Mr. Bedford was a friend of the family and stepped in to console her. Shame it didn't work out for him like it did for the architect. Shortly after their marriage, Mr. Bedford took her to Ascona, where he dreamed of writing an essay on the Italian corporate state. He truly admired the progress being made here. They had a son whom she didn't really want, who's probably now living in England. Mr. Bedford divorced his first wife for her, but theirs was by no means a happy marriage. He didn't understand her painting, nor did he wish for her to consort with the local nudists; he imposed a life on her that was too tedious for a true artist. When she asked if she could go abroad with a Scottish naturist, the beast almost slapped her. In short, their marriage was annulled and all the expenses were divided between Bedford and his successor."

"Don Clemente Caponsacchi," chimed in the bald, bespectacled man, who had been waiting his turn. But his portion of the story was cut short by the arrival of a briny oyster vendor and two strolling musicians who plunked out a tune on their guitars, and then passed around a hat. The roll-down gate was noisily raised and lowered again before calm was restored to the corridor. "Don Clemente," he went on, wiping his spectacles, "worked constantly, always traveling by plane from Rome to Constantinople, forcing Donna Odilia to lead a life that was far too worldly for her. She craved solitude, didn't like the mayhem of Rome, and she detested artists. She wanted children, lots of them, but he did not share this desire. You say she used to paint? How odd...On top of that, her husband spent too much time with politicians, too many party officials, while she, when I knew her, well, you know what I mean, heh, heh..."

"Heh, heh," the two cops said, winking and nodding.

"Oh, not in that way, I was just saying. Anyway, Don Clemente was not the best fit for such a refined woman. A legal separation was drawn up, but they continued to live under the same roof. Later, the separation was annulled, even though they went their own ways. Odilia suffered a severe nervous breakdown. I believe that's when Dr. Pinzauti came to her aid."

"Perhaps he wanted to win her back?" the man in the panama asked, shucking some fava beans and sprinkling them with salt.

"I would hope not, although I can't deny that he may have wanted to save her from a brute like Caponsacchi, who, in the meantime, was diddling one of his typists. But that would've been like going from the frying pan into the fire."

"What a dame!" one of the cops said in admiration, before calling out to his partner, who had disappeared down the stairwell.

"They're coming up!" the other cop replied, reemerging. "They're going to the concert at the Teatro Comunale. They were just talking about it and looking at the poster."

"Maestro Östenwald is conducting; it's sure to be an interesting concert," whispered the fellow who had known Mrs. Bedford.

"Fit for a queen..."

"Queen?" the bald, bespectacled man said with some confusion. "Ah, you mean Donna Odilia. Can someone please explain why creatures like her always wind up in the hands of people who don't know how to appreciate them? While we, or at least I . . ."

"Here she comes," said the man at the end of the row who had dared to call her Berta. "Who is the man in gray? Is that Don Clemente?"

"No, Don Clemente steers his own ship. Moreover, I believe the Saturday rule applied only to the first husband. Goodnight, all, I must take my leave. I just can't bear to see her in the company of yet another brute."

SLOW

I PUT IN an application for membership to the Slow Club because a local chapter had just opened in my city. Among the details of my vita, I have included that I get around on foot, possessing neither a car nor a driver's license. As a matter of fact, the club seeks "to counter the stresses and strains of modern times,"[53] not with prescription drugs or herbal liqueurs, but through what one might call a practice, a decisively anachronistic way of being. The association has its headquarters in a small villa with a vaguely Palladian atmosphere; it has no telephone and its rooms are furnished in styles that range from Tudor to Biedermeier. It is heated with wood-burning stoves, and the newspapers arrive with a few years' delay, which required protracted negotiations with various administrative offices that resulted in particularly unfavorable prices. The secretary, while showing me around the clubhouse, points out that the most recent portrait is that of La Belle Otero[54] and that the youngest poet with work admitted to the library is the eighteenth-century libertine Giorgio Baffo.[55] An old Alsatian cuckoo clock presides over the reading room. At the bar, one can order only chamomile tea, a tisane, or mandarin punch. Permitted games include checkers, tombola, and snakes and ladders; chess is not allowed, for it requires excessive intellectual liveliness. The Slow is a gentlemen's club and is not for persons who talk a lot or tend to proselytize, such as public officials and priests.

While admiring the binding of a collection of *Scena illustrata*, I happen to overhear a whispered conversation between a few members. Here are some of the fragments I recall.

First member. "Our brother Wickers, from the Chicago chapter, who is studying the life cycle of the snail, maintains that it simply cannot be compared to ours. If a gastropod were to see us in our entirety, it would not be able to understand anything about us; it would perceive us like the flash of a supersonic jet, our movements and sounds would be indistinguishable. Wickers has sent us his research via delayed express mail. I predict that in about two years it will be available for consultation in our library."

Second member. "Yesterday a relative of mine got married. You will receive the announcement in a couple of months. She got engaged in 1914, but having received the news that her father had been seriously wounded during the war, she made a vow to the Virgin Mary not to marry until she had finished embroidering something like four hundred liturgical chasubles. Even after her father recovered and her fiancé returned safe and sound from the front, the young woman still refused to break her vow. Just one month ago she completed the final chasuble, and so her fiancé, unintentionally reliving the story of Isaac, was able to bring her to the altar after faithfully waiting for thirty-three years."

Third member. "Do any of you remember Carlo Marinelli, my university friend? He died near Gorizia, in 1916, just a few days after hearing from his young wife that she was expecting their first child. Carlo had replied at once, but because of some snag or another, his letter only reached its destination the other day, which is to say, thirty-seven years late. You can imagine the anxiety of his now gray-haired wife when she recognized his handwriting. Among the tidbits of news and expressions of affection, Carlo wrote to ask his wife to baptize the child with the name Glauco, if it was a boy, or Margherita, if a girl. A bit too late! The girl, now a wife and mother herself, had been baptized with the name of Anna, but in a strange twist of fate, Anna is actually expecting a child, so the paternal wish will come true, albeit after skipping a generation."

Fourth member. "In a matter of days, I shall serve the board of directors a verbena tea with a very special porcelain tea set. It was purchased in China in 1819 by Admiral Lonefield, one of my wife's ancestors. The admiral, impressed by the skill of certain local artisans, ordered a series of hand-painted teacups and saucers. 'With pleasure,' the head of that group of modest artisans replied, 'but we do not create things in batches, especially for a man of your stature. Give us a little bit of time, not much, just a couple of years, and you will have the most beautiful set in all of England.' Sir Roger Lonefield was surprised but accepted the offer, leaving a more than satisfactory down payment, and set off for home. However, on the return trip, his frigate, *The Green Bird*, sank off the coast of Liberia, and none of the crew or passengers survived. A month ago, in January 1953, my wife, the last descendant of the Lonefields, received a large crate marked 'Fragile,' inside of which, under heaps of cotton, leaves, and moss, lay a set of marvelous porcelain pieces, some of which even depicted the admiral's likeness and his achievements. Experts hail it as a miracle. And we did not have to cough up a dime. 'The sum paid by the Admiral Lonefield,' the accompanying letter explained, 'yielded such a high return after 133 years that it more than covered all expenses, even considering the devaluation of our currency.' A few words of apology followed for the additional delay, deriving from the search for the Lonefield heirs; a delay that they felt was compensated, the letter continued, by the loving care and artistic skill employed by the best Chinese painters, chosen to complete the arduous task."

I wish I could have kept listening, but already a few of the waxen faces had started to get up from their chairs to observe the newcomer with suspicion, and the cuckoo poked its head out six times to mark the hour (cuckoo, cuckoo, cuckoo, cuckoo, cuckoo, cuckoo) in an exasperating lentissimo, at which point everyone said, "It's getting late," and they all stood to leave.

"In a few years you will receive news regarding your application," the secretary said, accompanying me to the door. "If you manage to stay out of the papers, it is very probable that you will not be blackballed. I have arranged a carriage for you."

Sure enough, in front of the door, a horse-drawn phaeton driven by a coachman in livery was waiting to take me back to the city.

PART III

THE BAT

IT WAS around midnight and the man was just about to turn off the light when a sinister fluttering shadow, a scrawl across the walls, a rapid zigzagging ray, passed over his head and disappeared behind the curtain that concealed the washbasin. A sudden and piercing shriek filled the room.

"*Un pipistrello*!" a woman's voice cried out, in sheer terror. "What sort of hotel have you brought me to? Get it out! Get that ugly beast out of here!"

She dove under the bedsheets, afraid of being brushed by the swooping beast. Her words muffled and convulsive, she suggested that he go after it with a stick, or better yet, an umbrella, keep the window wide open, turn the lights off. Maybe the streetlights would lure it out...

Dressed in his pajamas, a towel wrapped around his head for protection, the man lumbered up and down the room in the dark, tripping over chairs, waving a rolled-up magazine ("Use the umbrella!" she continued to scream, but they didn't have an umbrella), all the while mumbling and emitting inarticulate sounds. Coming across a switch on the wall, he flipped it, creating a luminous wave of light that radiated outward from a transparent seashell positioned high on the ceiling.

"It must have left," he said, trying to appear calm, and making his way towards the window to close it. But suddenly, a viscous whoosh grazed his forehead, and the shadow flitted wildly about on the wall for a moment, then settled on the unreachable peak of a dark armoire.

"Help!" the woman shrieked, peering out from under the pillow that she held over her head. And then, more calmly, no longer seeing the squiggle on the wall, "Did the monster leave? Tell me it left."

"I'm afraid not," he said, trying to soften the harsh truth (the shadow quivered as if it were building up pressure, about to take off again). "But I'll chase it out now. Cover your head, and don't be scared."

He climbed onto a chair, repositioned the towel around his head, took aim, and hurled the magazine onto the armoire with a loud thud, creating a cloud of dust from which flew the small beast, in a jagged and agitated path, a brief parabola that ended with it flinching at the bottom of a wicker wastebasket.

"Help, help!" she continued to scream, in a frenzy. The man, now armed with a Moroccan slipper and with a rug for a shield, approached the wastebasket cautiously and said calmly, "I'll take care of it. I'll flip the basket over and take the creature prisoner. Don't get worked up, no need to make a scene."

When he thought he was in range, though he clearly wasn't, he gave a kick to the basket that, according to his calculations, ought to have turned it upside down without spilling its contents, but the basket merely tipped over, scattering eggshells, ashes, and used matches, as the darting shadow took flight from those relics toward the alabaster seashell on the ceiling, which shone like a pearl in an oyster.

"Nothing doing," the man confessed, sitting down on the side of the bed. "It doesn't want to leave. Don't get upset. Let me rest for a moment, and then I'll continue with the hunt."

"Ring the bell!" she called out from under two blankets. "Call the maid, she's the one who opened the window, that Potiphar's wife! Let her handle this vampire..."

"Calm down, dear, we're not in Italy. At this hour, no one will come. But we could, now that I think of it, we could..."

"Call the porter!" she moaned from deep below. "Throw something over your head, lie down next to me—don't uncover me, though!—pick up the phone and talk to him, you're the one who's good with languages."

"Good with languages..." he mused, half lying down on the bed, half suffocating under the rug. "How in the devil's name do you say *pipistrello*?" (Someone at the other end was barking "Hello? Hello!")

"*Pipistrello, chauve-souris*, maybe 'bat!'" came her sunken voice.

"Ah, I see that reading romance novels actually does you some good," he said peeking out from under the rug. Then, bringing his mouth to the receiver: "*Allò allò: pipistrello, chauve-souris*, maybe bat! No, I'm not crazy. (He says I'm crazy!) *Chauve-souris*, maybe bat, in my room. Please come, *per favore*. Help! Help! *Au secours! Allò, allò!*" (Imprecations and nonsensical words flowed forth from the funnel-shaped receiver, followed by the sound of the line being interrupted with a click.)

"What did he say?" asked the padded voice.

"He'll come right away. Well, not right away, but he is coming... or should be coming. Actually, I'm not sure he understood. Be patient, dear!"

He got to his feet with a pluck and decisiveness that astonished him. Letting the rug drop from before his eyes, he sat down on a chintz armchair, the only one in the room. The flustered shadow continued to vainly flap about in the alabaster seashell, breaking up and obscuring the light at intervals.

"Wait a moment," he went on. "Are you sure that 'bat' is the word for *pipistrello*? Are you completely sure? Yes? Well, it does makes sense, even that ass of a porter said the word 'bat' a number of times. Calm down, he's on his way now with a broom—yes, broom, that's what he said—and he'll take care of it all. Hold on, come to think of it, didn't we first meet in a restaurant called the Bat? I seem to recall dark wings on the front door..."

"Oh, that's right," the tearful voice filtered up from deep below the subsoil of the blanket fibers. "Yes, the Bat..."

"How strange," he continued, keeping an eye on the oversize shell. "Something you might not know about me is that the only animal I've ever killed is a bat. They said it was impossible to hit, because of its erratic flight, that all it would take is one tiny buckshot and down it would fall, just one hole in its sticky wings. But who has aim like that? Everyone had a go: two, three, four of them, but none of them hit the bat; actually, even more bats flew out. There were so many of them it was as if they were laughing at us. Then I fired a shot, almost at random. It was the first time I ever fired a twelve-gauge. And the bat fell, dropping to the ground like a crumpled handkerchief, quivered a bit . . . then died."

"Eek!"

"Actually, they're not that ugly, you know? At the end of the day, they're just mice with cobweb-like wings. They eat mosquitoes and don't hurt people. And mine, unfortunately, wasn't dead, it quivered, just like this one is doing."

"Eek!"

"Don't cry, that other beast, the porter, will be here soon. We'll have to give him two or three shillings, maybe more, depending on how long the hunt takes. Don't cry, it won't cost that much. So, actually, this is not the second, but the third important bat of my life. The first: well, now you know the story. The second is you, sort of . . . don't be offended! And this is the third, the one that came out of nowhere. And to think this is how we show our welcome, by hurling magazines, slippers, and rugs at it. The creature is probably half-dead already and will soon be finished off with a broom. I truly hope we're doing the right thing, but I'm not sure we are, not sure at all . . ."

"Eek!"

"Come now, don't cry. I was just saying . . . Let's see, the only solution is to put it outside. If only it would get trapped in that cage of a wastebasket again. Then I could toss that dark soul out the window, cage and all. Hmmm, let me think . . ."

He threw himself down on the bed and wormed his way under the blankets until they were tête-a-tête. "And what if . . ." he whispered in her ear, "what if it's my father who's come to pay me a visit?"

With an exclamatory shriek, she jettisoned all blankets and pillows and sat straight up in bed. Her thoughts were no longer on the dark creature fluttering inside the large shell.

"You've completely lost your mind," she said, looking him straight in the eye. "Come on, let's get dressed and go downstairs. They'll give us a different room, or we can walk around in the garden for a bit.

It's hot and everyone's gone to bed. I'll talk to the night porter. Your father? Why? And why as a bat?"

"I don't know," he replied, on the verge of tears. "It's the only animal I've ever killed, aside from a few flies and ants, I mean. The only one, and my father was particularly upset about it. I think he comes back to see me, every so often, in various disguises. 'We'll meet again somewhere or other,' he said to me, the day before he died. 'You're too foolish to manage on your own. Don't worry, I'll find a way, I'll take care of it.' I had almost forgotten his promise. But when I see one of these beasts flying around, I aim my finger at it, and bang! it falls to the ground like a rag. That's when the memory of him comes back ..."

He then took aim at the seashell, setting in motion the creature's rapid and fearful flight. First it smacked the ceiling, then it flew out the window, swallowed up by the thick darkness and a heavy sirocco. She screeched again and dove back under the pillows, just as someone knocked at the door.

"Must be the porter," the man said, hurrying over to close the window and yelling, "One moment, please. One moment." Then, under his breath, "See if you've got a half crown, some change, but not much, after all, the oaf didn't do a thing."

He took the coin from her, opened the door, and stood there talking in a hushed tone for quite some time. Wide-eyed, she stared at the now lifeless seashell and thought back to the restaurant with the dark wings on the door. Then, remembering suddenly how a few years earlier her desire to see a performance of Strauss's *Il pipistrello*[56] had saved her from death, from the bomb that destroyed her home, she shuddered once more and threw herself onto the pile of blankets with a surge of convulsive laughter.

ANGIOLINO

IN THE darkness of the room, there's an unlikely sound: a soft, percussive rattle from the depths of a leather suitcase. One must be awake and alert to detect it; a single sigh, a yawn, a creak of the bed, even a padded footstep down the hall could muffle the sound, and it would go unheard. But such a thing almost never happens. At eight thirty in the morning, even on the darkest days of winter, when the hotel is still silent, the couple keeps vigil, waiting to be roused by the small, square, Angelo-brand alarm clock they keep hidden in their suitcase, enclosed in a nice red case. If they kept it on the nightstand, its luminous phosphorescent hands would glow in the dark, but he can't stand the faint ticking of that mechanical little heart, and she despises being so close to that constantly shining trail of light. It adds a certain uncanny feeling to the room, a soupçon—she says—of something spectral, which she cannot get used to. Besides, it's better to let time pass without checking it every second. The only solution is to bury the alarm clock at the bottom of the suitcase and wait wide-eyed to be awoken. Rarely does it ring without being heard, finding them both asleep. He suffers from insomnia and she sleeps little. So what happened? A quarrel ensues. "Bad Angiolino," says the man, shaking the red leather case and holding it up to his ear. "Did you do it on purpose? Have you lost your voice? Or," he says (turning to his wife with a scowl), "did you forget to wind him?"

"I've been winding him for twenty years, at the same time every night. Occasionally, I even get up to double-check. He must have rung while you were snoring. His voice has grown soft with age and is only getting weaker. But, if you pay careful attention, you can still hear him."

"Me? Snore?" he replied, pulling the pine-cone-shaped electric razor away from his chin. "You know very well that I'm always awake at four o'clock. He must have rung when those three black gals next door made that hellish racket. You didn't hear them? The Paprika Sisters! When they come back in the wee hours even the walls tremble."

"Last night they came in at four," she says, wiping Angiolino's glass face with the hem of her nightgown. "The baby must have rung at nine. There's no other way."

Someone knocks at the door. A hotel waiter enters carrying two cups of coffee and a daily paper that seems full of news. There's a moment of silence. Once they are alone, the annoying buzz resumes, the man returns to shaving the nape of his neck. He then unplugs the cord from the socket, stretches out on the bed, and opens the paper. He sits up with a start.

"Baby?" he says. "What baby! It's idiotic to call this poor wheezing alarm clock a baby. The Angelo is not a baby, it's a clock."

"You're the one who said he's like a son. He's been traveling with us for more than twenty years. I forbid you to hurt his feelings." (At this point, she picks up Angiolino, kisses him, puts him tenderly back in his plaid drawstring pouch, and places him at the bottom of the suitcase.)

"That's enough!" he says in exasperation. "This infantilism has to end. No more spurious babies, no more good things in bad taste, no more dewy Crepuscularism.[57] Life is hard. We have to see things for what they are, face the facts. Shall we try? We can start this morning, right now."

"Fine, let's try," she says, sighing in resignation.

But he, who has already gone back to reading the headlines, bursts out laughing.

"Well, well," he says, stirring his espresso. "Blackie Halligan has died: hero of the Pacific, wounded in combat, and decorated for his courage. You know who he was? The carrier pigeon who saved the lives of three hundred men."

"And so our pact begins," she says with irony. "You fail to mention if war is about to break out, whether Cardinal Mindszenty was drugged or not, or anything concerning the North Atlantic Treaty. All it takes is a pigeon to set you off."

"We'll start our pact in half an hour. Oh, to hell with it! We've been sharing inanities for thirty years, we can't be expected to stop just like that, from one moment to the next. Not even *they*, despite having won the war, take things so seriously. Unfortunately, Italy has become a land of bureaucrats and pedants. Where did this notion of us being incurable anarchists come from? We're formalists, reactionaries, and obstructionists, even in the smallest of matters. To attribute a human personality to a pigeon or even an alarm clock is a case of innocent animism, and animism is the most respectable spiritual position a human being can embrace, as well as the most logical. For man can neither step out of himself nor take his own measure."

Not entirely satisfied with the smoothness of his shave, he plugs the razor back into the socket. She is reading an English-language magazine.

"What does 'highbrow' mean?" she asks, looking up at him. "It says here that in America there are millions of readers, but only twenty-five thousand of them are highbrows."

"Let me think. It means supercilious, readers with fine taste, *emunctae naris*.[58] And what are they proposing to do with them? Shoot them?"

"No, quite the opposite. They're trying to find ways to increase the number. They want at least 1 percent of the population to be highbrow readers. That way, rare books, abstruse books, books without exciting twists or brutal crimes, would have a million and a half readers. And the other 99 percent of Americans could go on reading their usual stuff. Heaven for all."

"What if . . ." he wonders, checking the smoothness of his cheeks, "What if we were highbrows of life, rather than art? You read nothing but senseless magazines, and nowadays I only read murder mysteries.

We're rough-hewn, coarse. But in our daily life...we're different. Angels in our suitcase and prodigious pigeons in the sky; that's what we need."

"We?" she says bitterly. "Speak for yourself. I've done everything I can to make you more callous. Terrible days lie ahead. The Angelo was personal, a private flirtation. I should've gotten you a Roskoff, they're like steamrollers. I warn you: you're going to have to toughen up if you want to be taken seriously."

From the bottom of the suitcase comes a barely perceptible trill, a mere dust mote of sound that lasts a few seconds and then dies out. He jumps out of bed, and, in great excitement, they both lunge for the plaid bag. Then they remove the alarm clock, shake it, caress it, and look it straight in the face at great length.

"Nothing broken," he says, embarrassed at hearing his voice crack. "It was set for nine fifteen, not nine. The small hand slipped forward. Starting tonight, I'll do the winding, if you don't mind." He then goes and stands in front of the mirror to see if he really does have the face of a member of the one percent.

"What if...we start our pact tomorrow?" he mumbles, looking back at her.

Without saying a word, she nods her head slightly and places Angiolino back in his pouch.

RELICS

"I can't find the photo of Ortello," the ailing woman said, rummaging nervously in a box where she kept clippings, old letters tied together with a ribbon, and a few holy cards that she didn't dare destroy (you never know...). "You don't even recall who he was."

"He is, or was—if he died—a horse, a beautiful horse who won the Grand Prix at Longchamp. I remember him perfectly well. His photograph was in there, I'm sure of it. You never saw him race, but you were obsessed with him for a while. And that's how he ended up in your private reliquary, except now he's escaped, apparently. It was a newspaper cutting, it must've blown away with the wind."

"Ah," she said arranging her dry-leaf-colored hair. "You talk of *my* reliquary as if it were a mania that doesn't concern you. I should've imagined as much. It would appear that the wind has blown away something else..."

"The okapi?" the bald man asked with a start. "Impossible, look again."

"Yes, the okapi: that odd animal, half goat and half pig, whose memory you wanted to enshrine. Gone, with the horse. It seems as though your memory works perfectly when it comes to matters that concern you."

"Half pig?" he asked, getting worked up. "Anything but! More like half donkey, half zebra, half gazelle, or half angel. A unique specimen of its kind, belonging to a species thought to have been extinct for centuries. I wanted to go to London just to see him at the zoo. An animal that trembles with fear at the sight of a human being, far too delicate to be around brutes like us. I wonder if they've managed to keep him alive; impossible to marry him off. He was unique, you hear? Unique."

"Lucky him," came the barbed reply.

They were quiet for some time thereafter. She was lying on a chaise longue, looking at the frescoed ceiling and its allegorical scenes of animals and gods, but not depicting the kind of animals or god to which she felt close. He was staring out the window at a twisted poplar and its wind-ruffled tip. Further in the distance, the snow-covered slopes of the Alpine foothills were visible. Then it started to rain and the panes were soon streaked by large drops. It was almost dark, the nymphs and swans on the ceiling were about to be swallowed up by the shadows. They realized this only when the hotel maid came in to bring them tea and switched on the chandelier with a delicate touch. A discreet light was cast over the reproduction furniture. Even the sound of the rain appeared livelier.

"Ah, a bit of light," he said, helping her wrap a shawl around her shoulders. "Talking in the dark does no one any good. Sometimes all it takes is a light being switched on to give clarity to our thoughts. You're not being nice today."

"No, I'm simply taking stock of our memories, the only thread that connects us to each other after so many moons. In the meantime, those two have gone missing from the box, whether it's due to negligence on my part or yours. And yet so many others that should be stored in the reliquary of our minds apparently no longer exist in yours, if I'm to judge by your coldheartedness, your marmot-like silence."

"Me, a marmot?" he protested, passing his hand over the stubble of his bald pate. "Speaking of marmots, let's test your memory, shall we? Where did we see one, pray tell?"

"Near the Abbey of San Galgano. A hunter had one. Do you remember how he even offered to sell us his own son? A beautiful pink baby. He thought about it, talked to his wife, and went as far as saying, 'Don't worry, we'll make another, what's the harm?' But we didn't take the baby. It would've cost us too much later on . . . to support him."

"Impressive memory. But actually that was a simple marten and, moreover, a dead one at that. The marmots, the three marmots..."

"In a small grotto, under a boulder near the Gornergrat funicular. They were dancing happily about, waving their paws and greeting the travelers. They felt safe. But there weren't three, it was a large family: father, mother, and children. Milk or lemon?"

"Plain," he said, taking the cup. He then looked around and, noticing that the maid had left, nonchalantly asked after a moment of silence, "And... the fox?"

"The red fox in Zermatt, you mean? At first it was hiding in its little den, in its cage. It didn't want to come out. I said to myself: I'll count to twenty, if it comes out, then come what may, and if it doesn't... then to hell with this man. And so I counted slower and slower. At nineteen, the fox scampered out."

"And so you decided to marry me," he said, blowing on his scalding tea. "I see, and far too clearly. There are always unexpected surprises, even after all these years..."

"Oh, don't complain, I counted slowly on purpose. I probably would've taken an extra-long pause after nineteen. I'm the one who made the fox come out... with my thoughts. Sure, a bit of a trick was needed; I had to slow the tempo, the way some musicians do."

"Since we're in confession mode, I'll admit that when Mimì had to go back into one of her jars, in Vitznau, I said to myself: If she appears in the one on the right, then whatever happens, happens, but if she appears in the one on the left, then... well, you get the idea. Mimì, the white and yellow guinea pig, remember?"

"Perfectly well. And Mimì came out of the magician's sleeve and appeared in the jar on the right... Our union does have a solid foundation, doesn't it? Care for a biscuit?"

"No, thanks. Actually, she appeared in the one on the left, but the experiment was repeated three times and you won, two to one, which was enough for me. No trick needed."

"A fox and a guinea pig... interesting godparents. They must've passed away long ago without knowing the mess they caused. Our life is a menagerie, or, better yet, a seraglio. Do you really think I've lost them? All our dogs, cats, birds, blackbirds, turtledoves, crickets, worms—"

"Oh, those worms!" he said, almost indignantly.

"Yes, worms, and who knows what else. And their names? Buck, Pallino, Passepoil, Pippo, Bubù..."

"Lapo, Esmeralda, Mascotto, Pinco, Tartufo, Margot..."

He would have gone on, maybe even inventing a few, but he stopped when he noticed that she had closed her eyes with fatigue. He picked up a *torcetto* from the plate of biscuits and brought it to his lips. Then, almost without thinking, he reached for the shoebox and began to rummage through clippings, photographs, and old letters. From what appeared to be an empty envelope, two creased pieces of paper fell out, newspaper photos: a bold, high-strung colt, and a sensational animal with a lost gaze, a cross between a Bedlington terrier and a badger, a sow and a roe deer, a goat and a Pantelleria donkey; maybe it was a mistake of nature, a typo overlooked by the Great Typesetter, but a sight for sore eyes, an ineffable promise for the heart.

"The okapi! Ortello!" the man exclaimed. "I found him! I found them both!"

But she continued to sleep. Outside, the rain was beginning to taper off. He gently placed the clippings on her folded hands. "I'll go for a stroll but I will leave the light on so that when she wakes up, she'll see them right away," he thought, as he tiptoed out of the room.

THE RUSSIAN PRINCE

"To the Pied de Porc," Carlo said to the taxi driver. In reply to the man's request for a more specific address, Carlo added, in bad French, "It's on a street that intersects with rue de l'Odéon, when we get there, I'll show you where to go."

The driver set off, grumbling. White-haired, with a mustache and a chauffeur's cap. But his eyes...

"Did you see his eyes?" Adelina asked. "They're like the ocean, simply magnificent. He must be a Russian nobleman, maybe a prince."

"Russian? Why? And how would you know?"

"There are more than fifteen hundred Russians driving taxis in Paris, practically all of them blue bloods. Make sure you tip him well. Better yet, we should converse with him a little." (Turning to the driver, who kept his foot on the accelerator, she said, "It's hot this evening, monsieur, *n'est-ce pas*?")

"Bien sûr, madame," the alleged prince grunted, missing a reckless cyclist by a hair.

"Not very forthcoming, is he?" Carlo said. "Let him drive in peace."

"He's a very refined man, I noticed right away. I'll shake his hand, yes. Do you think fifty francs will be enough of a tip? I'm almost embarrassed, I don't want to humiliate him."

They were approaching rue de l'Odéon, but Carlo, who was looking out the window, could not see anything that looked like a pig's foot; the place had been described to him only in the vaguest of terms. The driver, slowing down, looked back at them with a quizzical glance.

"A bit farther down... a little farther... maybe on the right... no, wait, turn left here," Carlo said, but he saw no sign with a pig on it. The driver's grumbling grew louder.

"What a scene you're making!" Adelina exclaimed. "He's being so very patient with us. Good thing we found a true gentleman."

"He's a boor!" Carlo remarked. "After all, I pay what's on the meter." The car zigzagged up and down several streets, turned around, and then went up all the roads running both parallel and perpendicular to it, but with no success. At a certain point, the driver got out of the car and spoke with a small group of construction workers on a street corner. Then he got back in and drove off with the conceited air of someone who knows where he's going.

He drove for another quarter of a mile, turned down a dark, deserted street and stopped in front of a poorly lit sign that read "Au Pied de Cochon."

"Voilà le porc," he said, turning toward them.

"But this isn't it!" Carlo burst out. "They described it to me in a completely different way: a small, tree-lined square, *une place*, the front window filled with oysters, pheasants, partridges. And besides, it was *porc*, not *cochon*," he said, turning to the driver, "Je cherche le porc, pas du tout le cochon."

"Eh bien, monsieur," said the driver, opening the car door for them. "C'est bien la même chose: c'est toujours de la cochonnerie."

Carlo wanted to respond sharply but Adelina grabbed his arm. They got out, Carlo paid the driver 320 francs, Adelina topped it off with another fifty, and the white-haired man drove off, ignoring, but not ignorant of, her farewell.

"What a *rustre*," Carlo said pocketing the change. "He dropped us off where it suited him, not us."

"What a charmer: *C'est toujours de la cochonnerie*! Can you imagine an Italian or French taxi driver coming out with a quip like that? A Russian nobleman, for sure. And, besides, what did you expect? That he'd know all the Parisian *gargotes* by heart? You should've given him the exact address."

"Russian, my foot! He's a roughrider from the Camargue, a con man through and through."

"Well, you're an idiot."

"Well, you're a silly fool!"

"Well, I'm not hungry anymore."

"Well, neither am I."

Without realizing it, they found themselves sitting at a small table. The restaurant was sad, empty, and probably overpriced.

A waiter brought them the menu. "Hors d'oeuvres? Escargots?"

Crying, she admitted that, yes, she ate snails.

WOULD YOU TRADE PLACES WITH...?

FROM THE earliest hours of the day (the earliest hours for bathing, that is, namely, ten or eleven in the morning), they are out and about, in the pine grove or at the water's edge. They observe, scrutinize, listen, and, every so often, make a mark in a pocket notepad. But their most fruitful hours are in the late afternoon, when people come together in small groups to chat and confide in one another, ultimately spilling any secrets they might have.

"Would you trade places with him?" Frika asks Alberico, pointing to a hairy lawyer wearing shorts, bent over his playing cards. His loud and self-assured voice, which not even the breeze could dispel ("Black canasta!" and "I'm forced to play a wild card"), caught her attention.

"Me? Instantly," Alberico replies, making a mark in the memo pad.

A woman walks by wearing a skimpy bikini and gold sandals. Statuesque in her beauty with hair dyed red and blond, she drives down from Busto every year, in her large car, with a child and governess.

"Would you trade places with her?" Alberico asks.

"What kind of question is that! Immediately," Frika says, and makes a mark in the notebook.

An elderly woman with peroxide-blond hair ambles past them on the beach, a white poodle trailing behind her. The dog is long-haired on top, but its belly and legs are shaved bare; both shaggy and balding, it has visible patches of pink, flea-ridden skin, and beady, black eyes that peer out from under its ruffled mop. "Come on Cheap, come along, sweetie," the old woman calls, and she goes on to say that Cheap is like a son to her, but if she had to do it all over again, she wouldn't, seeing how much work it is, but what can you do? He's here now, and he lacks for nothing. When he's left on his own, he cries and grows depressed, poor Cheap. He's better than any Christian, he has liver disease but could still live another ten years, poor Cheap. "Come along, sweetie pie, come to Mommy."

"Would you trade...?" Frika asks.

"With her?" Alberico replies, appalled.

"No, with Cheap."

"In a heartbeat," Alberico answers, and makes a check mark in the notepad.

"I'd even trade places with her," Frika adds. "At least she has Cheap." She makes a single check mark, and then adds a second.

They've reached the shoemaker's stall on the corner, which is shaded by a thick cluster of dusty holm oaks. She gives him her sandal and he gets to work using some cord and a cobbler's knife. From above comes a long, sweet, painfully melancholic, joyous song. A flicker of light in the dark.

"A great tit," the shoemaker says. "I've heard it for years, but have never seen it. It's the last beautiful thing on earth."

They listen in rapture. Alberico makes a check mark in the notebook.

"With the shoemaker?" she murmurs.

"No, with the bird," he says. "But, come to think of it, why not?" He makes another mark.

She nods but adds only one mark, for the great tit.

Several years have passed since they married. Maybe only their Wagnerian names kept them together, but, anyway, it's too late now. And so it goes, for hours on end, on land and at sea, at the table and in the street, in bed or stretched out on deck chairs. Late at night they calculate who has racked up the most points, which of them is unhappier, who would more willingly trade places with someone else...

A DIFFICULT EVENING

THE FIRST time that he, in a moment of intimacy, called her—who knows why?—a *pantegana*, his lovely *pantegana*, she hadn't been too suspicious.

"Pantegana? What's that? A creature, a toad, a flower?"

"Yes," he had replied. "A creature of sorts: a sweet, furry, little thing, a kind of ferret or weasel or chinchilla..."

But that evening, after passing under the Rialto bridge and turning down a dark canal, the gondola was rocked by a sudden splash. From her relaxed position, blissfully cradling her face in her hands, she sat up.

"What was that?" she asked.

"A pantegana," the gondolier replied, in a heavy Venetian accent.

The tragedy unfolded in a matter of seconds.

"A rat!" she said, wide-eyed, staring at the eddies forming in the putrid water of the canal. "A filthy water rat. How dare you..."

"Me?" he stammered, sensing the approaching storm. "A rat? What are you talking about? Look," he said (as the eddies disappeared), "it's not a rat, more like an otter or beaver, and with such pretty fur..."

The eddy had vanished, but soon another, even louder, splash was heard. As the gondola passed in front of a shrine with candles that illuminated a small statue of the Madonna, she saw the slimy, swollen body of a pantegana, with an obscenely long, ridged tail, wending through the water amid sawdust and lemon rinds, its snout punctuated by a pair of grimy eyes at one end and long, dripping whiskers at the other, its claws scrabbling frantically through the rubbish in the canal.

"A pantegana! How horrible!" she screamed. "Go closer, let me get a better look."

The man turned toward the gondolier with an imploring gesture and the hope that he might press on, but a quick flick of the oar turned the gondola toward the filthy rodent. For a moment it was dark and then a beam of light from a window illuminated the vortex created by the small, paddling monster. She peered at it myopically.

"Are my eyes like that?" she cried. "Do I have whiskers like those? Do I have pee-colored fur?"

"No, of course not, Signora!" exclaimed the gondolier.

Her companion short of breath tried to sidle up to her. "You must understand, it's a term of endearment, a Venetian pantegana is something else entirely. Yes, that's a disgusting rat, but what I was referring to, I thought..."

He stopped short, seemingly calmer. The pantegana had leaped out of the water and disappeared down a sewer. The gondola glided on in darkness toward the Bridge of Sighs, just a short way off. She was crying silently.

"Admittedly," the man said, trembling nervously, "here, in these sewers... but in other places, you see, where the water is—"

She interrupted him, icily. "As soon as we get back to the hotel, call for a launch," she said. "I'm leaving tonight. I'll let you know where to send my luggage."

THE RED MUSHROOMS

LATE IN the evening, they would gather in the empty stockroom of the shop to fantasize and plan the most opportune way to celebrate the fall (and ideally the death) of the Tyrant. And since all four of them were gluttons, or at least gourmets, the envisaged saturnalia always took on the form of the most appetizing and succulent banquets. As men with no political ambition, and with the fall of the scoundrel seeming both remote and unlikely, waiting to pick up the spoils was out of the question.

"When *he* dies," Abele said softly (you never know, the walls have ears), "we'll have paella Valenciana, escargots à la Bordelaise, and a soufflé au Vieux Prunier. It will be my treat that day, naturally. I'll bring in the top chef in town."

"If they manage to skin him alive," muttered Egisto, looking around suspiciously, "I'll prepare a lobster bisque so delicious that not even the Heavenly Father has ever tasted one quite as good. As for wines, don't get me started, because down in the cellar . . ."

"If he has a heart attack," Volfango cried out (but they quickly covered his mouth so he'd pipe down), "I'll prepare cappelletti the way they're meant to be, followed by a nice, crispy, spit-roasted, suckling pig, with rivers of Lambrusco, a whole tidal wave . . ."

"When he croaks," Ferruccio yelled, leaping to his feet, bug-eyed and gasping for breath, "we'll need more, so much more! A one-course meal, the kind that makes your mouth water, some kind of stew, yes, a venison stew, served with . . ."

"With?" the other three inquired.

"With a lovely dish of sautéed red mushrooms, splashed with

verdicchio, and braised with half a potato, half a tomato, a celery heart, a pinch of ginger, a splash of rum, a sprinkling of fennel seeds, then, after half an hour over low heat, a light veil of cream, and a drop—no, not a drop, only the mere idea—of balsamic vinegar, and last, but not least..."

"And last, but not least?" Abele, Egisto and Volfango asked eagerly.

"And last, but not least...wait, there's more...and last, but..."

Ferruccio ransacked his memory, then thrashed his arms in the air, unsteady on his feet. They caught him just in time and helped him over to a sofa. He had gone white as a sheet and seemed not to be breathing. Abele checked his friend's pulse and then shook his head.

"Call an ambulance immediately," he said. "Looks like he's a goner. I should've known, just talking about these things brings bad luck."

CRUMBLING ASH

The pontoon bridge that led to the front row seats facing the Isolotto dell'Indiano was not far off, but unfortunately it did not appear accessible to everyone. Some moments earlier, a few VIPs in dark cloaks had passed by, welcomed with weak applause and obsequious greetings from a group of valets who dispersed the dark with smoky torches and pocket flashlights gripped like automatic pistols. The boats were then shifted to impede access to mere mortals. The sky was cut through by vast and luminous beams from searchlights; swells of people crowded the Isolotto, which glowed under large floodlights: directors armed with loudspeakers and whistles could be seen running about, along with telephone operators, electricians, correspondents, and other so-called specialists. My approach to the pontoon must have aroused some suspicion, because one of the fire handlers came toward me, pointing a narrow tube with a menacing blue light in my eyes.

"Papers," he said sluggishly.

He stared long and hard at my identity card, glancing up to compare me to the photograph, and then drily issued his orders. "That way," he said, pointing me down a path that led to the parapet that ran along the river.

I soon found myself standing near a low wall under a weak streetlight, far from the crowd, far from the bridge of big shots, and next to a woman with red hair who seemed intent on observing the movement of a snail along the wall. She must have been around thirty or thirty-five. The man she was with, who had just lit a thick Minghetti cigar, looked some years younger. They spoke animatedly but the rumble from the low-flying aircraft that were disseminating spiraling pamphlets onto the crowd prevented me from catching their words. The performance, a "mass spectacle" titled *18 BL*, had begun: a motorized land and air performance for *One, No One, and One Hundred Thousand*[59] spectators, which, according to the press release, would definitively break the back of bourgeois theater.

I didn't watch the events taking place on the riverbank very carefully, and, for a while, I just sat on the wall, lost in my own thoughts, until a loud clamoring made me look up. In the distance, amid trees and bushes, a horseshoe-shaped table laden with food appeared, the word PARLAMENTO written across it in block letters. All the spotlights were aimed at the banquet and the banqueters, who were soon overcome by a rapidly advancing incursion of tanks from the shadows, intent on crushing the obscene parliamentary charade, apparently with the objective of overturning the table and dumping it in the Arno.

"It's stuck," she said, barely lifting her gaze from the snail, which had reached the halfway point between two edges of the wall.

"Yes, it is," the man said, puffing on his Minghetti.

The table was, indeed, blocked by some unforeseen obstacle, and the tanks that had plowed through it and tossed it in the air were now unable to push it into the river, causing the audience to jeer and laugh. In the meantime, the Social Democratic hogs who had been sitting at the table ran off this way and that, like so many tiny ants, chased down by the bold armored trucks. One of the spotlights fizzled out and the show seemed to lose momentum. But then other airplanes flew overhead, the light came back on, and choreographed scenes were acted out on the riverbank to the accompaniment of tubas and drums.

"I don't understand why…" the woman with red hair lamented, and then she stopped because the small, dappled snail had also stopped, shining in the light.

"It isn't the first time we've discussed this," the man said, puffing like a steam engine.

I stepped to one side, out of discretion. The sky clouded over and threatened rain. A few frogs managed to squeeze in their wheezing whistle amid the ruckus from the riverbank. Under a multitude of blinding lights, large plows and other outsized farm equipment started to till the once sterile lands of the empire. At the sound of the directors' whistles, luminous ears of corn rose up, cotton plantations flourished, torrents of oil flowed steadily into productive pipelines, while nymphs cavorted and pseudo Russian ballerinas danced. Sirens wailed and fireworks exploded. The audience suddenly went quiet, worried by a few large drops of rain that made the lights on the stage flicker. I went back to the wall.

"What's happening over there now?" she asked in a calmer voice, pointing to the Isolotto, but continuing to watch the snail, which had resumed its slimy slither along the wall.

"I believe the League of Nations is on fire," he said, checking the program and taking another puff. He then smugly observed the long arc of white ash on his cigar; it had yet to fall.

"Leave it," she said. "I have an idea."

The wind grew stronger, lights and strange shadows flitted across the island. Taxis sounded their car horns on the Lungarno, beckoning to passengers, as the audience's swift departure threatened to become a stampede. Two men coming from the pontoon bridge, accompanied by an officer from the carabinieri, rushed past us.

"Not an ounce of order," one of them said. "A complete fiasco. There's going to be hell to pay, for sure. Even Galeazzo[60] was disgusted."

"So, what's this idea of yours?" the young man with the cigar asked, reaching for his hat from the parapet.

"Just an inkling I had. Don't move."

An airplane roared over the din of one hundred thousand spectators. I tried to distract myself but heard a sudden cry and saw the red-haired woman throw her arms around the man's neck and burst into convulsive sobs. The ash from the Minghetti had fallen and the cigar embers were burning brightly. The snail was gone.

"It rounded the corner!" she said, clutching him. "Only by half a second, but it rounded the corner..."

"Half a second? What corner? What on earth are you talking

about?" the man asked, bewildered and looking over at me as if for help. The blubbering woman seemed incapable of uttering a single word of explanation.

"I beg your pardon," I intervened. "It would seem that the snail managed to round the corner *before* the ash from your cigar crumbled, that's all..."

"Oh, is that so? Before the...? And what is that supposed to mean?"

"Ah, that's a secret I cannot divulge. However, I would guess that this kind lady endowed its passage with some special, private meaning, a sort of vow or wish...perhaps something that concerns you, dear sir. Am I right?"

The woman nodded, a bewildered half smile spreading across her face, as she continued to sob and clutch at him.

The man with the cigar appeared even more intrigued and tried to comfort her. Then he turned back to me. "Excuse me, but how did you know this? Do you read cards? Are you a magician?"

"Worse. I'm a journalist."

The couple walked off, glancing back at me once in a while. I followed behind, slowly, in an effort to avoid another parade of party officials. There was a loud rumble of automobiles. The first cars had already reached the Viale dei Colli and were visible in the distance, the luminous dots of a mobile rosary.

THE DIRECTOR

HALOED, almost merging with the early morning mist, the man who resembled Amerigo stood perfectly still on the sidewalk, staring at me. I gestured noncommittally, then reconsidered, but my uncertain greeting didn't go unnoticed.

"So, you recognize me?" he said. "It really is me, Amerigo."

(Damn, I thought to myself. Why did I think he was dead? Misinformation, I guess, one of those stupid bits of news you don't bother double-checking... Thankfully, he hasn't heard about it.)

"How are you?" Amerigo continued. "You're just the man I was looking for, along with a few others. I'm only passing through for a couple of days. I shouldn't tell you why, top secret and all that, but I'll never forget the service you did me that June in Vallarsa, when you gave me leave the day before the counteroffensive. I know you didn't intend to save my skin—quite the opposite, actually, since you didn't really like me—but precisely because of your inexplicable aversion to me, you wanted to be completely fair. So, to you I owe my life, my first encounter with Y., a true stroke of luck that happened on those few days of leave, and all the rest that followed. Don't thank me, just hear me out (and most importantly, don't utter a word of this to anyone or your name will fade into obscurity). We're shooting a film about the next fifty centuries, a film that the involved parties will see, or rather, experience, for the fraction of time that concerns them, anyway. You, as a living being, belong to the previous film in the series—not a bad film, not at all, just a bit dated, a tad démodé, too many close-ups, too many tracking shots, too many divas. The new story is much more coherent, more fluid, it moves at a brisker pace. And the music! Wait till you hear it! As loud as a cannon and as subtle as a whistling thrush. But that should come as no surprise. They've got their ear to the ground up there, they follow all the trends. We do, after all, have a far vaster selection than you ever will."

"Right," I stammered, stepping back toward a wall that was plastered with posters advertising Road Safety Day. "Right, admittedly, up there...a greater selection, more variety..." I noticed that one of the posters read LIFE IS SHORT, DON'T MAKE IT SHORTER.

"Now," he went on, "It's not a question of assigning you a new role. Yours is about to end, and it wasn't exactly brilliant. I know, I know, it's not your fault! During your lifetime, celebrities were in fashion and you just weren't cut out for that kind of thing. You would have been better off in this new film, but, like I said, I can't do anything about it now. You were born too early. Don't get upset! I can secretly squeeze you into the new film, give you a role that exists in the memory of the new actors. If I remember correctly, you write, don't you? At least, you used to. No wishful thinking now, a role like Homer's is out of the question, judging from the briefing notes we've compiled on you, which are far from exceptional. And I highly doubt they will assign you long-lasting fame (in any case, no more than fifty centuries) such as Callimachus enjoys, thanks to his two hundred readers a century—and what readers! Nor can I guarantee you posterity based solely on the merit of your works...I know, you may well deserve it, but my hands are tied. The briefing notes are what they are, and yes, the people who wrote them may well be imbeciles, I would concur, but I can't just toss them out the window. This new film is a sequel, a revisitation of the facts, impossible to start tabula rasa. One day, perhaps, but for now we have to be patient. I, too, will soon be succeeded by new directors, who will be far worse than I. So, what do you say? Are you interested in a bit part? No one will read your books in the new film, but you'd be remembered as an actual person, as someone who lived in another time period. How about becoming a character in a libretto of an opera, a secondary role, of course, someone like Angelotti in *Tosca*? I think he actually existed. Or would you prefer to link your name to a steak, like Monsieur

Chateaubriand? Or, if you'd rather, we could name a kind of pin after you, or a necktie knot, or a hairstyle, or a new species of dog. I know you were fond of a few mutts in your day. We could invent a breed and name it after you. But we have to do it fast. If I hadn't run into you, I'm not sure you would've ended up in my treatment. Any thoughts? Suggestions?"

I took a few steps forward in the fog, faltered, and Amerigo caught my arm. A green light behind me turned fiery red and a river of cars came rushing toward me, then screeched to a halt, thanks to the sound of a whistle. A policeman in a black overcoat hurried over to me. "You're breaking the law!" he yelled. "Onto the traffic island, move it!"

"What about him? Is he... breaking the law too?" I asked, glancing at Amerigo, who had hopped onto the island with us.

"Him, who?" the policeman asked, pulling out his pad to write me up. "Are you drunk?"

Apparently he didn't see anything in the fog where I saw the face of the man who had smiled at me more than thirty years earlier in Vallarsa.

THE WIDOWS

ALL MY best friends are dead. Their wives, who were neither younger, fitter, nor more deserving of survival, live on, and continue to perpetuate the memory of their husbands. Wrapped in their mourning crepe, decorated with trimmings and lace, and fawned over by magistrates, the widows chair committees, cut inaugural ribbons at exhibitions, smash bottles of champagne on the hulls of ships, edit proofs of books written by the deceased, retrieve cremation urns, confer scholarships, and keep alight the wicks that would prefer to extinguish themselves for lack of oil. "Leave us in peace!" the feeble voices of the departed whisper from underground. But the widows press on, and if shadows of oblivion appear while they sit at a card table playing canasta in the pine groves facing the Apuan Alps, they hunch over their hands and say, "Keep back! *Non praevalebunt!*"[61]

The dear widows have chosen not to stay on in the city during the summer to safeguard their scorching relics. Instead they've gone off to the seaside and to the mountains to watch alpinists climb the Matterhorn through their binoculars, float like fin whales on the calm waters of the lido, eat goulash at the Hungarian shack on Cinquale beach in Versilia. They recognize each other instinctively, huddle together and gab...gab about those who have preceded them to the kingdom of heaven. They're multilingual, worldly, reserved, haughty, detached. And if they've remarried, they preserve the cult of their *first*.

"*Mein Mann,*" says one; "*mon mari,*" says another; "my husband," adds a third. And a fourth whispers into the ear of a fifth: "Even in private, you know what I mean, he always wanted me to keep my *th*ockings on . . ." (She spoke with a slight lisp.)

All my best friends are dead, and I alone remain to rail against the cult upheld by the dear widows. I remember my friends in my own way, while boarding a tram or drinking an aperitif; I see them in the expression of a dog, in the contour of a palm tree, in the arc of an exploding firework. Sometimes I even catch a glimpse of them in the litter that the sea pushes gently out to Calambrone, in the dregs of a glass of old Barolo, in the leap of that cat last night as it chased after a butterfly in the piazza. No one said "my husband," and my friends were happy, alive with me.

THE GUILTY PARTY

IT WAS almost three o'clock in the afternoon. Federigo had returned to the office just a few minutes earlier. Standing at a lectern that came up to his neck, he started to draft a letter of reply to an unknown individual from the distant city of Seattle, Washington, who wrote to inquire if the podiatrist Fruscoli could still be found on Via del Ronco, as had been true twenty years ago. To be perfectly clear, Federigo did not run a tourist information office but rather a kind of *bottega*[62] that catered to English and Americans (as well as Italians), a lending library of books, from theosophy to crime novels. In truth, this bottega was hardly a bottega at all, but actually a long-standing institution that had gotten along perfectly well on its own for more than a century, ignored by the authorities. However, in the past few years, local "officials" had decided to involve themselves in its operations, turning it into a semipublic, semiprivate institution that was hard to define and even harder to run. Federigo, heedless of this new era, continued (noblesse oblige) to reply to strangers from Seattle and elsewhere, keeping alive a gracious tradition that had, until that day, been preserved within the four walls of the old bottega.

And so, Federigo stood at his lectern, working. There were no other furnishings in the office (a high-ceilinged, narrow, cold, mere hole-in-the-wall that was once a chapel), other than the lectern, a letterpress, and a few stacks of files. Facing Federigo, and busy scribbling away, was an old employee in a wool cap, an honest, pug-nosed fellow who was the bottega's thrifty treasurer and Cerberean overseer. The rest of the institute could be seen through the glass that separated it from the chapel: a nave with stained-glass windows, drapes, and bookshelves that reached halfway up to the ceiling. Off to one side, near a counter, stood another old man in a wool cap, who was always gesticulating and often drunk; he was in charge of book distribution, and was assisted by a few clerks. On that particular long-ago afternoon, almost no one came in, except one of the regulars, the blind octogenarian Lady Spelton, who let herself be led to the counter, where she proclaimed "Murder!" and slipped the latest thriller into her purse, then gave a Fascist salute, and disappeared. It was almost three o'clock, as I already mentioned, when lo and behold, something quite unusual happened. From down in the damp cellar, accessible via a stairwell situated in the main room of the crumbling institute, came the warbling of a telephone. Federigo rushed downstairs and held the receiver up to his ear. A few blunt words: Count Penzolini was expecting him.

Federigo threw on his threadbare overcoat, wrapped a scarf around his neck and, a moment later, he was crossing the vast medieval piazza presided over by the municipal palazzo and its imposing tower. His feathers were not at all ruffled by this unusual summons. Lacking entirely in prophetic capabilities, he was not the kind of person who could hear the grass growing beneath his feet or predict the unpredictable.

He paid five lire to use the palazzo elevator (his position entitled him to a 75 percent discount) and alighted shortly after, in the count's empty but well-heated antechamber. Two footmen in white stockings and livery stood at a window that was ajar, tossing breadcrumbs to a few shivering pigeons. When Federigo told them that the count was expecting him, they professed to be busy and carried on feeding the birds. Then one of them stepped forward and told Federigo to wait his turn.

Nobody else was waiting and no sounds came from the count's office. It took longer than expected, nearly two hours. The attendants continued to toss crumbs onto the windowsill, as staff members passed through occasionally, papers in hand, and did their part to aid the city's feathered friends too. Now and then a car horn blared from the piazza below. The view through the windowpanes of bell towers and the spires ablaze in the sunset offered a respite to myopic Federigo.

It must have been five o'clock when a murmur was heard from behind the closed door. Perhaps Count Penzolini had finally taken up his position. An envoy in gold braid approached Federigo.

"Your turn," he snapped.

Federigo entered, slipping a little on the waxed tiles. The count's office was vast and unadorned. No documents lay on his desk, as was the custom of the time, but several portraits of important men hung on the walls. Resting on a tripod next to the window was an ebony sphere[63] that revealed—from whichever direction one looked—the imperious profile of the Unique One,[64] the only man worthy, in those years, of the honor of being addressed with a capital letter. It was, in fact, a historic model of his face, a shape created with a patented mold that had become very popular. Count Penzolini stood behind his desk. He looked to be about forty years old: tall, clean-shaven, with grey, fishlike eyes, and only a few insignia on his lapel. A number of framed mottos hung on the wall: "Keep visits short" and "To live is not necessary" and a third one, with a longer phrase, possibly even more menacing, but which Federigo did not have time to decipher. The count raised his arm in salute and our visitor feebly imitated him.

"You called for me, sir?" Federigo asked shakily. He wasn't sure why, but he had begun to feel anxious.

"Have a seat," the count said. He opened a drawer, took out a sheet of paper, and started reading it. Then he looked up but stared off into the distance, out the window.

"I need to speak to you," he said coldly, "about a matter that concerns the institute under your direction, which I have the honor and responsibility of presiding over as mayor of the city of X. Some time ago you were informed by certified mail that it was my intention to establish closer ties between our association and the local section of Mysticism, whose headquarters are in the same building. A few days ago, the administrative board examined the problem. It was during your absence... a justifiable absence, I presume."

"Most certainly justified," Federigo said. "I obtained five days of leave for a family funeral from you, sir."

"Fine, let's say it was justified," the count conceded. "It was actually useful, as it allowed us to discuss an anomaly in your situation with greater calm. The matter is crystal clear. Ten years have gone by, Signor P., since this city assigned you a task, one that is far from negligible, without asking you, as would have been opportune, for any specific political allegiance. Perhaps Marquis G., my predecessor, placed too much faith in your sensitive nature and thought you would have kept up with the changing times on your own. Now, even if you were willing to do it, it is too late. Surely you understand just how problematic it is that a man lacking the basic... requisite of belonging... ahem, ahem," (the count coughed without clarifying further) "should hold the reins of a cultural center that must align fully with the directives of our section of Mysticism. I do not wish to discuss the reasons that led to your... disengagement. They are not up for discussion. I am here to inform you that as of next Thursday you will stand down and hand over all responsibilities to your successor, who will be introduced to you in a matter of days. The books are in perfect order, I imagine. And if not, no more than a couple of hours will be needed to set them straight."

"Actually, the books are not in order," Federigo stammered. "I haven't been paid for eighteen months. Moreover, in the last trimester, I paid the employees out of my own pocket... while waiting for the funds to come in."

"Ah," the count said. "And you did not inform us of this situation?"

"I sent at least a dozen memorandums, sir."

"Of course, of course," the count acknowledged. "You will receive your final payment as soon as possible. As for your severance pay, a letter of resignation would simplify matters enormously. By choosing to step down, you will not be exposed to any unfavorable comments, you see? In your so doing, the institute's administration will be absolved of any obligation and may even agree to grant you a small bonus, a tangible recognition... am I perfectly clear?"

"Thereby obtaining," Federigo spoke with an unfamiliar audacity, "a considerable savings on my severance pay."

"Peu de chose," Count Penzolini added dryly. "You now belong to a semipublic corporation that has not been duly recognized as such. Consequently, we have taken appropriate measures. I await your letter of resignation."

"And if you should not receive it?" Federigo asked, surprising himself ever more.

"In that case," the count concluded, raising his arm in sign of dismissal, "we will aim low. Don't fool yourself."

Federigo raised his arm and did an about-face. He descended the steps of the municipal building and soon reached the church-library, now empty. The unfinished letter to his unknown correspondent in Seattle lay on the lectern. Federigo picked up his pen, cleaned the nib by dipping it in a glass of hunting pellets (one of the inventions of that thrifty Cerberus), and went on to write, in bad English, "As for Mr. Fruscoli's shop, I beg to inform you ..." He concluded the letter, sealed the envelope, put a stamp on it (paid for out of his own pocket), and reflected melancholically on how the tradition of noblesse oblige within those four walls had come to its definitive end, how no future letter from Seattle would ever receive a reply. He then locked the front door with his bunch of keys and made his way, his head hung low, under the porticoes and toward the post office.

MARMELADOV'S SECOND PERIOD

A FEW DARK cypress trees in the background, in the foreground a large haystack and two or three smaller yellowish sheaves buried in a lettuce-green field; on the right, close to the most irritating sheaf, sat a dog, looking at a line of white lead, the cloudy sky. I hate cypresses and I detest haystacks. All the Romantic trees, with the exception of the oak, laurel, and willow, leave me less than indifferent. Haystacks, sheaves, and long stretches of plowed and farmed land don't inspire me in the least. Nature speaks to me when it is rugged and untamed, but when it is portrayed as lovely, dewy vales that have been overly cultivated, I become decidedly hostile. I prefer weeds and thorns to fields of golden wheat. While I greatly admire the Tuscan countryside, I only feel completely at ease in the area surrounding the Abbey of San Galgano, where you can still find marten hunters. I prefer a meadow of wildflowers to a farm, the woods to tilled soil. And if I were to reprint Foscolo's poem *Le grazie*, faced with the ambiguous variant "i colti di Lïeo" or "i colli di Lïeo," I would opt for the latter, the hills rather than the sown fields, without worrying about the original manuscript (after all, it's hardly legible).[65]

How then had I come to purchase a painting that portrayed—and so poorly—aspects of nature that were unbearable to me? And yet there it was, in my room. I had an ornate silver frame made for it, inside of which the pointy tips of the cypresses and the obscene yellow sheaves appeared even more ungracious. With its clashing colors, artless rendition, and a few poorly hidden corrections (a gasometer in the background, hurriedly erased, traces of which could still be seen), the painting had bothered me for years. Having left Florence long ago,

I rarely slept in that room, but as soon as I returned and set eyes on the painting of the cypress trees and haystacks, I felt unhappy. I tried covering it up with a newspaper and a towel, but the painting was still there, fermenting and fidgeting under that temporary camouflage.

I admit to purchasing it for five hundred lire from the painter, Zoccoletti. It was the best piece in the show. I had stopped to look at it and foolishly had commented, "Nice, nice … maybe I could …" and Libero Andreotti, who was there with me, had encouraged me. "Why don't you buy it? You can pay for it over time, it doesn't cost much." Zoccoletti, who was standing nearby, had seized his opportunity, "I'll have it sent to your home, you can pay me whatever you want," and so, one fine day, the painting arrived, unframed. Libero Andreotti was a sophisticated man and I wouldn't dare accuse him— now that he is no longer with us and can't defend himself—of over-valuing Zoccoletti's work. But, at the time, Andreotti was reconsidering his bohemian lifestyle in Paris and most likely the cypress trees and haystacks had aroused not altogether unpleasant feelings. It must be said, too, that Zoccoletti was a genuine soul, a dilettante, both as painter and as dealer, incompetent at making money from his art or anything else. I saw him twice a day at the café and if I hadn't accepted Andreotti's invitation, I simply don't know how I would have sustained Zoccoletti's expression of silent reproach under those disheveled eyebrows.

And so, the painting ended up in my room, but from the very first day it failed to fit in. It was ugly, downright ugly. Not even Millet or Fattori could have made me appreciate that subject, style, angle, or setting, much less the ungrateful and miserable Zoccoletti!

I tried to forget about the painting and I lived through several dark months under the influence of that landscape. From the window I could see a few cypress trees and some farmland, a cypress tree here, a cypress tree there, but I decided to convince myself that Zoccoletti would neither take away nor add anything to my life. And so, time passed …

Until one night, when I turned on the bedside lamp and the painting seemed so odious that I decided then and there to get rid of it. I couldn't just throw it out the window; I would have to remove it from the frame, a feat beyond my strength, because it seemed to have been cemented into the silver casing. I wasn't up to the task, it required equipment and tools, and the skill of a gravedigger. I was also afraid of ruining the frame, which had cost more than the painting itself. Then there was the problem of what to do with the canvas: if I left it out on the street, it might find its way back to its creator; if I set it on fire, it would stink up the house. Was there no middle ground?

Yes, there was a solution, and I reached for it like a lifeline. Zoccoletti's painting wasn't protected by glass, so I could easily paint over it, taking full advantage of the nice silver frame as a starting point. Under the new painting, the old one would continue to live on, not destroyed, just buried. On my deathbed I would be able to say to my heirs: There's another painting under that one, and with some careful sponge work, it could reappear. And if, in the meantime (who knows, anything is possible), Zoccoletti had become famous, his painting embellished with the remnants of my dabbling and tinkering would only make it more precious and less tasteless. A four-handed painting, the most precious, the rarest Zoccoletti ever . . .

I leaped out of bed, threw open my closets, and found an old palette, a brush, and a few tubes of dry paint. Luckily there was a lot of white lead. I squeezed a generous quantity onto the palette and spread a white shroud over the much-loathed landscape. The result was encouraging: the frame could breathe, it was free, maybe the painting would take shape on its own.

I started to trace some contours on the white field. I trusted in fate, trying to extract color from tubes that had already been squeezed dry. Soon it was a tangled mess of creepers, crowned by a reddish blob that could pass for a rising or setting sun. But nothing significant appeared on the canvas, no spot, no line that said: Here I am, follow me, develop me. I was out of luck, the painting wasn't taking shape. I had nothing to inspire me: no vases, no bottles, only the bed and two chairs. At two in the morning, I stopped painting and went back to sleep, discouraged. The next day I left Florence and gave no more thought to the unfinished canvas.

A few months later I went back, and just before dawn I was woken by distant barking—distant, but bothersome and incessant nonetheless. I opened the window and looked out onto the street. I went into the kitchen and looked out at the convent garden next door. No dog could be seen or heard. The howling came from my bedroom, but there were no dogs in my house. Could the barking come from the dog in the Zoccoletti painting that I had buried under a layer of white lead? I rejected the absurd idea, but when it happened again the following night, I pressed my ear up to the canvas and, convinced that *the barking came from within*, I dipped a rag in paint thinner and energetically rubbed the unfinished painting in a south-southwesterly direction, in search of the dog. I worked diligently until, under a blob the size of a coin, less than an inch in diameter, the dog appeared, yelped once, and then sat still, under the creepers, without jumping off the canvas. Worn out, I threw a towel over the painting and thought of it no more. From that night on, I was able to sleep in my room without being awoken by barking. Nothing would have led to my making peace with the obscure painting—not even the news of Zoccoletti's death, which I read about in a local newspaper—if it hadn't been for a visit, when I was back in Florence for a few days, from a well-known collector and expert in contemporary art. Noticing the painting on the floor, facing the wall, he rose from his seat and turned it around, studied it for a long time, and said, "Interesting...very interesting, beautiful, actually. Who's it by?" The canvas was signed with a single letter *M*, but after Zoccoletti's death, I could look at that painting and say to myself, like Calaf in *Turandot*, "il mio mistero è chiuso in me,"[66] and all it took was an instant for me to invent a name and reply with confidence.

"It's a Marmeladov, from his second period, before he joined the 'Primatist' movement.[67] And yet it reveals the first signs of his change, as you can see. I've had it for more than twenty years, but I just recently had it cleaned."

"A strong piece, definitely very strong," the critic said. "I wish I had a photograph of it for my magazine. This primitive dog, this *Urhund*, surrounded by this tropical thicket, is ever so slightly representational, just a hint, really. I like transitional works, pieces that bridge one period and the next. Who did you get it from? It can't be easy to find a Marmeladov from this period. I've seen two, in Bern, and while I'm not saying that this is one of his best, if you ever want to get rid of it, I think we might be able to make a deal. With a little goodwill, we could meet halfway…"

The painting stood in a ray of sunlight, beautiful. A few polychromatic arrows, a fiery globe, and, almost skewered with zigzagging lines, the little black dog, its nose in the air, the same dog that had barked so hard before being reborn as a Primatist.

"Beautiful," I agreed, somewhat timidly, "and to think it doesn't even bark anymore."

"What's that?"

"It was a defect…or rather, an attribute of the painting. The dog used to bark all night. But now it has been corrected; it's been a while since it last barked. And still, I need to keep an eye on it. Would you mind if we hold off on a deal?"

He left shaking his head, unhappy and suspicious; he would soon learn that the Primatist movement did not include anyone by the name of Marmeladov at any period of his life. When I went back to my room, the ray of sunlight was gone and the painting had fallen asleep, cold and inexpressive. I understood then that I would never be able to throw it away or bury it in the basement. Poor old Zoccoletti's dog had found an owner and, until the little fellow was shuffled off to some ultramodern museum, unfortunately, that owner was me.

POETRY DOES NOT EXIST

CURFEW had sounded, and the two men who out of precaution were staying at my house had just returned. One of the two nocturnal visitors, or "flying guests," was my friend and longtime conspirator Brunetto, a physicist and researcher in ultrasonics. He was the stable, or semi-stable, element in the clandestine arrangement, while the other was more of an interchangeable "flying ghost," one of a series of phantoms who were always careful not to reveal their real names.

It was the onset of the somber winter of 1944, and the city was an endless nightmare of raids and reprisals. That evening's phantom went by the name of Giovanni. He was gray-haired and seemingly mild mannered, but it was said that he had compelling reasons to steer clear of his own home. It was cold and the two guests were sitting next to the radio, warming their hands at an electric heater, when the inside phone line rang from the concierge's desk downstairs.

"Careful, a German is on his way up," the concierge said.

There was no time to lose. At my signal Bruno and Giovanni disappeared into the small, dark bedroom. Having turned the radio dial back to the local station, I moved closer to the front door, waiting for the bell to ring. What would my friends do? And what about me, how would I get out of it? There was no rear exit and the German was probably not alone ... The doorbell rang softly, then more insistently. I let a few seconds pass, pretending to come from down the hall, unfastened the chain, and opened the door. The German walked in: a young man, around twenty, nearly six feet tall, with a hooked nose like a bird of prey, eyes that were at once shy and frenzied, and a longish crew cut. He removed his cap and, after verifying my identity in faltering Italian, aimed, as if with a musket, a thick roll of papers at me.

"I'm a literary," he said (surely he meant a littérateur), "and I've brought you the poems you asked for. I'm from Stuttgart, my name is Ulrich K."

"Ulrich K., your name is not new to me," I replied, showing how immensely flattered I was, while ushering the man (a sergeant) into the room where the radio was located. "What an honor. How may I be of service to you?"

I was completely in the dark for a few moments but gradually found my way. He had written to me two years earlier about his translations of some Italian poets, and I had replied, or rather had found somebody to reply for me, asking for the collection of Hölderlin's poems, which at the time were unobtainable in Italian bookstores. He explained that the book was also out of stock in Germany but that he had managed to type out nearly three hundred pages for me. He regretted that it was drawn from the Zinkernagel edition, not the Hellingrath, but I could reshuffle the work as needed, it wouldn't take more than a few months, nothing really. What did I owe him? Not a pfennig, he was much obliged to have served *sein gnädiger Kollege*. If anything, maybe I could type out the work of some of our most illustrious modern poets for him. (I broke into a cold sweat, and not just at the thought of the effort.) He had only recently arrived in Italy and was stationed in Terranuova Bracciolini, where he worked as an accountant in a food supply unit. A small crew, they initially feared local hostility, but then things started to look up and, in spite of the curfew, they even managed to organize a few concerts in the main piazza. Lurking among them were three or four professional musicians. He, too, played an instrument, I'm not sure if it was the flügelhorn or the fife. His vocation in life? At first, he studied philosophy but he refused to accept that philosophical speculation was a kind of snake swallowing its own tail, a constantly pirouetting form of navel-gazing. He had felt the need to explain the meaning of life, but couldn't. He had ended up in the hands of a teacher who disassembled others' systems of thinking, revealing their aporias and internal contradictions where the only—and ultimate—certainty was anguish, shipwreck, checkmate. The student had asked whether it was worthwhile to free oneself from the old metaphysics, if by chance Dasein, the existential self in flesh and bones, was a hypothesis just as intellectualistic as the Cartesian cogito. The teacher, somewhat annoyed, had kindly shown him the door. (A glass of wine? Why not, maybe even more than one, join me, please, thank you, *bitte, bitte schön.*) After that, he had turned to poetry, but not to the vulgar belletristic kind, and even here things got confusing, and rather quickly. Ancient poetry is basically inaccessible. Homer was no ordinary man, and all that deviates from what is ordinarily human seems essentially extraneous. Greek lyrics were not the fragments that have reached us, and so we lack the right perspective to judge them; where can we find the sacred element necessary for understanding the great tragic poets? We can forget about Pindar, since we are no longer part of the mythical, agonistic, and musical world that made his existence possible, and the same goes for the oratory and didactics of the Latin writers. Dante? A giant, but reading his work is basically a pensum; after all, the Ptolemaic man lived in a box of matches (and spent ones at that!), so a completely different ball game for us. Shakespeare? Huge, but his limitlessness conveys too much of his naturalistic approach. Goethe, meanwhile, is quite the opposite: sailing down the river of full-on neoclassicism, his theory of naturalism is nothing more than a controversial conquest.

"And the modern poets?" I asked, pouring him the last drop from a straw-wrapped jug of Chianti Gallo Nero.

"Oh, the moderns, my illustrious colleague," Ulrich continued, in his eyes a glint of excitement. "We are the ones who create the moderns, thanks to our collaborative efforts. But there's always an element of instability, and we're too involved to be able to pass judgment. Believe me, poetry does not exist. When it's old, we can't identify with it, when it's new, it repulses us the way all new things do, having no history, no character, no style. And what's more, well, what's more is that a perfect poem would be like a flawless philosophical system, it would be the end of life, an explosion, a collapse, while an imperfect poem is simply not a poem. We're better off grappling with . . . the ladies. But you know what? Over in Terranuova, they don't trust us. A real pity." (And then, in French, "*C'est dommage.*")

He got up, peered into the jug to see if it really was empty, and then bowed, wishing me an enjoyable reading of his Hölderlin. I didn't have the heart to tell him that as of a couple of years ago I had stopped studying German. Out in the corridor, he put his cap on askew, causing a lock of hair to tumble out, and bowed once more. A moment later, he was swallowed up by the elevator.

I stood outside the small bedroom and opened the door quietly. They were waiting in the dark.

"Did your German leave?" Bruno asked. "What did he say?"

"He said that poetry does not exist."

"Ah, I see."

Giovanni rolled onto his side and began to snore. The two of them slept on a tiny cot.

PART IV

THE MAN IN PAJAMAS

I WAS WALKING up and down the corridor in my pajamas and slippers, stepping over mounds of dirty linens heaped here and there. It was a first-class hotel because it had two elevators and a dumbwaiter (almost always out of order) but no storage closets for used sheets, pillowcases, and towels, so the cleaning ladies had to pile them up where they could, in unused corners. Late at night, in those same unused corners, I'd appear, and because of this, the cleaning ladies didn't like me much. However, after handing out a few tips, I obtained their unspoken consent to stroll wherever I pleased. It was past midnight. A telephone rang softly. Was it coming from my room? I was walking quietly in that direction when I heard someone reply from Room 22, the one next to mine. I was about to turn in, when the voice, the voice of a woman, said, "Don't come up yet, Attilio. There's a man in his pajamas pacing up and down the hallway. He might see you."

I heard a garbled mumbling from the other end. "Who knows?" she said. "I have no idea. Some poor devil who's always shuffling about. Don't come up, please. I'll let you know." She put the receiver down with a heavy thud and I heard her step toward the door. I sped off urgently, as if on skates. At the end of the hallway was a sofa, a second pile of linens, and the wall. I heard the door of Room 22 open. I turned and saw the woman peering at me through a crack. I couldn't just stand there, so I headed back slowly. I had about ten seconds before I would pass her door. In a flash, I examined my options: (1) return to my room and lock myself in; (2) ditto, with one variation: inform the lady that I had heard everything and that it was my full intention to appease her by turning in; (3) ask her if she really cared to receive Attilio or if I were merely a pretext to exempt herself from an unwelcome nocturnal bullfight; (4) ignore the telephone conversation and continue with my walk; (5) ask the lady if she would consider substituting me for the man on the phone, for the purposes set out in number three; (6) demand an explanation for the term "poor devil" that she had applied to me; (7) . . . my mind struggled to elucidate a seventh option. But by then I was standing in front of the door to her room: two dark eyes, a red *liseuse* over a silk blouse, and short, curly hair. No more than a glimpse, and she slammed the door shut. My heart was beating fast. I returned to my room only to hear the telephone in Room 22 ring again. The woman spoke so softly that I couldn't understand what she was saying. As stealthily as a wolf, I stepped back into the hall and managed to detect a few words. "Absolutely not, Attilio, absolutely not . . ." Then the sound of the receiver being hung up and steps taken toward the door. I leaped toward the second pile of dirty linens, reevaluating options 2, 3, and 5. Again, the door opened a crack. I froze but couldn't possibly stay where I was. Yes, I am a poor devil, I thought to myself, but how does she know that? And what if my pacing actually saved her from Attilio? Or saved Attilio from her? I'm not cut out to be a referee, much less take that role in anyone's life. I headed back to my room, with a pillowcase caught on my slipper. The opening widened, the curly head of hair peered out further. I was only a few feet away. I kicked off my slipper and stood to attention. Then, in an overly loud voice that echoed down the hall, I said, "I'm done with my evening stroll, Signora. But what makes you think I'm a poor devil?"

"We all are," she said, closing the door quickly. The phone rang again from within.

AT THE BORDER

I CAN ONLY recount the initial part of the journey, and it was preceded by a bad accident. I had left my friends' house on Via delle Carra and managed to find a taxi rather quickly, which I hoped would take me to Piazza Beccaria. At an intersection near Porta al Prato, I saw a green Chevrolet heading straight at us. Both drivers had all the time in the world to step on the brakes if only they had had an inkling of common sense, but neither of them did, as they were equally convinced of having the right of way. The distance between the two cars diminished swiftly. "Yet another stupid accident," I said to myself, closing my eyes. After a blink that lasted an eternity, there was a violent collision, I was tossed around the dark interior of the vehicle like a die in a dice cup, and I found myself lying on the ceiling of the car, which had evidently flipped over. Light filtered in through a broken window, together with voices from a crowd that had gathered. The two charioteers began to argue animatedly, the onlookers took sides, and nobody seemed to bother with me. "But there's a man inside," a merciful soul finally said. Someone tried to pry open the car door that was holding me up, which led to me rolling out onto the street before bouncing to my feet. At this point the altercation between the two drivers had reached its climax of injurious cursing; I had time to dust off my jacket as well as possible, pinch myself to make sure I was alive, and hop on a passing tram. The tram was half-empty; most everyone got off at the Porta, including the ticket collector, who stepped out to have a smoke. All the same, the vehicle left again rather quickly, without him, and after a few minutes I realized I had reached the outskirts, but on the opposite side of the city from what I had intended. We came to a stop at a rain shelter, where I heard the tram driver say, "End of the line," inviting me to disembark. A moment later the tram left again, empty, and I remained alone at the stop. It was spring but already quite warm. It must have been six o'clock in the evening, judging from the light. How odd, I thought it was much later. As I felt around for my wristwatch, I saw a Sardinian donkey cart coming toward me along a small path, driven by a young man wearing pajamas and a featherless alpine trooper hat. Sitting comfortably next to him was a small reddish dog of indeterminate breed that kept barking at me.

A rotation of the brake disc, a tug on the reins, and the cart came to a halt. The pup leaped down, elated, and rushed over to me, bright-eyed and panting, while the young fellow in pajamas came toward me with a wan smile and outstretched arms.

"Don't you recognize me?" he asked. "I suppose that's to be expected after such a long time. It's me, Nicola."

"Nicola?" I repeated disoriented. "Nicola...who?"

"Nicola is the last name, my dear friend. I'm the aspiring alpine trooper who left the marching battalion with you in Negrar to join the volunteers on Mount Loner and Mount Corno. Don't you remember? That's understandable, our friendship lasted only a couple of days, but it was the final one for me, and that's probably why it had such a lasting impression. I got here shortly afterward, hit by shrapnel from a fuse. All sorts of shards of metal rained down on the bed of the Leno, remember? Ah, but you were part of a different battalion, maybe you never even heard about it..."

"Nicola...of course...I remember it perfectly well," I replied, stunned. "How very kind of you. A fuse, right...I read about it in the division's bulletin. Nicola...so nice to see you again!"

"And I didn't come alone. Here's Galiffa, your favorite pup when you were a child, and Pinocchietto, the donkey, the one you always fed sugar cubes, in Vittoria Apuana. Good company, right?" he said, with a disturbing chuckle.

"Galiffa...Pinocchietto..." I said, teetering unsteadily. "I'm sorry, but how do you know about them? I mean, didn't you ... end up here ... on your own?"

Both the donkey and the dog joyfully licked my hands in a sign of recognition. I had no sugar cubes on me and felt completely unprepared for this meeting. Nicola laughed with an air of superiority and motioned for me to climb into the cart.

"I'm stationed at the sorting office, at the Border," he continued. "And when I heard your name, I asked to see the film of your life right away. I had already seen it a few times, it was complete, up until today, and I wanted to be ready so that I could pick you up on time. (There's a lot to do here and we're short-staffed ...) Actually, your arrival caught me off guard, otherwise I would've come with all the animals from your personal ark: Fufi and Gastoncino, Passepoil and Bubù, Buck and Valentina ... But don't worry, you'll get to see them all soon."

Really! Even Valentina, I thought to myself. (He must be talking about the turtle who used to come into the kitchen to snuggle with Buck, the German shepherd ... How many years ago was that?)

"I was hoping to bring Mimì in the same jar the magician used to keep her in, but it was getting late and I wanted to be on time. But you'll see Mimì. Giovanna is taking care of her."

"Mimì in the jar ... yes, of course ..." (Probably the guinea pig I saw eons ago in Maloja; but who was Giovanna? An animal or a human being? I felt my heart skip a beat. Giovanna ... could it possibly be *her*?)

"That's right, Giovanna," Nicola confirmed, urging the donkey forward through flourishing fields of what appeared to be castor plants. "She's also at the Border, and even finds time to take care of the zoo."

"Dead?" I wondered aloud, looking down at the ground, the donkey cart bumping along, the two of us jostling on the cramped bench. I tried taking a drag from an extinguished cigarette and found it oddly tasteless. "And ... how is she?"

"Alive," he admonished dryly. "Or rather, the tables have turned for her, too. Just like for me . . . and for you. But you can say *dead*, if you prefer."

"Oh, I see," I mumbled. The certainty of it all made my chin drop to my chest. When I looked up again, we were passing some pavilions where scores of women stood waiting in long lines. The surrounding countryside was colorless and in the distance I could see a cluster of remarkably white houses.

"It hit you hard, didn't it?" Nicola said, with a strained smile. "I know. At first you still feel attached to the stories of the past. It was the same for me, back when I was among the living. Among the dead, I mean. Back in the Anteborder, where you just came from. Sometimes I used to dream and when I'd wake up, I could still remember my dream, and then, eventually, even that memory faded. That's exactly what's happening to you now: a leftover fragment from earth is still awake in your mind, but it will fall asleep soon, it won't be long. Later, when Giovanna lets you see the film of what you once called your life, you'll have a hard time recognizing it. Apparently, this is the way things are until we reach Zone I, where Jack and Fred often go. You recall Fred, don't you? The man who painted your portrait in Spoleto. They say that those memories fade too, and that we get other ones. To tell you the truth, Giovanna and I could have already reached the next destination. I think that over at the Center they agreed we were overqualified, but who's to say . . . We make ourselves useful at the Border. Giovanna is precious to them as an interpreter; she's always had a knack for languages, and I can assure you that there's a real need for that around here. Of course, there would be lots for her to do in Zone II, especially over at the Institute of Superior Entelechies, where the process of dematerialization begins. But the news we get from there is not very encouraging. It appears that they're much stricter about membership and they say it's hard to find accommodation. Your father had promised to report back, but nothing so far . . . And that's why we decided to extend our stay here."

Nicola whipped the donkey along as he talked. The town, perched elegantly on a hilltop with stairs going up and down, eventually came into view. The trees of the valley were low and uniform and the sun seemed fixed on the horizon. I threw the cigarette butt to the ground.

"What about me?" I asked, beginning to perspire. "Will I have to stay with you?"

"Of course, at least for the time being. It all depends on Fred. Poor Fred, he was always so very jealous of you. At the end of the day, he's not a bad fellow, but he's of little use in this life. I imagine you know that he got here after brawling with some drunks. Oh, but how he remembered Giovanna! When we saw the film of Giovanna and Jack trapped inside that sealed freight car, Fred screamed like a madman. He wanted to be the only one to receive them. It was thanks to you that we all became friends. They'll feel bad about not coming to meet you. But what's a person to do? This is one of the perks of working in the arrivals office: we monitor thousands of individual films. This evening, if you want, we can project a part of yours. We can choose a harmless scene, one that doesn't cast any shadows on anyone, especially not Fred. Me, I can handle anything. I always get the short end of the stick, even if I'm the oldest one here. And Jack is so kind . . . so very tolerant."

I crossed and uncrossed my legs. Galiffa licked my hands affectionately and the donkey pricked up his long ears with each flick of the whip.

"Nicola," I managed to mumble softly. The cart turned down an avenue lined with what looked to be horse-chestnut trees, at the far end of which a row of immaculate white houses blocked all further view of the countryside.

"Yes?" Nicola replied, cracking his whip merrily in the air.

"Couldn't this whole business be postponed? This meeting, I mean? I'm sure you understand. For me, the score was settled long ago. I worked hard for so many years to try and forget about these . . . friends. I tried so hard I almost thought I'd lose my mind. Fate spared me the news about the sealed freight train. And now, you . . . No, no, it's too much, too much . . . I just wanted something to be *finished* in my life, you see? Something eternal, because it was so very damned finished.

I can't start over again, Nicola, I can't. Please, take me to my mother, if she's here."

"You'll be able to communicate with Zone III later on. The last bit of news we received from her was good. But then again, memories there are extremely limited, I have to be honest. Stay with us for a decade or so. You'll get used to it. See how young I look?"

Pinocchietto stopped in front of a building. From an open window on the ground floor came the sound of someone tapping on a Noiseless typewriter. Nicola jumped down from the cart and offered to help me. Galiffa was fast asleep in my arms, content.

"She's working overtime," he whispered to me. "Come on now, muster up some courage. She hasn't changed. Forgetting is too easy. Do as we do . . . Live anew."

ON THE BEACH

THE YELLOW postcard I found this morning on the beach where I normally lie in the sun, next to the newspapers and the lounger, and just a few steps away from the umbrellas of the Hunger Pensione, informs me that a package has arrived from the United States and is waiting for me in town. If not claimed by the twenty-eighth of the month, it says, the precious bundle will be given to the Red Cross. A package from whom? And for me? My legitimate curiosity is quelled with a letter rerouted from Florence, also from overseas, which clears up all doubts. It's from Miss Bronzetti, who remembers me fondly and decided to send me sweetened cocoa powder and other delicacies. She hopes her greetings find me well, sends her best wishes, and recalls how very patient I had been with her cat that used to steal meat from the butcher's shop on the ground floor of my apartment building. Other pleasantries follow, the promise of more packages, and the initials A.B.

"A.B." I mumble to myself. "Why, yes, of course . . . Her name was Annalena or Annagilda or Annalia."

I turn to Antonio, who is walking barefoot back to his beach chair, leaving deep prints in the sand. He must have heard the whistle of the postman on his bicycle and gone to meet him, leaving my mail in my spot. As the person who had introduced me to practically all my acquaintances over the past few years, Antonio would surely know more about it than I.

"Anactoria or Annabella," he confirmed. "I remember her well. She lived near San Gervasio but was from Vercelli or thereabouts.

She taught at a college in Wisconsin, or maybe Vermont, but she was on sabbatical at the time, wintering in Florence."

A sudden flash, a memory, a flare in the dark. I recalled a modest apartment in Le Cure, a spinster's impressively tidy home, full of cheap reproductions and oleographs—Botticelli's *Venus*, Masaccio's fresco at the Carmine church, Gozzoli's angels—and books, heaps of them, hardcovers, books from libraries, impersonal and with intimidating titles (*Misunderstood*, *Kidnapped*, *Upstarts*...), alongside a selection of our own flowery classics that provided foreigners with an overview of the Renaissance: carnival songs, a nice little Dante with parallel English text, and a collection of thirteenth-century canticles. And amid all that stood Annabella, or Anactoria, a petite, thin, tenacious Piedmontese, who spent twenty or thirty years teaching the cult of our language (or the suspicion of it) to generations of young women in the United States, thereby fortifying her bond with Italy, her homeland, through thick and thin, year in and year out, with no regard for the fluctuating barometer of either politics or history.

"Anactoria...of course, I recall perfectly," I say to Antonio, trying to sound convincing. "How very kind of her. I'll write back at once, even before sending someone to pick up the package. What a pain, though, to have to deal with it from here...I'll have to sign some kind of form, send my identity card, and who knows what else..."

To be honest, I'm crestfallen. I think about the tricks the mind plays on us, on our bottomless well of memory. I thought I had always done right by myself. And, in terms of others, I figured that an infinite number of now-faded things lived on inside me, finding their ultimate goal and purpose in my heart. In other words, I thought I was rich but now realized I was actually destitute. Someone I had forgotten about entirely had caught me off guard; I live on in the mind of Anactoria or Annalena, I subsist in her, but not she in me. Fine, but how does a memory just vanish? I was aware that I kept locked away in the treasure chest of my memory a multitude of possible ghosts whom I avoided evoking precisely out of the fear of reawakening specters who were not always welcome but nevertheless kept surfacing in my consciousness, somehow enriching it. Reminiscences like those—unreleased spores, firecrackers set off a moment too late—can be easily explained or justified. But what about facts that sprout *ex abrupto* from seemingly inert gray matter? What about when an absence suddenly becomes a presence? I've always believed in a kind of relative forgetfulness, an almost voluntary process, a form of Taylorism,[68] really, with the mind sending everything that cannot be of service off to early retirement, while still holding on to the end of the thread. But here, it was different. Anactoria or Annabella had been suppressed in my mind for four, five, or six years and had now returned because it was her "will" to return. She's the one who chose to grace me with her presence; I had not reawakened her while fumbling about, like an amateur, in search of lost time. She's the loving one, the worthy intruder who, while digging into her past, had come across my specter and tried to reestablish, in the best sense of the word, a "correspondence."

"The cat's the thing," I said to Antonio, "that leaves me perplexed. First of all, there has never been a butcher on the ground floor of my building. And then, I would have given the kitty a name, I always remember the names I give to animals."

"There was a cat," Antonio declared. "A female. She liked to be held, stroked, and petted, and would howl terribly if she didn't get enough attention. She must have fallen out the window or run away a few days after her owner left, together with the girls, I think: Patricia ... and the others."

"Oh, Patricia! I've often thought about her. But for some reason, not Annalena ..."

The light blazes across the Apuan Alps between one late August storm and the next. The bathers start to vanish, but a number of yellow, green, and orange umbrellas still stand open on the damp sand. I can't seem to get as much sun as I'd like, and from behind my sunglasses I watch the last peddlers stroll past the empty bathing huts. I can hear their droning, disheartened cries of *lampi, lampini, lamponi,* as they sell their gelato and cold drinks. Next comes the poodle leading the blind man, a dark, Velázquez-like figure with a concertina that wheezes forth the evergreen "Bésame Mucho." It must be getting late.

"Of course, I remember perfectly, my mind is a steel trap. Even though she was technically on her winter break, Anastasia—Anactoria, I mean—was in charge of chaperoning the young ladies from Miss Clay's college when they made their way down to the city from Villa del Giramontino. Six or seven young heiresses who came here to be cultured. They studied art history, music, dance, the history of Fascism, and other esoteric subjects. In the spring, there was an awards ceremony at the villa, presided over by the prefect and three or four ringleaders from a local political party. The young women were all eager to meet them, with Miss Clay downright enthusiastic about it. Some of the men were even nobility, one may have had an American wife. It must have been at one of those parties that I first met Mr. Stapps. Patricia, the sneakiest of them all, said she had a soft spot for him. When she left Villa Giramontino to stay with a noble family in the city, Anactoria was asked to keep an eye on her. She accompanied Patricia to museums and concerts at both the theater and the Boboli Gardens, ensuring that on all other evenings, the young lady went to bed at the same hour as the chickens. But come midnight, Patricia was out and about with Mr. Stapps. Poor Anactoria, if she only knew... Or maybe she did know but preferred not to pass judgment. It was her fate to watch others burn the candle at both ends while she ... well, she was simply too old to dance the Java. She must've lived alone thirty or forty years in a one-bedroom apartment on a lush green campus, in that wasp's nest of women, eating in the dining hall with her young ladies sometimes, but, more often than not, on her own, frying up some eggs and bacon on the electric stove in her kitchen. Every six or seven years she managed to come home, to Italy, but over time she had grown detached from it, and often acted very American ('Things like that don't happen back home...'), only to suffer great homesickness when she got back to that patch of green, entirely uninspired by the student productions of Shakespeare, the concerts given by second-rate German singers, or the conferences of French scholars on tour. I do understand. It wasn't very courteous of us, Antonio. We should have written to her first or, better yet, we should have taken better care of her when she was here..."

"Have you lost your mind?" Antonio asked in surprise, looking up from his paper. "You're still thinking about that poor lady? Send her a postcard and be done with it. Who remembers her anyway? We don't even know her name!"

"We might not know her name, Antonio," I said indignantly, "but I remember everything perfectly, I can assure you. The only thing that doesn't add up is the cat. Everything else is as clear as day, even the things that Anactoria-Anastasia never mentioned, not back then, and not now. Just think of the tall tales that must have reached her ears after the first war, when we let ourselves be governed by that gang of thieves. Think of the soundness of her judgment in a situation that was made so much more difficult by her being thousands of miles away, not to mention the brainwashing propaganda. Anactoria didn't give a hoot about revering His Excellency, I remember well. Nor did she share in the political resentment of any of her beaux, unlike most of her sheepish colleagues, who lost their way. She was purity and justice incarnate, Antonio. We realized it too late. She thought with her own head, like me... and better than you."

Antonio stands up, yawns, and stretches. A few large drops of rain start to fall on the sand and the wind picks up, darkening the *Reseda odorata* growing around the pine trees. The last of the vacationers hurry onto the terrace of their pensione, Hunger, where there is a sudden bustling of maids. The lifeguard hastily closes up and puts away the remaining beach umbrellas. I didn't hear the bell, but it must have been past one o'clock.

"It's always too late for you," Antonio said. "But you can still make it up to Attanasia. Now, shall we go see if the food at the hotel still lives up to its name?"

STOPPING IN EDINBURGH

IN EDINBURGH, a city where the main squares are called *crescents* and are shaped like half-moons, there stands a polygonal church with an inscription that extends all the way around its perimeter, a message much longer than the slogans that were pasted to the walls of our villages until as recently as two years ago. The endless legend, which wraps all the way around the church and keeps the visitor looking upward from one wall to the next, does not celebrate any earthly leader or other glory in our transient world. Proceeding by way of skillful exclusions and negations, the coiling spiral of golden letters (or was it made of stones in a kind of mosaic; who can recall?) seeks to inform absent-minded passersby where the celestial one cannot be found, where it is pointless to look for him: GOD IS NOT WHERE... And to tackle the next face of the polygon, the reader has to take a few steps: GOD IS NOT WHERE... And all the places where life is good, easy, or congenial, places where God might actually be, or at least be sought out, are then enunciated in a long list, always with the recurring reminder that God is not here, or there, or even there...

One summer's day I found myself circling that tangled knot for quite some time, tracing and retracing my steps, wondering with growing angst and a sense of dizziness, "For God's sake, where is the Almighty?"

I may have actually muttered my question out loud, because an elegant gentleman crossing the crescent just then, a man whom I later learned was a colonel on leave from the Highlanders, came up beside me and firmly denied that the solution to my question was anywhere inside or outside those Presbyterian walls, written or unwritten.

"God is not here, sir," he said with a serious and knowing air, pulling a small Bible out of his pocket and reading a few verses out loud. A number of people stopped to listen; a few women and two or three factory workers formed a circle around him. Then the cluster grew, with one of the newcomers taking a Bible out of his own pocket and starting to read from it, expounding his rebuttal of the colonel's comment. Soon, there were three or four jabbering clusters, each one with its own referee, a natural-born arbiter who gave (and took away) the floor, summarized the pros and cons of each argument, and attempted reconciliation and mediation where, most likely, none was possible. Staunch Presbyterians, lax Arminians, Baptists, Methodists, Darbyists, and Unitarians; lukewarm and indifferent bystanders; men, women, and young people; the middle class and the working class; employees and proprietors; everyone listened or spoke with a strange glow in their eyes. Disconcerted by having involuntarily kicked that mystical hornet's nest, I took a few steps toward Princes Street, the broad avenue lined with buildings on one side only, leaving an impressive view (at least for a Scotsman) of the three-hundred-foot-high fortress, with its castle. Princes Street is dotted with private clubs, whose exclusive circles are further protected by double-glazed windows, behind which the outlines of austere butlers in livery can be seen. That regal road is always windy and often empty, but alongside the grander buildings, busy side streets lead down to other crescents and squares, each with its own church and park. GOD IS NOT WHERE... Then where was he? Had they ever actually found the Celestial One? I suddenly felt terribly anxious and started to scold myself for never dealing at any length with this specific issue in my own country, in all these years.

When I made my way back to the crescent, only a few people were left. The old colonel came up alongside me again, pocketed his Bible, and commented heartily on the development of the debate. I didn't ask him for the outcome, as I probably wouldn't have been able to extrapolate it from his torrent of words, half of which I failed to grasp.

THE PAINTINGS IN THE CELLAR

THE BORA started to blow just as B. and I came out of the Revoltella Museum. We were making our way toward the Garibaldi café when a tall and thin young man, his gabardine raincoat flapping in the wind, passed by in a hurry, slowing down only to wave hello. Although there was nothing remarkable about him, I turned to B. and asked, "Who's that?"

"Oh, no one," B. replied indifferently. "Just a Futurist."

Two or three years later, in Trieste again, I went to see an exhibition of works by Giorgio Carmelich, who had recently died of consumption in a German sanatorium. The catalog included a few biographical notes on the artist, how he had passed away at the age of twenty, and some comments on the works he had left behind. Before me was his opera omnia, a total of about thirty pieces: pastels, gouaches, and drawings—though mostly pastels. The art of the deceased was not terribly interesting, but I wasn't much of a talent scout, at least not in terms of painting. Nonetheless, I asked my cicerone from Trieste for more information. His answer surprised me.

"Don't you remember that young man, the Futurist we ran into two years ago in the piazza? That was Carmelich," B. replied.

I say his answer surprised me, because I recalled the encounter perfectly but didn't understand why we should both remember it so clearly. I looked hard and long at his relics. I wouldn't call them works of art exactly: stylistically they were a cross between the Munich Secessionist period and recent Central European Expressionism, dealing with subjects and themes that were almost literary. They were permeated with a macabre obsession with realism, that "smell of horse meat" typical of Kafka, Ungar, and other writers from Prague, who were in vogue in Trieste: skulls, deformed figures, abstract still lifes, and metaphysical cityscapes, tempered into small pastels done in strident tones and chalky textures. But the painter was dead, his fairy tale had ended, and something both pathetic and sincere emanated from his first (and last) "solo" show, something that went well beyond the problem, at times insignificant, of what art is and is not; he was dead. I had seen him, Carmelich, the Futurist, when he was very much alive, fighting his way through the bora, he had waved, I had asked who he was, and now I remembered him, and yet I couldn't say why... How would I ever be free of that dead young man? The result, less than a half hour later, being that I left the exhibition with two of his pastels under my arm, paying a paltry sum for them, even for those days. And thus, my career as buyer began—and just about ended—at least as it regards art. I was certain I had purchased the two best pieces in the show.

The pastels traveled with me to a city where art had, and still has, other roots and a more human aspect. They clashed immediately, both with the house and the environment, which ought to have welcomed them, and they resisted adapting to walls that were too foreign and unfamiliar. Eventually, we, the paintings and I, found a sort of modus vivendi of reciprocal tolerance. The larger and louder of the two pastels—the one depicting Prague buried under snow, with a few men in top hats and swallowtail coats standing next to the towering monument to Jan Hus, and confetti-colored buildings with pointed roofs—found its place in what could be called a utility room, where the elements of an electric heater were always turned off, in the name of frugality, a place where only Agata, my personal factotum, ever set foot. I bravely hung the smaller pastel—a gondola in front of a Venetian palace, all lace and mullioned windows, and a shadow, the dissolving contour of an equestrian statue—in my below-street-level bedroom where I only slept and never went during the day. Positioned under a shelf stacked with books, it had no other painting to compete with. My real paintings, a couple by De Pisis, and, later on, a Morandi, were upstairs, on the floor accessible to visitors. The small Carmelich was out of bounds, like the English, who had yet to enter the city. I was the only one who saw it, and only when I turned on the lamp at night. One evening, I noticed a white cat sleeping next to it, on top of a step stool. But on all other nights, unless I was woken by the watchman doing his rounds of the building, I never saw it, and the cat never came back.

Several tranquil years thus passed for the two Carmelichs. I then underwent a complex change of residence, moving from the below-grade level to the top floor of a five-story building, which in Tuscany is considered a skyscraper. I had lots of books, a few other small paintings, trunks, crates, and suitcases, all crammed into a new apartment that was far smaller than the old one. After unpacking and settling in, I realized that the two Carmelichs were missing. I learned of their fate from all-knowing Agata; they had ended up in the basement of the building, with a lot of other useless things. Initially, I felt some remorse, but this was soon lessened by a new event: the war, the second great war of my life, which forced me to pack away in the basement all the furniture and paintings and books that I cared about a great deal more than the two pastels I had purchased so many years earlier. My aim (and in this I was successful) was to safeguard my things from the bombs that swarms of aircraft were dropping on the outskirts of the city. The railway station of Campo di Marte was nearby, and if the bombers missed their mark, even by an inch ... Best not to dwell on it. Only the most essential pieces of furniture remained in the half-empty apartment, together with piles of discarded books, practically all of which were complimentary copies or volumes of poetry. But the finer objects, including the paintings by De Pisis and the little Morandi, were safe belowground, wrapped up the best it was possible. Who had time to think about things like that, anyway? Other worries, other hopes, filled our hearts. Only now has the problem presented itself again, after Liberation, after having had to evacuate our buildings for eleven months in order to provide refuge to a number of mysterious bearded men equipped with false papers and charged with top-secret missions. I went down to the basement and helped Agata haul up furniture and shelves and papers. I opened crates, knocked over piles of dusty books, and even had a mousetrap snap shut on my fingers in the dark. Slowly the empty apartment filled up; my books, the best paintings, and the prints of Manzù all saw the light of day, while the miniatures of Prague and Venice by Carmelich remained at the bottom of a trunk, their glass shattered, their mounts speckled with mildew.

("So, what're we gonna do with them?" Agata wanted to know, rubbing her hands together impatiently.) What can we do, my sly old Agata? I wish I had an answer. Blessed be the day I handed over my large Bolaffio to a respectable art collector, who was able to give it a decent and stable home; even though, as a result of my gesture of "*cieco disamore*," a celebrated poet from Trieste[69]—a poet, and thus susceptible—shot an arrow in verse at me, out of anger. But what to do with the tiny Carmelichs? Can I, the final custodian of that young man's secrets and sadness, just let them die? Or should I persevere (as has always been my weakness) and attempt a second chance for all that life has so cruelly cast aside and diverted from its intended course? I stand in the doorway to the pantry and feel a gust of cold air. The gondola and the monument to the great Protestant reformer glimmer at the bottom of the trunk. Twenty years, and it seems a day. I see a tall, thin young man cross the blustery piazza, his overcoat flapping around him, as he waves to us and I distractedly ask, "Who's that, Bobi?"[70]

("Oh, no one, just a Futurist," he replies, and we press on, toward the café.)

ANGST

I'M VERY sensitive to the Stimmung, the mood of Nordic cities, and the sight of Zurich, blanketed in snow, with its pointed neo-Gothic pinnacles, streets covered in an armor of ice, large automobiles silently gliding by, colors shifting in the neon lights, all so spectral, empty, and yet teeming with life (at least until five o'clock in the afternoon), held me captive at the double-glazed window. It was around four o'clock, so only one hour of life left. My breath was slowly fogging up the glass. The room was overheated but the thermometer outside read -22°C. The telephone rang. It was the hotel porter.

"Frau Brentano Löwy is here to see you," he stated. "She says she has an appointment. Shall I show her up?"

"Yes, please do."

Probably one of those turbaned intellectuals who congratulated me after my talk yesterday evening. She had requested to meet in private so she could interview me for a popular illustrated magazine. Her specialty was great men *en pantoufles*. In the event of a shortage of great men, she contented herself with slightly lesser ones, as long as they were interesting. A few indiscretions, a touch of color, a photograph, and the piece was done. She was a professional interviewer, gifted with intuition and sensitivity, and apparently quite well paid. She knocked on the door and walked in, wearing a light-blue turban with a red feather, a close-fitting suit, and an expensive fur, which she immediately removed. She had dark hair, probably dyed, and was of an indefinable age, somewhere between thirty and sixty.

"Tea?" I offered.

She accepted. I rang and ordered tea for two in the room.

"I don't have many questions, Signor Montana," she said. "Here's the rundown: Are you favorable to the union of European states? If so, do you favor a federal union with partial renunciation of individual sovereignties or simply a defensive covenant, an alliance that shares a common army? Do you find UNESCO's peripheral action useful? Are you for or against the execution of MacGee, the black man accused of raping an American woman? Who would you nominate for a peace prize? Do you think women's rights in Italy are sufficiently protected? In terms of existentialism, do you consider yourself more of an atheist or a Christian? Do you think that figurative art still has its place in the visual arts? Are you for or against euthanasia? Do you believe that a common European language is an urgent necessity? And would a 3 percent contribution from the Italian language be sufficient?

She stopped, took a sip of her tea, and then started again. "Simple things, really. And just a few personal questions: Do you like animals? Which animal is your favorite? Have you done enough to fight for animal rights? Have you actively fought against vivisection? Do you prefer cats to dogs, or vice versa?"

She fell silent and peered at me through her glasses. The chimes of a pendulum clock broke the quiet.

"I always thought I preferred cats to dogs," I replied, apologizing for beginning with the simpler questions. "Later, the exaggerated devotion of certain women to their tribes of cats sparked my interest in dogs. But my conversion is a recent one and it is due to the fact that dogs (far more so than cats) live on in our memory; they want to survive within us. Theoretically speaking, I am against the notion of living on, and believe it would be immensely dignified if both human beings and animals receded into eternal nothingness. But in practice—through inheritance—I'm a Christian and I can't escape the idea that something of ourselves may, or even must, endure. My dog Galiffa, here, let me show you a photo, died more than forty years ago. In this photograph, the only one I have of him, he sits next to a friend of mine, who is also dead. Thus, I am the only person who still remembers that joyful mutt with reddish fur. He loved me and, when it was too late, I loved him too.

"Passepoil," I continued, "was my second dog. He was a Scottish terrier, though of questionable pedigree. We never cared much for each other, so I gave him to some friends. I don't have a photograph of him, but he may remember (up in the Elysian Fields for dogs) how I rescued him after an automobile accident. My third dog was Buck, a German shepherd. He was a good dog and very fond of a turtle I had, with whom he shared his meals. When he caught distemper, I sent him off to some farmers in Val di Pesa, near Florence. But that same night, he escaped and made his way home, a trip of fifteen miles or so. The distemper got worse, and a lethal injection put an end to it. I didn't see him when he was dead. You mentioned euthanasia, Frau Brentano, well, that covers that. Pippo, my fourth dog, was a purebred schnauzer. He was born in a villa belonging to Olga Löser, a country house surrounded by olive trees and home to eight Cézannes. His old owner has since died, while I live on. Pippo lives on, too, in a city in the Marche. He was very touchy and never forgave me for having given him away. But at a certain point in my life it was impossible for me to keep a dog."

"Oh, life!" said Frau B.L., sighing, "Life in Italy! I have such marvelous memories of *il bel paese*. I spent quite a lot of time there. A charming country, but the men—if you only knew what a struggle—always lying in wait! Are you like that too? Or are you different?"

A tear ran slowly down her cheek, trickling with difficulty through her cakey face powder, her beady eyes scrutinizing me.

With a muffled voice I uttered a few words. "Yes, Frau B.L. I'm different, very different" (I perceived a twitch, disappointment maybe), "well, maybe not all that different," (then, fearing hostility), "but ultimately, yes, different, different from everybody else." I was sweating; each word felt like an unpardonable gaffe.

The telephone rang. "Frau Brentano's car is here," the porter announced.

"Thank you for your interesting remarks, Signor Fontale," the lady said, pulling out her lipstick. "I will be sure to point out your... differentness."

She left, nodding her head. After some time, I received a clipping of the article. There was no mention of dogs or of men hiding in ambush; it only mentioned a certain Herr Puntale and the very modern problem of angst.

THE ENGLISH GENTLEMAN

I KNOW a gentleman who spends his Christmas holidays in Switzerland in order to practice a sport of his own invention, that of "the fake Englishman." I can imagine why he has chosen to interpret this role outside England. In the British Isles, the English are an ordinary commodity, they care neither for themselves nor for foreign visitors, and they barely manage to be properly English even in their own homes. No, to act out this role, an entirely different setting is needed, a world that is refined, neutral, and in appearance plush but actually quite uncomfortable. Feral (deep down inside), terribly busy, and overly troubled, Albion is actually the last country in the world where one can reap the benefits of being English.

It may well be that the fake Englishman (whom I've been trying in vain to emulate for years) wasn't able to hide his true identity from the sharp-eyed concierge at the hotel reception, but no matter. Once he handed over his documents, the game could begin. And the game itself consists of eschewing all sporting events, spending the day in the lobby, having tea and cake at the requisite hours, and accepting the set menu without making a fuss, even if it includes those deplorable dishes that Italian guests (after swearing picturesquely in Roman dialect) manage to have replaced with juicy, grilled tenderloin or zebra-striped paillard.

For example, if one night the hotel restaurant is serving Irish stew, that sweetish concoction of over-boiled mutton with canned peas and carrots, the fake Englishman will drive his fork into each and every chunk of the old beast, into every single pea and carrot, and consume them with the same devotion he pretends to have for his daily meal of smoked kippers and oatcakes at home.

The fake Englishman smokes Dutch cigars and drinks the coffee that he is duly served, and never asks for it freshly brewed. Ensconced in an armchair, he spends his afternoons reading articles about the Bernese oligarchy of the 1700s, and the great Gibbon's opinions on the matter, scrutinizes all the news in the *Gazette de Lausanne*, including the obituaries, and ends his days leafing through a book from the hotel library, the least offensive he can lay his hands on, something by Wilkie Collins or Ouida. The fake Englishman is polite to everyone but talks to no one; he utters little except the occasional '*kyou*, as a form of gratitude, when addressed by other foreigners or by waiters. In the evening, the fake Englishman dons a tuxedo and wears it with nonchalance, as if he's had many years of practice. On New Year's Eve the fake Englishman attends the *réveillon* but does not dance, either because he doesn't know how to or because he doesn't know anyone.

He asks for a bottle of brut champagne on ice, allows a colored paper hat to be placed on his head, toots his horn in unison with the others, and sits blissfully in his chair, covered in streamers. Just before midnight, when the orchestra quiets down, the room is darkened and everyone stands to raise their glasses, when corks pop and people embrace and say cheers, the fake Englishman also gets to his feet, raises his glass and makes a silent toast, perhaps to his own health or to someone far away. Later, when the dancing starts again, he takes his leave with great dignity, whispers '*kyou* to those who make way for him, mutters a second '*kyou* to the elevator attendant who opens the door for him, and with great dignity allows himself to be swept up to his room.

The following day, dressed in a proper gray suit, he is among the first guests to come down for breakfast. He appears to be completely at peace with his small continental breakfast which includes neither porridge nor standard-issue sausages and quite content with his tea and buttered bread. The hotel is deserted: the others are still sleeping or have already departed for the funicular in their winter gear, dressed like bears. The fake Englishman makes himself comfortable in an armchair and removes a bookmark from an old, unreadable novel. He watches the snowflakes dance like butterflies at the window, tries to light a cigar with a lighter that's broken, of course, then strikes a safety match, a sweet spiral of smoke unraveling around him. The fake Englishman leans his head back, reads, swims through the smoke, sleeps, dreams. Tomorrow he will leave. For where? Only I know the answer.

I don't know the man's name, but I've seen him walking down city streets, transformed into a long-winded and short-tempered Milanese. I don't know if he's aware that for years now I've been trying in vain to imitate him. And I don't know if he's ever been to England, or if he found it as exquisitely boring as I did. I do know that if there was ever a club of fake Englishmen, he should be named president and I, vice president.

THE FLIGHT OF THE SPARROW HAWK

IT'S RAINING incessantly. Beyond the courtyard, beyond the zig-zag of rooftops, the tangled cluster of branches of a tall, leafless tree. Concealed and revealed by blustery sheets of rain, it looks almost like a deeply engraved etching or a faded pastel. A black dot suddenly drops out of the sky and lands on the tree's highest branch, a thin and crooked bough that bends with the weight. It's a large bird, not a tiny thing, judging from the curve of the branch and the black mark the winged creature stamps against the gray sky. Another bird cuts across the curtain of rain—a sparrow or swallow—a much smaller dot in the sky. No, that bird up there is no sparrow or pigeon; it plummeted down in an erratic flight, dashes of light visible between the fringe of its wings. Now it's turning its head to peck at its tail, which appears to be incredibly long, the bough swaying like a swing. It seems to grow even larger, upon careful observation, practically obscuring from view the tangle of branches. The tree itself is enormous; it must be a few centuries old, how many hundreds of windows look out at it? Maybe I'm the only one who noticed the celestial visitor. Then again, maybe not ... Sure enough, if I strain my inner ear, I hear many other voices, voices I've never heard before and surely will never hear again.

"It's a carrier pigeon, a lost magpie, a duck," the residents from the fourteenth floor of a brick-colored building call out, almost in chorus.

"Could it be a kestrel? I can't quite see its beak. Hand me the binoculars, Adalgisa," says a naturalist nestled in his mezzanine-floor apartment on Via Borgospesso.

"It's Edgar Allan Poe's raven," says an old painter on Via Bigli who illustrated that poem thirty years ago.

"'Thou wast not born for death, immortal Bird!'" says a bald man from an attic on Via Verri who twice failed to attain a professorship in English literature. "Who wrote that? Keats or Shelley? Pasqualina, dear, bring me that yellow book, won't you? The one on the mantelpiece. Was it a skylark or a nightingale? This one is as fat as a hen. 'Thou wast not born for death...' Damn it all! And to think that they interrogated me about that very poem..."

"It looks like a peacock. But how on earth did it get up there?" remarks a butler on Via Sant'Andrea. "Come and take a look at it, Annetta. Oh, come on, don't be such a prude, let's have a little fun, the family's out for the day, anyway. Have you ever eaten peacock?"

A garbled noise is heard, a smack (perhaps a kiss?), a little spat.

"It's a sparrow hawk," says a woman from a rooftop behind my own. "Young, happy... and free. It can go wherever it pleases. It's not bothered by the storm; it has no troubles, duties, or worries. It flies as it lives. Soon it will reach Codogno, then Parma, then Sicily. When it wants to land, no one bothers it for its papers. It eats what it finds—grass, mice, insects—and drinks an elixir of rose petals that's sweeter than the best Chablis. It's a god dressed in feathers, but a god nonetheless. It's a sparrow hawk, I tell you. Oh, how I wish I were one."

"Are you joking?" says a man, apparently from somewhere nearby. "Sparrow hawks live on mountaintops, they end up stuffed, they can't possibly be happy. I bet that's nothing more than a jay, a poor old jay that will soon be shot by some hunter. Inedible, to boot. What's that? What are you mumbling about? Better an hour of freedom than a lifetime of subjugation? Such sentimentalism! You see what happens when you don't keep busy, how you feel disoriented, more dead than alive? Humans have to invent all sorts of obligations for themselves, piling one problem on top of the next, just for the pleasure of overcoming them. Mankind nurtures unhappiness so it can be faced in small doses. A state of mild unhappiness is the sine qua non for intermittent moments of joy. Pedantic? Me? You silly fool! What would you do up there, on that tree branch, soaked to the bone... without me? You want to go to Codogno? Sicily? Oh, really? You do? Go on, then, off you go! Let me see you fly!"

A gust of wind rattles the windowpanes and shakes the tree. The sparrow hawk suddenly takes flight, its outline a heraldic emblem in the sky, only to dive between the tallest rooftops. It has resumed its journey. The branch continues to quiver. The rain intensifies. I hear scraps of an argument but don't understand it. And then I recognize the same man's voice.

"You're right, I apologize, it was a sparrow hawk: a strong, free, marvelous sparrow hawk. I understand that you wish you were one. I wish I was one, too... but with you. That's the difference, the tiny difference. What's that? Not such a tiny difference? It was a sparrow hawk, sorry. I don't know why I denied it so adamantly. I really don't know that much about birds. By now, it has probably reached Casalpusterlengo, or maybe even the Po. It was a sparrow hawk, you were right. I plead for forgiveness, have pity..."

Another gust of wind, a strange sound (maybe a kiss). Then, in less than a whisper, "With milk or lemon? I never remember. We spend so little time at home... A pretty bird, though. By now it has probably reached Piacenza and is flying over Piazza dei Cavalli."

NEW YEAR'S EVE DINNER

"MAY I inquire whether the reservation was made by telephone?" the maître d' asked, consulting his register. "Your name, please. Pantaleoni? Yes, of course, table fifteen, centrally located, but far from the orchestra, just as you requested."

"The menu, please."

"Here you are, sir. Potage Parmentier, sole meunière, guinea hen en brochette with red radicchio Trevisano. Peach melba and a glass of spumante: domestic, naturally."

"All that for 4,500 lire," the customer scoffed. "Well, I can't say that creativity is your forte. I'd like something better."

"Monsieur wishes to dine à la carte? A fine idea. Here's the list. There's a vast selection."

Signor Pantaleoni hunched over the ornate scroll, furrowing his brow. Then, pounding his fist on the table, he demanded, "I'd like a word with the people in charge, the chef and sommelier. There are too many things written here. I want to know what I'm up against."

The maître d' shrugged and walked off, reappearing soon after in the company of the head chef, in a white toque, and the wine steward, with his precious leather-bound volume.

"My friends, I've summoned you for a consultation," said Signor Pantaleoni. "No matter the cost, I want to dine like a king. I'm somewhat undecided: I see I could start with vodka and caviar on toast, but if you won't take offence, I'd prefer a plate of Tuscan beans *al fiasco*, as dictated by tradition. Do you concur, Chef? Just a small plate, served lukewarm, and, on the side, a bowl of consommé with a drop of sherry. Tocón will do nicely, dry and slightly bitter. You have Tocón, do you not, garçon? What an angel. Now let's move on to the main courses. I'll admit that your grilled Adriatic turbot sounds very tempting. But is it really fresh from the Adriatic, or does it come down from Basel, like your dreadful sole? If you truly recommend it, I'll accept the challenge. *Alea jacta est* for the most precious guest of the lagoon: simply grilled, with lemon and parsley, or with tartar sauce, you be the judge. And now I'm torn between something roasted or something stewed. Roast woodcock or boar cacciatore? Hmm. Would it be possible, mon cher ami, for you to prepare a stew of lamb offal with porcini and potatoes? It's a dish that needs to be cooked slowly in an earthenware pot, and don't forget to add a touch, just a sprig, of calamint. Do make a note of it, Maître. Now, on to the problem of dessert. Personally, I would forgo it, but social conventions demand otherwise. Let's have the crêpes suzette. No one knows how to make them anymore: Let's see what you can do. Thank you, Chef, off you go. Sommelier, I'm all ears. A white Valtellina would go nicely with the fish, don't you think? I'm not quite sure about the light red wine to accompany the offal. A rosé d'Anjou? Let's give it a try. And with dessert, a nice bottle of Roederer brut or Charles Heidsieck, vintage, of course. I'm counting on you. And that leaves you and me, Maître: time to settle up."

"No hurry, monsieur. We can get to it later."

"No, I'm sorry, but I'd like to pay straightaway."

The maître d' seemed rather surprised. He went to consult the wine steward, took several notes, and returned a few minutes later, presenting his customer with a very detailed bill.

"Twenty-three thousand, five hundred lire," remarked Signor Pantaleoni, "including taxes and service. *Optime.* Here's twenty-five thousand, and keep the change. One more thing…"

"Yes, sir."

"To be entirely clear, the cook can spare himself the trouble of preparing this banquet for me, unless you and your staff would like to treat yourselves to it, while drinking to my health. All I want on my table is a plate with a few walnut shells, a cup of chamomile tea, and an empty bottle of spumante. In front of the other guests, I want to appear to be someone who has already finished dining. To be quite honest, as you might have detected, I'm not at all interested in my meal, I'm interested in theirs. Do you understand?"

"?"

"I've always enjoyed food, and eventually I became a refined gourmet. But now, at this point in my life, the only pleasure I have left is watching other people dine. Those who know of my weakness call me the Clairvoyant. But, truth be told, I'm no meddler. I'm an epicurean moralist. Since man cannot be studied in all his aspects, I've chosen the most regular and pleasurable one: eating. From the way people eat, from the choices they make, and from their behavior during this daily ritual, I can draw conclusions about the general order of the world; I can understand the final cause of things. Is that clear?"

"?"

"I understand your objection. Why not just invite a number of people over for dinner and observe them at my home? First, it would be much more expensive. Second, because a guest is not a free man, he cannot choose what he'd like to eat, making him both restricted in his movements and conditioned in his reactions. Third, my guests would inevitably represent only one segment of humanity, and not necessarily the most interesting one. I suppose I could take up work as a waiter in a restaurant or go strum a guitar in a trattoria, but then I wouldn't be able to observe with such care. The only way open to me is the one I have chosen: to buy the right to sit at a table and watch as dozens of succulent meals are consumed. If the carving of some rare fowl or the deglazing over a burner should trigger my salivary glands, I can always pretend to receive a phone call and go observe more closely. And to this end, my dear friend, I beg of you: at my signal, please send a server to inform me of a long-distance call, so that I can get to my feet, walk past the more interesting tables, and take in the show, down to the last detail, making my way back and forth very slowly. I identify with others to the point of experiencing indigestion, or even feeling drunk. Precisely because of this, my doctor advised me not to overdo it. At a certain age, even a clairvoyant has to be mindful. Ah, here come the first guests! I entrust this delicate matter to you, *cher* Maître and would hate for anyone to catch on. Prepare my table as requested and make sure to call for me at my signal. Be at the ready, like Spoletta in *Tosca*. 'Indi . . . ai miei cenni!' I'm in your hands, *cher* Maître."[71]

"Not to worry, sir. Your wish is my command."

THE CONDEMNED

IN ONE of those small zinc tubs used for soaking dried cod, a lobster (or "bug," as they are often called) was protruding from a few inches of water, not unlike the one whose praises were sung by Lewis Carroll in his *Alice*. The color of its shell was somewhere between shark gray and moldy green, its eyes were two tiny black spheres glimmering at the ends of two rods, and its large claws were tightly tied with twine. If someone reached out to touch it, the lobster would carefully observe the trajectory of the person's finger and then lash out, as if to sever the phalanx with a rapid clench of its claw. But the twine restrained it from pinching, and the razor-sharp shears fell back into the water. We were in Trieste, at a fish stall on the waterfront. The sky was overcast and it had started to rain.

"It'll be in the pot within the hour," said a man in glasses, "and yet it keeps trying to attack. Just goes to show that the aggressive instinct dies hard in both humans and animals."

"I'd say it's more of a defense mechanism," said a man in a beret. "It only pinches people who want to eat it. Hard to blame it."

"Nonsense," said a third man. "Heaven knows how many oysters it's cracked open with those loppers. Oysters, clams, mussels. Crustaceans love mollusks."

One by one, the three men reached out their fingers. Each time they did, the lobster raised, and then dropped, its harmless weapon. Its eyes showed alarm but no bitterness.

"I think it's just playing, like a cat," said the second man. "It doesn't want to hurt anyone. Even cats scratch when they play. It probably doesn't realize it's condemned to death. All it realizes is that its claws aren't working."

"It knows perfectly well what's about to happen," said the first man. "And it has no intention of selling itself—or, rather, its shell—on the cheap. When it's boiled, the shell will turn a crimson, cardinal red. And the claws are the best part, tender and a bit gelatinous; the rest can be rather stringy."

Everyone started smacking their lips and then moved along to make room for a new group of commentators.

"An example of the classical *homard*, which the French prefer to spiny lobster," a thin young man commented to an elderly gentleman. "It's very expensive there: in Paris *homard à l'américaine* is on all the menus."

"That's a malapropism! The original name was *homard à l'armoricaine*," said the elderly gentleman. "When I was sous-chef at the Ritz, that's how we wrote it on the menu. Ah, the good old days!"

"Ohh, look at that big shrimp!" a child said. "Can I touch it, Daddy?" And before his father could reply, the child stuck his little finger in the tub, right between one of its claws, freeing them from the twine. The lobster closed its pincers gently around the child's finger as if in a caress, only to then release its prey. "Careful!" "Don't touch it!" people yelled, but the child's finger wasn't scratched in the slightest. In the meantime, the fishmonger rushed over and picked up the crustacean in order to retie the knot, but with a flick of its tail, the lobster shot to the ground and, inching forward by dint of its claws and its hard flippers in a series of hiccupping hops and bursts, like a combustion engine on the fritz, it scooted toward the dock to throw itself back into the sea. A brief chase ensued, followed by a skirmish around the fugitive. After a few seconds it was bundled up in a piece of yellow paper and tossed onto a scale, curling and uncurling its tail all the while. Who wanted it? The vendor offered it at a discount, just to be rid of it.

Everyone watched as the customer who purchased it walked off with his clickety-clacking, oddly shaped package.

"Is he going to end up in the pot?" the child whimpered. "Why? He just wanted to play with me."

"Yup, into the pot—alive!" someone said to the child.

"No, no pot. Heaven forbid!" exclaimed the elderly sous-chef. "Baked in the oven and then drizzled with a nice cognac sauce. But who even takes the time, these days?"

And with that, he opened his umbrella and strolled off in the company of several others, reminiscing about bygone menus at the Ritz.

THE SNOWMAN

IT'S COLD, Saint Moritz is buried under snow, the radiator works like a dream, and I'm strolling around (my room) in pajamas. I don't like skiing, ice-skating, or hiking, not to mention sledding; the mountains bore me in the summer and are unbearable in the winter. I come here at year's end to see the performance my friend Herr Kind[72] organizes, to receive a noisemaker, a party hat, a pressed cardboard donkey, and other such trifles, and to enjoy the sight of families embracing as they uncork bottles of champagne. But above all, I come to see the statue, or, rather, the enormous snowman that Mr. S. builds in front of his hotel, located across the street from mine. From my window I can admire the snowman: almost ten feet tall, he wears a feathered hat, has a cigar in his mouth (with the ash about to crumble), two carrots for ears, two onions for eyes, and three turnips for jacket buttons. He's a cross between Churchill and Grock.[73] But it's his onion eyes that attract me most. From the moment I first saw them they stirred in me, through mental association, the most lachrymose of sentiments. The enormous bogeyman is crying, of this I am certain. He's the only one in the midst of all this merrymaking truly capable of crying. He sheds stinging, red tears, drops as large as billiard balls. No one sees them except me. He's never the same snowman, each year he is made anew, but for me he is always one and the same. He doesn't cry just because he has onions for eyes, he cries for other reasons that I can't explain but that seem pointless to ponder. And when a fresh flurry of snow blankets him and his eyes become caked and powdery, he no longer resembles Churchill, but only Grock.

And that's when I hear him say, "Are you enjoying yourselves? Go on, have a good time. I weep for all of you, as I wait to melt, so these onions can fall into the slush of the street."

I've never encountered Moby Dick, the white whale, but I've seen Grock several times now, and, while standing at the window, fogging it with my breath, I try to speak to the awe-inspiring snowman.

"Let me join you, Maestro," I say to him, "Let me take part in your irrepressible, all-encompassing, universal weeping. I came here expressly to see you, though I may not be worthy, and yet I may be the only one here who understands why you weep. Let me melt into your slush, as I too have onions for eyes, a turnip for a nose... Please, Maestro, let me..."

A light knock at the door, and the maid enters with my tea. She's a plainspoken Tuscan and disinclined toward mysticism.

"See?" she says, catching me spellbound at the window. "They put up that scarecrow again this year."

"So they have," I say coolly. "That big old snowman. Why bother?"

BUTTERFLY OF DINARD

THAT TINY saffron-colored butterfly—the one that visited me every day at the café, bringing me (or so I thought) your news—would it return to that cold and windy square in Dinard after I left? It was unlikely that the chilly summers and shivering orchards of Brittany could generate so many sparks, much less all of them the same size and color. Perhaps I had encountered not the butterflies but *the* butterfly of Dinard, raising the question of whether my morning visitor came just for me, deliberately ignoring all the other cafés in order to see me at mine (Les Cornouailles), or if my little corner was merely on its daily flight path. In other words, usual morning stroll or secret message? To dispel all doubts, the day before my departure I decided to give the waitress a generous gratuity, along with my address in Italy. She was to write me one way or the other: if the winged visitor returned after my departure, or it was never seen again. I waited for the small butterfly to land on a vase of flowers, then pulled out a hundred-franc note, a piece of paper, and a pencil, and I called the girl over. Stammering, in a clumsier-than-usual French, I explained the situation; not all, but part of it. I was an amateur entomologist and wanted to know if the butterfly would be back, how long it could tolerate the cold. I then fell silent, perspiring with anxiety.

"*Un papillon? Un papillon jaune?*" asked the graceful Filli, staring at me with big eyes, à la Greuze. "On that vase? I don't see anything. Have another look. *Merci bien, monsieur.*"

She pocketed the money and strode off, a *café filtre* on her tray. I lowered my head and when I looked up again at the vase of dahlias, the butterfly was gone.

TRANSLATORS' NOTES

1   *La gran via* is the title of a popular Spanish operetta by Federico Chueca (1846–1908) and Joaquín Valverde (1846–1910), often performed in Italian theaters in the early 1900s. *Boccaccio* is the title of an operetta by Franz von Suppé (1819–95).

2   After Leopold II (1835–1909), king of Belgium and the Congo Free State, saw the dancer Cléo de Mérode (Cleopatra Diane de Mérode, 1873–1966) perform at the Opéra de Bordeaux, he was so enchanted by her that he was given the nickname "Cleopold."

3   Saint Benedict Joseph Labre (1748–83). A French pilgrim of humble origins, Labre moved to Rome, where he was much loved by the people but died in poverty. He was canonized in 1881.

4   *Il Caffaro* was a conservative newspaper founded in Genoa in 1875. In *Il secondo mestiere*, Montale recalls his father buying the paper and mentions that the editor wore a monocle.

5   "Not a dime for a bed, not a dime for a meal, I might as well ..."

6   The Gothic Line was a defensive boundary created by the Germans during World War II that extended from the Tyrrhenian coast between Pisa and La Spezia, over the Apennines, to the Adriatic coast between Pesaro and Rimini.

7   *Carregún* is a Ligurian dialect term for a chair with armrests.

8   *Criada* is the Spanish word for servant or maid.

9   *Caras y Caretas* was an Argentinian literary magazine that included satirical cartoons, and it was widely read in the 1920s. *Scena illustrata* was a popular Italian magazine founded in the late 1800s with a focus on art and culture.

10 *Cocorita*, in Argentinian Spanish, is a word used to describe someone who speaks a lot, an impertinent chatterbox. In English, a type of wavy parakeet native to Australia is called a cocorita.

11 See note 1.

12 Montale combines two titles by Cervantes, *El casamiento engañoso* (*The Deceitful Marriage*) and *El ingenioso hidalgo don Quijote de la Mancha* (The Ingenious Gentleman Don Quixote of La Mancha), forming the exclamation "The ingenious marriage."

13 For *Il Caffaro*, see note 4. *Leila* is a novel written by Antonio Fogazzaro (1842–1911) that describes life in Genoa during the belle epoque. "Zazà, piccola zingara" is an aria is from *Zazà*, an opera by Ruggero Leoncavallo (1857–1919) performed for the first time in Milan in 1900.

14 "Ridi pagliaccio" is an aria from *Pagliacci* (1892) by Leoncavallo. "Niun mi tema" is an aria from *Otello* (1887) by Verdi. "Chi mi frena in tal momento" is an aria from *Lucia di Lammermoor* (1835) by Donizetti.

15 The reference is to the poet Ugo Foscolo (1778–1827), author of the unfinished poem *Le grazie*.

16 Singing in the mask, sometimes known as forward placement singing or mask resonance, is a method traditionally used in bel canto. This technique involves using abdominal breathing combined with chest and head voice to obtain a fuller sound.

17 Jules Lemaître (1853–1914) was a French writer and critic, renowned for his publications on Rousseau and Racine. Edmond Scherer (1815–89) was a French critic, theologian, and politician, as well as one of the editors of Henri-Frédéric Amiel's *Journal intime*. Amiel (1821–81) was a Swiss writer, philosopher, and critic. All three were admired by the young Montale, as indicated in his *Quaderno genovese*.

18 As narrated in the story, Montale aspired to sing bass but was told by his music teacher that he could only sing the slightly higher register of baritone. The first characters he alludes to are bass voices: Boris in *Boris Godunov* (1874) by Mussorgsky; Gurnemanz in *Parsifal* (1882) by Wagner; Filippo II in *Don Carlo* (1867) by Verdi; Osmin in *Entführung aus dem Serail* (1782) by Mozart; Sarastro in *Die Zauberflöte* (1791) by Mozart. The second grouping of names are low baritone voices: Jago in *Otello* (1887) by Verdi, and Scarpia in *Tosca* (1900) by Puccini. The third group cited are baritone voices: Carlo V in *Ernani* (1844) by Verdi; Valentino is Valentin in *Faust* (1859) by Gounod; Giorgio Germont in *La traviata* (1853) by Verdi; Belcore in *L'elisir d'amore* (1832) by Donizetti; Dr. Malatesta in *Don Pasquale* (1843) by Donizetti.

19 An aria from *La favorita* (1840) by Donizetti.

20 *I Lombardi alla prima crociata* (1843) is an opera by Verdi.

21 Amonasro is the king of Ethiopia in the opera *Aida* (1871) by Verdi; Mignon is the protagonist of the comic opera *Mignon* (1866) by Ambroise Thomas; Principessa Eboli is a character in Verdi's *Don Carlo* (1867); Nemorino is from *L'elisir d'amore* by Donizetti.

22 Valentino is Valentin in Gounod's *Faust* (1859); Josef Kaschmann (1850–1925), a baritone of Istrian origin, made his debut at the Teatro Regio in Turin in 1876 in Donizetti's *La favorita*. He was particularly appreciated for the intensity of his dramatic performances.

23 Unlike the story, Montale actually resumed his singing lessons with his teacher, Ernesto Sivori, after his World War I infantry training in Parma.

24 In Verdi's *Aida* (1871), Ramfis is the high priest who blesses Radamès, captain of the Egyptian army. The two characters join together to sing "Immenso Fthà," an aria of invocation to the god Fthà.

25 In Verdi's *Rigoletto* (1851), Sparafucile is an assassin hired by the hunchback jester, Rigoletto, to kill the Duke of Mantua.

26 Montale bases the character of José Rebillo on the avant-garde composer, pianist, and painter Alfredo Berisso (1873–1931). Born in Argentina but of Ligurian origin, he resided in Genoa. His works include a piece titled *Ninfea morente*.

27 *La Prensa* was an Argentine newspaper founded in 1869. For *Scena illustrata*, see "Donna Juanita."

28 *Ebrea* is the Italian title of *La Juive* (1835) by Jacques Fromental Halévy (1799–1862). "Se oppressi ognor" is an aria from this opera.

29 *L'Africaine* (1865) is an opera by German composer, Giacomo Meyerbeer, and is famous for the arioso "Beau paradis," sung by the character of Vasco da Gama.

30 "Home, Sweet Home" is an aria from *Clari, or the Maid of Milan* (1823), by John Howard Payne, music by Henry Rowley Bishop. Adelina Patti (1843–1919) was a soprano of Italian origin who was said to have sung "Home, Sweet Home" at the White House for Abraham Lincoln in 1862, forever linking the song to her name.

31 Francesco Tamagno (1850-1905) was an Italian tenor who received accolades for his interpretation of the role of Otello, in the opera of the same name by Verdi.

32 The reference is to the character of Tonio who plays the role of the clown Taddeo in the opera *Pagliacci* (1892) by Ruggero Leoncavallo.

33 "Il lacerato spirito" (The lacerated spirit) is an aria sung by the character of Jacopo Fiesco in Verdi's *Simon Boccanegra* (1857), set in Genoa. In

fact, Montale chose this aria for his first singing lesson audition. It is worth noting that the opera was performed at the Teatro Comunale in Florence on May 9, 1938, on the occasion of Hitler and Mussolini's visit to the city.

34 Cap-a-pie means from head to toe. This is a direct reference to Shakespeare's *Hamlet*, where the ghost of the king of Denmark is described as "Armed at all points exactly, cap-a-pe" (act 1, scene 2).

35 *Gli ugonotti* is the Italian title of the opera *Les Huguenots* (1836) by Meyerbeer. The character of Marcello (Marcel) is a Huguenot soldier in the service of the Protestant nobleman, Raoul de Nangis. The siege of La Rochelle (1627–28) marked the end of the Huguenot rebellion.

36 Marco Praga (1862–1929) was an Italian playwright and critic, son of poet Emilio Praga. One of his identifiable features was his pointy mustache.

37 Dulcamara is the doctor in Donizetti's *L'elisir d'amore*. Alcindoro is the state councillor in *La bohème* (1896) by Puccini. Both these roles are for bass voices.

38 See note 16 for "singing in the mask."

39 In Verdi's *Nabucco* (1842), Zaccaria is the name of the character who plays the pontiff.

40 "Giudizi temerari" (Rash judgments) is an aria from *La forza del destino* (1862) by Verdi.

41 "Del mondo i disinganni" (The disillusions of the world) is another aria from *La forza del destino*.

42 The reference is to the character of Méphistophélès in Charles Gounod's *Faust* (1859).

43 Tomáš Garrigue Masaryk (1850–1937) was the first president of Czechoslovakia. Edvard Beneš (1884–1948) succeeded Masaryk as president, continuing to govern from London while in exile during World War II.

44 A *buca* is a typical Florentine trattoria usually located in a below-street-level wine cellar.

45 A pastiche of English, Italian, French, and Brazilian Portuguese, the general meaning of the phrase is: "A letter from you is most desired."

46 The *Scoppio del Carro* is a traditional Easter event that takes place in Piazza del Duomo in Florence, and originated in the twelfth century. During the course of the celebration, a mechanical dove lights a wick that causes the "carro" (a towerlike structure packed with fireworks) to explode.

47 Eduard von Hartmann (1842–1906) was a philosopher who expanded on Arthur Schopenhauer's principles of pessimism.

48 *Calcio storico fiorentino* is a competitive sport similar to rugby. Players dress in medieval garb and the games take place in several historical piazzas in Florence.

49 Max Reinhardt (1873–1943) was a renowned Austrian director, famous for his production of Shakespeare's *A Midsummer Night's Dream* at the Boboli Gardens in Florence on May 31, 1933.

50 This is a reference to the Caffè delle Giubbe Rosse in Florence, where a group of intellectuals, artists, and poets gathered in the 1930s and 1940s. As suggested by Niccolò Scaffai in his notes to the recent reissue of *Farfalla di Dinard* (Mondadori, 2021), in this story Montale playfully alters the names of members of this group: Montale (Mondelli), Mario Luzi (Guzzi), Ottone Rosai (Funai), Arturo Loria or Antonio Delfini, both from Modena (Lunardi), Piero Bigongiari (Piero Lampugnani), Giorgio Zampa (Gamba), and Sandro Penna (a possible inspiration for various characters).

51 "Miss Otis Regrets" (1934) is a song by Cole Porter much appreciated by Montale.

52 "Ne daignait rien voir" ("would not offer one look round") is a line from Baudelaire's poem "Don Juan aux enfers," from *Les fleurs du mal* (1857), as translated by James Elroy Flecker (New Directions, 1955).

53 "To counter the stresses and strains of modern times" is the translation of the slogan *Contro il logorio della vita moderna* used to advertise Cynar, an iconic Italian liqueur made from artichoke leaves and other herbs.

54 La Belle Otero is a reference to Carolina Otero (1868–1965), a Spanish cabaret singer and dancer.

55 Giorgio Baffo (1694–1768) was a Venetian poet who was famous for his licentious sonnets written in dialect.

56 In Italy, Johann Strauss' operetta *Die Fledermaus* (1874) is often sung in Italian and is known as *Il pipistrello*.

57 "Good things in bad taste" (*le buone cose di pessimo gusto*) is a reference to Guido Gozzano's poem "L'amica di nonna Speranza" (1850). Gozzano (1883–1916) was one of the figures of Crepuscularism, a movement formed by early twentieth century Italian poets whose work was characterized by its nostalgia and unadorned style, a reaction to the florid, ornamental manner in vogue at that time.

58   This expression, which means witty, with a keen nose, is from Horace's *Satires* (I, 4, 8).

59   *One, No One, and One Hundred Thousand* is a reference to the title of Luigi Pirandello's novel *Uno, nessuno e centomila* (1926).

60   Galeazzo Ciano (1903–1944) married Mussolini's daughter, Edda. During the Fascist regime, he was named undersecretary of state for press and propaganda, and later minister of foreign affairs. In July 1943, during the Fascist Grand Council, he voted against his father-in-law and was brought to trial on a charge of treason, found guilty, and executed by a shot in the back.

61   The Latin expression *Non praevalebunt* (shall not prevail) is from Matthew 16:18 (KJV): "thou art Peter, and upon this rock I will build my church; and the gates of hell shall not prevail against it."

62   This is an allusion to the Gabinetto G. P. Vieusseux, a prestigious reference library in Florence.

63   The sculpture by Renato Bertelli, *Profilo continuo del Duce* (Continuous profile of Mussolini), 1933.

64   The reference is to Mussolini. The "Unique One" is a term that the German philosopher Max Stirner uses to describe an individual in his controversial 1845 text *The Ego and Its Own* (also known as *The Unique and Its Property*), which in turn inspired Mussolini's authoritarian regime.

65   Due to Ugo Foscolo's obscure handwriting, two variations exist of a single line in his poem *Le grazie* (1812). One reads "i colti di Lïeo" (the sown fields of Dionysus) and the other "i colli di Lïeo" (the hills of Dionysus) where *Lïeo* comes from the Greek *lyein*, to dissolve, an epithet for Dionysus, the god of wine, who dissolves the suffering of mortals, thus liberating them.

66   "Il mio mistero è chiuso in me" (My secret is hidden within me) is a line sung by Prince Calaf in Puccini's *Turandot* (1924).

67   An allusion to suprematism, the art movement started by Kazimir Malevich in 1913.

68   Taylorism is a management theory developed by the American engineer, Frederick Taylor (1856–1915), which focuses on improving workflow and industrial efficiency. Here Montale is alluding to the mind's capability of storing memories in a systematic manner.

69   The poet in question is Umberto Saba. The story goes that Montale purchased a painting by Vittorio Bolaffio from Saba but then gave it to a friend of theirs, Bruno Sanguineti. When Saba saw the painting at San-

guineti's home, he wrote a poem that appears in *Il canzoniere*, which includes the line *"cieco disamore"* (blind unlove), playfully scolding Montale for his unloving gesture.

70   Roberto Bazlen (1902–1965), writer, editor, and close confidant of Montale.

71   In Puccini's opera, *Tosca* (1900), Baron Scarpia instructs Spoletta to watch for his signal.

72   Perhaps a relative of Silvia Kind (1907–2002), a famous Swiss harpsichordist.

73   Grock is the stage name of Swiss-born Charles Adrien Wettach (1880–1959), an internationally famous clown.

OTHER NEW YORK REVIEW CLASSICS

For a complete list of titles, visit www.nyrb.com.

DANTE ALIGHIERI Purgatorio; translated by D. M. Black
HANNAH ARENDT Rahel Varnhagen: The Life of a Jewish Woman
DIANA ATHILL Don't Look at Me Like That
POLINA BARSKOVA Living Pictures
ROSALIND BELBEN The Limit
HENRI BOSCO The Child and the River
DINO BUZZATI A Love Affair
DINO BUZZATI The Stronghold
CAMILO JOSÉ CELA The Hive
EILEEN CHANG Written on Water
AMIT CHAUDHURI Afternoon Raag
AMIT CHAUDHURI Freedom Song
AMIT CHAUDHURI A Strange and Sublime Address
LUCILLE CLIFTON Generations: A Memoir
RACHEL COHEN A Chance Meeting: American Encounters
COLETTE Chéri *and* The End of Chéri
E. E. CUMMINGS The Enormous Room
JÓZEF CZAPSKI Memories of Starobielsk: Essays Between Art and History
PIERRE DRIEU LA ROCHELLE The Fire Within
FERIT EDGÜ The Wounded Age *and* Eastern Tales
MICHAEL EDWARDS The Bible and Poetry
BEPPE FENOGLIO A Private Affair
GUSTAVE FLAUBERT The Letters of Gustave Flaubert
NATALIA GINZBURG Family *and* Borghesia
VASILY GROSSMAN The People Immortal
MARTIN A. HANSEN The Liar
ELIZABETH HARDWICK The Uncollected Essays of Elizabeth Hardwick
GERT HOFMANN Our Philosopher
MOLLY KEANE Good Behaviour
WALTER KEMPOWSKI An Ordinary Youth
JEAN-PATRICK MANCHETTE Skeletons in the Closet
THOMAS MANN Reflections of a Nonpolitical Man
EUGENIO MONTALE Butterfly of Dinard
ELSA MORANTE Lies and Sorcery
PIER PAOLO PASOLINI Boys Alive
PIER PAOLO PASOLINI Theorem
ANDREY PLATONOV Chevengur
RAYMOND QUENEAU The Skin of Dreams
RUMI Gold; translated by Haleh Liza Gafori
ANNA SEGHERS The Dead Girls' Class Trip
ELIZABETH SEWELL The Orphic Voice
ANTON SHAMMAS Arabesques
WILLIAM GARDNER SMITH The Stone Face
VLADIMIR SOROKIN Blue Lard
VLADIMIR SOROKIN Red Pyramid: Selected Stories
ITALO SVEVO A Very Old Man
MAGDA SZABÓ The Fawn
SUSAN TAUBES Lament for Julia
TEFFI Other Worlds: Peasants, Pilgrims, Spirits, Saints
YŪKO TSUSHIMA Woman Running in the Mountains
LISA TUTTLE My Death